Y0-DJN-763

Sylvia entered the darkened tent, lighted only by one wavering candle. Before she could ask about Miss Bitfort-Raines, the old woman reached out and took her hand, turning the palm toward the candle flame.

"You will marry a tall, dark man, my lady, and your life will be a long and happy one with many children."

The voice sounded vaguely familiar to Sylvia—but not like that of the old gypsy woman she had hired—and she tried to focus more clearly on the face in the shadows.

"Will I not marry a tall, dark *stranger?*" inquired Sylvia, determined to hear more of the voice.

"No, my lady, not a stranger, but a man you already know—and love," came the reply.

Sylvia, certain now of the fortune-teller's identity, reached forward and jerked away the scarves draped about the gypsy's hair and face, revealing Sir Charles's laughing eyes. She turned to leave, but he caught her hand and pulled her close to him in the darkness.

"Just what game are you playing at, my lady?" he demanded in a low voice, his lips next to her ear. "Why did you run away from me this afternoon?"

Sylvia struggled in his arms, but her struggle was half-hearted and all resistance stopped when Sir Charles's lips met hers. Her arms slipped around his neck and for a breathless minute she was only dimly aware of the orchestra playing and the people dancing outside the tent . . .

ZEBRA REGENCIES
ARE
THE TALK OF THE TON!

A REFORMED RAKE   (4499, $3.99)
by Jeanne Savery

After governess Harriet Cole helped her young charge flee to
France—and the designs of a despicable suitor, more trouble soon
arrived in the person of a London rake. Sir Frederick Carrington
insisted on providing safe escort back to England. Harriet
deemed Carrington more dangerous than any band of brigands,
but secretly relished matching wits with him. But after being
taken in his arms for a tender kiss, she found herself wondering—
could a lady find love with an irresistible rogue?

A SCANDALOUS PROPOSAL   (4504, $4.99)
by Teresa DesJardien

After only two weeks into the London season, Lady Pamela
Premington has already received her first offer of marriage. If
only it hadn't come from the *ton's* most notorious rake, Lord
Marchmont. Pamela had already set her sights on the distinguished Lieutenant Penford, who had the heroism and honor that
made him the ideal match. Now she had to keep from falling
under the spell of the seductive Lord so she could pursue the man
more worthy of her love. Or was he?

A LADY'S CHAMPION   (4535, $3.99)
by Janice Bennett

Miss Daphne, art mistress of the Selwood Academy for Young
Ladies, greeted the notion of ghosts haunting the academy with
skepticism. However, to avoid rumors frightening off students,
she found herself turning to Mr. Adrian Carstairs, sent by her
uncle to be her "protector" against the "ghosts." Although,
Daphne would accept no interference in her life, she *would* accept
aid in exposing any spectral spirits. What she never expected was
for Adrian to expose the secret wishes of her hidden heart . . .

CHARITY'S GAMBIT   (4537, $3.99)
by Marcy Stewart

Charity Abercrombie reluctantly embarks on a London season in
hopes of making a suitable match. However she cannot forget the
mysterious Dominic Castille—and the kiss they shared—when he
fell from a tree as she strolled through the woods. Charity does
not know that the dark and dashing captain harbors a dangerous
secret that will ensnare them both in its web—leaving Charity to
risk certain ruin and losing the man she so passionately loves . . .

*Available wherever paperbacks are sold, or order direct from the
Publisher. Send cover price plus 50¢ per copy for mailing and
handling to Penguin USA, P.O. Box 999, c/o Dept. 17109,
Bergenfield, NJ 07621. Residents of New York and Tennessee
must include sales tax. DO NOT SEND CASH.*

A Scandalous Charade

Mona Gedney

KENSINGTON BOOKS are published by

Kensington Publishing Corp.
850 Third Avenue
New York, NY 10022

ZEBRA BOOKS
KENSINGTON PUBLISHING CORP.

ZEBRA BOOKS are published by

Kensington Publishing Corp.
850 Third Avenue
New York, NY 10022

Zebra and the Z logo Reg. U.S. Pat. & TM Off.

First Printing: September, 1994

Printed in the United States of America

Chapter One

They stood together on the balcony for what seemed like hours, waiting patiently for the sea-freshened, cooling breeze from the Mediterranean to dispel the heat of the day. The stones were still hot beneath her thin sandals, and she was acutely aware of that warmth, as she was of each detail of the evening. The sunset had faded to a faint rose-petal glow, and distant stars had begun to glimmer in the gathering darkness.

She did not look at the man standing close beside her, but she could have described him so precisely that any artist could have painted him accurately. His dark hair sprang from a wide, intelligent brow and the line of his jaw was clean and strong. He could as easily have been a Roman patrician as an English gentleman. The white toga that he wore merely served to emphasize the similarity that already existed.

He had asked her what her costume for the ball tonight would be and she had told him that she would come as Cleopatra. It had come as no surprise to her when he appeared for dinner that evening in the guise of Marc Antony.

From behind them came the pleasant discord of instruments being tuned for the dancing. Never yet had he danced with her nor touched her in any way, and yet she was painfully aware of his arm, dark and strong, lying within an inch of hers as they leaned against the stone parapet of the balcony.

"And what will you do, Sir Charles, when you return to England?" she asked idly, quite as though the question were not of paramount importance to her.

He smiled—she could see the lift of his lips without turning her head to look at him directly—and took her hand, measuring it against his own. His answer, when it came, was much what she had expected.

"When I return to England, Lady Sylvia, I shall stand outside each evening at sunset and face the south and think of you."

Her laughter rippled through the warm night air until he had pulled her close and silenced her with his kiss. . . .

Slender white sails slipped along the rippling river, and in the distance the *muezzin* was calling the faithful to prayer. Minarets were silhouetted against the scarlet sunset, and the scent of sandalwood lingered in the warm evening air. All was as it should be, Sylvia reminded herself firmly, rejecting the unwelcome memories that suddenly threatened her peace.

She shook herself a little as she turned from the storybook scene, annoyed by her momentary weakness. She had little patience with those who indulged themselves in weeping over the past; particularly when the present offered so many pleasures. She smiled at the thought of how delighted one or two young ladies would be if they thought that she was wearing the willow for some long lost love.

"And I am certainly doing no such thing," she assured herself cheerfully, unthinkingly crushing the white jasmine blossom she had plucked from one of the shrubs. During the past few years she had been courted by a succession of eligible young men, English and otherwise, and had refused several flattering offers for her hand. Her time had been filled with balls and routs and dinners and with her frequent travels. No one of sound mind could possibly accuse her of wearing the willow for Sir Charles Redford.

Unfortunately, however, the heart-wrenching fragrance of the bruised petals in her hand carried her back to that other time as swiftly as any magic carpet, and the carefully buried memories came flooding back: Charles standing in the garden beneath the flowering acacias, watching with bright, appreciative eyes as she walked toward him for the first time, a string of jasmine blossoms threaded through her red-gold hair; Charles walking by her side through the Street of Gold, admiring the gleaming necklaces of hammered gold coins and fastening one about her throat, smiling as he said that it belonged with the vivid brightness of her hair and eyes; Charles holding her close in the moonlight at the temple of Karnak, the two of them feeling suddenly insignificant in that place that seemed to have been built for giants; Charles . . .

She pulled herself sharply from her reverie. This was indeed getting out of hand. Whether at her side or two thousand miles away, Charles Redford was the most aggravating of men. Try as she might, it seemed as though she could no longer put the past firmly behind her. Instead, it seemed to seep in at the corners of her mind when she least expected it. Recently she had found herself falling prey to such memories again and again, and it could be borne no longer. She was a person of action, not a dreamer, and it was most certainly time to remedy this situation.

She smiled to herself, suddenly sure of her course. All that was needed to cure her of what had been merely a young girl's infatuation was a strong dose of reality. Seeing Charles Redford again would undoubtedly put to flight these lingering romantic fantasies that troubled her.

Less than a month later, Lady Sylvia Danville stood on the deck of a ship, her back to the shores of Egypt and her face turned once again toward England, and a wave of exhileration filled her. Traveling always had this effect upon her, but she knew that the piercing sweetness of her pleasure was sharpened by the knowledge that she would soon be in London . . . and that Charles Redford might be there, too, if Whitehall had not once more sent him abroad. Nothing had changed between them, of course, but it would be satisfying to see him and to remind herself of just how fortunate she had been to avoid marrying him.

She leaned over the side of the ship and watched the waves leap into the air as the prow plunged through them, pushing away all thoughts of Charles. Above her the white sails billowed in the wind, an unexpected gift of the late afternoon. Grateful both for the movement of the vessel and the reprieve from the sultry heat of the day, she was cheered by the thought that the change in weather undoubtedly betokened a similar change in her own unsettled mental state. Breaking with the past brought its own heady kind of freedom.

It had been only a few weeks ago that she had informed her parents, the Marquess and Marchioness of Greystone, that she had decided to return to England for a visit. She had the most plausible of excuses, for someone had to escort Robert back to Greystone Park, and he preferred Sylvia's company to that of anyone else. If her mother and father suspected that there was any other motive for her journey, they had tactfully refrained from saying so, knowing that she would do as she pleased, and they had concentrated instead on the list of items they wished for her to purchase while in London and ship to them. They anticipated a visit of their own, but it would not be for several months.

"And do be certain, my dear, to have Povey get Robert the proper clothing as soon as you arrive in London," her mother had reminded her. "The climate is so much cooler and you don't want him to be uncomfortable. Povey will take care of that, of course—but you must pick out some toys and books, too, for there hasn't been a child in the nursery at Greystone Park since your father was a boy."

"And look for Denon's journal, my dear," the Marquess had added. "It is available now, and I want to see all of the sketches from his travels. I saw only a few when I met him in Nubia. And I have boxed all of my papers and some of the artifacts that I wish to catalogue before sending them to the Museum."

He regarded her with a worried gaze as he considered the welfare of his treasures. "Be most careful with those, my dear," he cautioned her, "and store them only in my study where the servants will not disturb them. We will go through them carefully when your mother and I join you at Greystone in the autumn. I daresay that we can have those taken care of by Christmas."

Sylvia had assured both of her parents that she would carry out their wishes in every particular, and her mother had added thoughtfully, "If you would only wait a few weeks, my dear, Carter would be back and he could take Robert to Greystone. Or he could at least travel with you. He would like to do so, I know, and Robert, after all, is his son."

Sylvia's lips had tightened. Now that she had made up her mind to go, she intended to leave immediately, and there was no knowing when Carter might arrive. He had been on such a journey when their beloved Laura had died suddenly of a fever. Carter had often professed his love for his wife and his child, but that had not kept him close to them. Laura, however, had never appeared to resent this, accepting it as a part of Carter's personality, pointing out to Sylvia that the Marquess was much the same.

He was actually even more of a wanderer than Danville himself, and, although he had worked with her father for several years, faithfully gathering information and antiquities, Sylvia had never felt that she had gotten to know him well. His visits were too brief, and he was always preoccupied by his work. She had never understood the fascination that he had held for Laura.

For a moment her thoughts lingered with her friend, who had been like a sister to her. The child of an Englishman and the only daughter of a wealthy Egyptian family from the fertile delta country, she had been orphaned when she was sixteen. Both of her parents had fallen prey to a fever, and Greystone, who had been a friend of her father's, had brought her home to stay with them until arrangements could be made with distant family members. Those arrangements, however, had never been worked out and, to their delight, Laura had remained with them.

Laura's father had had her educated in the English manner and once she had joined the Danvilles, she had shared Sylvia's governess. It was two years later that she met young Carter Blackwell when he first visited them in their home along the Nile. He had written to ask permission of Laura's English uncle, living in distant Yorkshire, to pay his addresses to her, and she had accepted him immediately. Together they had returned to the delta and the estate belonging to Laura's family. Sylvia and her mother had visited her there frequently, for Carter, who had originally come to Egypt because he, like the Marquess, was fascinated by the past, spent much of his time away.

Robert had been born a year after their marriage, and Laura, who never really recovered fully from his delivery, had died two years later. Sylvia had been present at her death, but Carter had been away upon another of his journeys. As she sat at Laura's bedside, she could not keep from resenting the man who had brought this trouble upon her beloved friend and then left her alone while he pursued his own interests.

Laura had taken her hand and held it to her own thin cheek, smiling up at her. "You mustn't be angry with Carter," she had said softly. "I knew when I married him that this is the way it would be. I truly don't mind, Sylvia, because I love him."

Her eyes had darkened as she looked across at the small bed where her son lay sleeping. "I know that Carter will be quite all right, Sylvia, for he has his other interests to occupy him—but you must promise me—"

And here she had stopped and clutched Sylvia's hand more tightly. "Carter will be away so often that it frightens me to think of Robert. You must promise me, Sylvia, that you will see that Robert is taken care of. If need be, take him back to Greystone where he will be safe. Will you promise me that?"

And of course she had promised, and Laura's grip upon her hand had eased. Finally, during the night, Laura had slipped away. Sylvia herself had made arrangements for the funeral, which was immediate, and she had sent a message to Carter and taken Robert back to her own home, trying to fight back her resentment of the absent husband and to see him through Laura's eyes.

Although Sylvia had not grown close to Carter during his marriage, she knew that her own father regarded him with approval after their travels together into the interior of Africa. In fact, after Robert's birth the Marquess had remembered Blackwell in his will, saying that he regarded the young man as a part of their family now that he had married Laura and established their family. And so Sylvia had tried to fight down her resentment at his absence from Laura and to regard him kindly for the sake of Laura and Robert.

"I am sure that Carter will come to Greystone when he wishes to see Robert, Mother," she responded crisply. "And you know that it was Laura's wish that Robert be taken there so that he would be properly cared for."

Regarding the silence of the Marchioness as agreement, she pressed her point. "We are gone too frequently for this to be a good home for him, and Carter is always away from the *ezba*. Laura's son cannot be always left in the hands of those servants, who are anything but reliable. And Carter told us to make whatever arrangments 'for the child' that we thought suitable. You know perfectly well, Mother, that he doesn't wish to be bothered with Robert, nor does Laura's uncle in Yorkshire wish to take him."

The Marchioness had been unable to argue this point, and knowing that at Greystone Robert would be under the careful supervision of Nanny Reese, who had cared for both Sylvia and the Marquess, she had conceded.

After making the decision to journey to England, Sylvia had felt quite lighthearted: taking action to solve a problem always comforted her. She had thrown herself into making the preparations for her journey with her usual vigor.

Then, as often happened in Egypt, the unexpected had occurred. It had been only five days ago, while purchasing a string of blue beads in one of the *souks* of Cairo. She was holding the necklace, admiring the brightness of the beads and thinking of the pleasure they would give her old nanny, now safely retired at Greystone and eagerly awaiting the arrival of Robert, when she had become uneasily aware of someone watching her.

Before she could put down the necklace and move away, a small, wizened woman swathed in a *milaya-lef*, the flowing black cloak worn by so many Egyptian women, had seized her hand and begun to search it carefully. Sylvia had been startled to meet the intent gaze of her bright, sunken eyes and to note the blue tattoos on her face. She had attempted to withdraw her hand, but the old woman had held it firmly and traced a pattern on the palm. As Sylvia watched in fascination, realizing that she had fallen into the hands of a local fortune-teller, the old woman murmured in a low voice, lifting her eyes to the heavens and her murmur to a shrill singsong. Finally Sylvia had been able to reclaim her hand as the woman lifted her hands to call upon Allah, and she and Povey, her elderly, disapproving maid, had hurried on their way.

"Did you hear what she was saying, Povey?" she had demanded when they were safely in their own courtyard once more.

"Well, of course I heard her talking, your lady, but as she was speaking in some heathen tongue, it meant nothing to me," replied Povey dourly, firmly ignoring the fact they were the foreigners in the old woman's country.

"What nonsense, Povey!" returned Sylvia briskly. "You have been here quite as long as I have, and I know that you have some knowledge of Arabic."

"Not enough to understand such an uneducated, superstitious woman, my lady," said Povey. "She is just like the gypsies at home, and you'll do well to ignore people like her."

Sylvia had turned upon her triumphantly. "There! I knew that you had understood her, Povey! Now confess it!"

Povey, rock firm in her rejection of superstition, had steadfastly refused to do so however, although she had watched her young lady with troubled eyes during the days that followed. Deprived of a confidante, Sylvia had turned the event over and over in her mind, and it had seemed to grow in significance each time.

"You seek love, lady," the old woman had crooned, her bright eyes studying Sylvia's face, even though she had held her palm firmly upward, as though to study it.

That, of course, could be said to any young woman, and Sylvia could dismiss that remark with ease. But the fortune-teller had continued. "But be most careful, lady," she had cautioned, her voice rising. "All is not as it seems to be. A dark man walks closely with you. Death walks with you—"

It was at this point that Sylvia had jerked away her hand, suddenly overcome by the heat and the closeness of the curious onlookers who crowded them, and hurried back to her carriage. She had since regretted her action, wishing that she had heard the rest of the old woman's fortune. She knew, of course, that she was not going to London to look for love: she was going to lay to rest the ghost of an old love.

So the fortune-teller was shooting quite wide of the mark there, but she wondered what in her life was not as it seemed to be. Although she naturally did not put great faith in those that told the future, she had heard a number of most uncomfortable stories while living in Egypt, stories which indicated that sometimes these fortune-tellers were astonishingly accurate. And Sir Charles Redford was indeed a dark man . . . and he had shown that he was capable of deception.

Now, rejoicing in the fresh breeze and the movement of the ship, Sylvia felt that she could finally dismiss the troublesome incident, and she tossed her parasol to the deck behind her, careless of the effects of the late afternoon sun on her complexion. Secure in the knowledge that Povey was resting in her cabin, she unpinned her saucy bonnet and sent it sailing to join the parasol. She had allowed herself to be bullied into observing these fashionable conventions only because Povey was suffering from her usual *mal de mer* and Sylvia had had no wish to take unfair advantage of her. Indeed, it had taken all of her persuasive powers to convince the unfortunate maid that she could not accompany her unruly charge to the deck.

"But you can't go out alone, my lady," she had protested, making a feeble attempt to rise from her bunk. "You know that it isn't the proper thing for you to do. You *must* remember that there are other passengers on board and they simply will not understand that you are accustomed to more freedom than young ladies have at home——"

Here she had sunk back to her pillow with a moan as the ship dipped unexpectedly.

"Now, Povey, it will be quite all right," Lady Sylvia had assured her, pressing a cold cloth to the maid's forehead and moving a basin closer to her bedside. "There could be no possible objection to my taking Robert out for some fresh air."

"Perhaps not," Povey had replied doubtfully, "although a child scarcely could be considered a chaperone. Do take Sally with you." Then, giving way to yet another sudden movement of the ship, she had retired abruptly beneath the covers, pausing only to beg feebly, "Pray *don't* do anything to overset the other passengers, Lady Sylvia."

"Of course not, Povey. Whatever could I do that would disturb people like Lady Pendicott and her daughter?"

Her unfortunate question did not have the soothing effect she had intended, for Povey emerged from her nest of covers looking harassed. It was apparent that *she* could think of a number of things that her charge might do to set tongues wagging. Years of experience had taught her that Sylvia would always do the unexpected—and do it in the most public manner possible.

"I think that I hear Robert," Sylvia had said mendaciously, quickly opening the door to the connecting cabin.

"I will be back shortly, Povey," she had called over her shoulder. "Do try to rest."

And she had gratefully made her escape. She felt no guilt that she had misled Povey into believing that Robert, who was slumbering quietly in his cabin, would be accompanying her. She had not, after all, actually said that he *would* be, and the deception was entirely for Povey's benefit. She would rest much more easily thinking that Sylvia was not alone. As for Robert, he needed his rest, and Sally, their housekeeper's youngest daughter, was sewing quietly at his side. They had no need of her.

Breathing deeply to drive away the last lingering mustiness of the cabin, she smiled and began a brisk walk about the deserted deck, rejoicing in her freedom. Scraps of lacy foam, looking like ladies' carelessly dropped handkerchiefs, dotted the deck, and drew her thoughts back to Povey's cautioning remarks. Now that they were returning to England for a time, she supposed that it would be necessary for her to remember that her countrymen—and women—did not always regard her actions with approval.

Resolving nobly that she would not deliberately do anything to distress the long-suffering Povey, Sylvia paused by a longboat and braced herself against the movement of the ship. Feeling that she had not yet walked away the stiffness of her limbs and irritated by her inability to exercise in their small staterooms, she took advantage of the secluded area and her grip on the longboat to swing one leg back and forth, then to turn and repeat the action with the other, holding her skirt just high enough to allow a little freedom of movement.

"Good afternoon, Lady Sylvia," said a clipped, chilly voice just behind her.

"Yes, is it not, Lady Pendicott," returned Sylvia as she glanced over her shoulder, undaunted by the basilisk gaze of the older woman and the wide eyes of her prim young daughter. "You should join me," she added, continuing her leg swings vigorously. "It is impossible to get enough exercise when you are on board a ship and this helps wonderfully."

"I am certain that it must do *something*, Lady Sylvia. One has only to look at your flushed countenance to see that you have been exerting yourself."

If her tone had left any lingering doubt about her profound disapproval, her next comment vanquished it altogether. "But I doubt that your mother would approve of such behavior, Lady Sylvia," she said coolly surveying Sylvia and then attempting a frosty smile. "I feel that I can say this to you since she is not present to guide you."

Sylvia paused for a moment, her color heightened by more than exercise, and met Lady Pendicott's gaze directly. Then she forced herself to smile brightly at this impertinent woman, certain that this would annoy Lady Pendicott more than anything.

"You are mistaken, Lady Pendicott. The Marchioness is the one who has taught me to take care of my health. During her years on the stage she found that exercise was most beneficial to her." And she resumed her leg swings with renewed vigor.

Lady Pendicott's lips thinned at this double-edged remark. She had no doubt that Sylvia was reminding her that she was the daughter of a Marquess while Lady Pendicott was the wife of a mere Baron. And the chit had the audacity to flaunt her mother's past even though everyone in polite society discreetly overlooked the fact that the Marquess had married his wife straight from the

London stage. How like the Danvilles to feel themselves above the dictates of society!

"Come along, Annabelle," she said, turning stiffly to her daughter. "It is time to dress for dinner." And, favoring Sylvia with the most cursory of nods, she moved away majestically, her daughter scuttling along behind her.

"I believe that you have seriously displeased her, Lady Sylvia," remarked an amused voice. Gerard Mannering and his twin sister Amelia, arm in arm and smiling appreciatively, stood just behind her.

"She is accustomed to calling the tune, you see," added Mannering. "Your obvious lack of deference must have come as a shock to her."

"Yes, indeed," agreed his sister, her expression suddenly serious but her eyes still alive with merriment. "Why, she told me only yesterday that I must never expect to be of interest to any gentleman of real consequence, for I have no title or important family connections, I shall never be an accredited beauty, and my fortune, while substantial, is not adequate to elicit a proposal from a member of the *ton*."

"How insufferable!" exclaimed Sylvia, her eyes widening in disbelief. "Surely the woman did not say precisely that, Miss Mannering! Even she could not be so ragmannered!"

"I assure you that she could be," replied her brother. "And before I could gather my wits to make a suitable retort to defend the honor of my house, my unnatural sister told Lady Pendicott that she was most grateful for her counsel and that she would, of course, renounce all hope of marriage and seek refuge in a nunnery. Then she very gravely asked the old harridan if she had a particular convent she would recommend!"

"And I believe that she was about to do so," chuckled Amelia, "but dinner was announced and so we all paraded in. Fortunately, we were not seated together."

Smiling, Gerard rescued Sylvia's abandoned parasol and bonnet and offered them to her with a brief bow. "I believe these are yours, Lady Sylvia. Or would you prefer that I hold them while you continue your exercises?"

Sylvia smoothed her skirt and accepted them with an answering smile, adjusting the bonnet carefully so that Povey would ask no unfortunate questions upon her return. The Mannerings accompanied her on one more turn about the deck before escorting her to her cabin, and Sylvia congratulated herself upon the good fortune of meeting the two of them again.

She had first met them in Cairo last fall and had enjoyed them then. They were a lively, handsome pair, dark-eyed and perenially cheerful. They were native Londoners who had decided that a year or so of travel would be a welcome change from their normal round of activities. It was unlikely that in England they would have found themselves in the company of a Marquess—or the daughter of a Marquess—but life in Egypt was much less formal. There the addition of another cultivated person from home, particularly two such charming ones, was always welcome.

"It had simply come to be quite boring in London," Amelia had confided to her as Gerard paused to exchange a few words with one of the other passengers. "And Gerard was longing for something different. He has so much energy, you know, that he simply must be up and going all the while."

She paused a moment, and then added cheerfully, "And even if Lady Pendicott is quite right and I never marry, I could never regret it, for I shall keep house for Gerard and travel about with him—until he marries, of course—and then I can help care for the children."

"Nonsense!" Sylvia returned briskly. "There is no need for you to dwindle into an old maid. I daresay you shall have many opportunities to marry should you wish to do so, and—should you not wish to marry—there will be other things for you to do aside from fetching and carrying for nieces and nephews."

Amelia had smiled at her. "That would be entirely true for you, Lady Sylvia, for you are a woman of position and wealth. For me, I fear, it is quite otherwise. My circumstances are comfortable, but I cannot imagine myself setting off alone as you have. But I daresay that you shall always do precisely as you please."

She paused a moment and chuckled. "I fear that you are what Lady Pendicott speaks of in horror as a 'strong-minded female.' She told me that she even suspects you of being a bluestocking, for she has seen you reading a rather heavy-looking book. She said it in the same tone she would speak of a man-eating cannibal."

Lady Pendicott's reaction was not an unusual one. To say that Lady Sylvia Danville was eccentric was somewhat like saying that the ocean was wet: it was an absolutely unnecessary observation. Nor was there any need for the curious to wonder how she came to be so; they had only to look at her father and mother.

Her father, the Marquess of Greystone, was an antiquarian who had spent his life wandering in Egypt and other far-flung lands. He was far more interested in the world of the ancient pharoahs than he was in the attempt of Napoleon to capture Egypt while he was pottering about the sands there.

In fact, Greystone's attention had been captured only when Napoleon had had his cadre of experts gather antique treasures to take back to France. Until then, he had dismissed with a shrug the Frenchman's pitiful attempts to conquer the ancient land, and he had been unmoved even when Nelson destroyed the French fleet at the Battle of the Nile. In his mind, these were relatively insignificant events in the vast scheme of centuries.

He had, however, been quite determined that the French would not strip the land of its priceless treasures. He had enjoyed the company of some of the French specialists in antiquities before their inglorious departure from Egypt, and he was aware of the value of some of their booty. In his eyes, finding the Rosetta Stone had been a far more significant event than the struggle between rival navies for control of the seas, and he had become involved in political matters only when it seemed that the removal of the stone to France was imminent. His relief had been great when the English representatives had claimed all of the antiquities acquired by the French and had sent them safely back to London and the infant British Museum. The Egyptians themselves, who doubtless wished to retain their own treasures, were naturally not consulted by either group—or by the Mamelukes who ruled them.

The Marquess was aided in all of his undertakings by his amiable and intelligent wife. Lady Sylvia's mother, who had once been the delightful Sarah St. Clair, friend, companion, and favorite actress of the brilliant Richard Brinsley Sheridan, had married Greystone against the wishes of his family and friends and had renounced her life on the stage to join him in his search for antiquities. It had been predicted at the time that such an outrageous mismating would never prosper, but it had; theirs was a strong and loving marriage, and their one child, the Lady Sylvia, had been born in the shadow of the Pyramids.

Some small-minded souls had been heard to remark that her birth and background explained a great deal: one could not expect a person born and reared in heathen lands ever to be a proper Englishwoman, particularly one of the Danvilles, who were noted for their careless disregard of the rules of the *ton*. Others, more charitable in their judgments, found her lack of concern about propriety delightful. Lady Sylvia had her critics and her admirers; few fell in between the two camps.

The lady herself took little interest in such matters; it was a matter of amazement to her that other people could have so little business of their own to occupy them that they would spend their time gossiping about her. Consequently, she regarded those who did so with a blend of amusement and irritation. Lady Pendicott, she knew, was but a small sample of what she could expect upon her return to London. She smiled to herself. It would undoubtedly be amusing.

"Shall we take one more turn about the deck, Miss Mannering?" she inquired cheerfully.

She reminded herself that Sir Charles Redford approved as little of her exercising in public as Lady Pendicott had. It was likely that he would also disapprove strongly of her casual acquaintance with the Mannerings. In fact, he had disapproved so strongly of virtually everything she did that it had been amazing that he had ever fallen in love with her.

Lady Sylvia chuckled to herself. Comparing Charles Redford to Lady Pendicott had a salutary effect: it tarnished the romantic glow that his memory was acquiring.

Lady Pendicott represented everything that annoyed her about polite society in London, and it would be well for her to remember that Charles was fully as annoying.

Lady Sylvia was pleased. The trip was already serving its purpose: her fascination with Charles Redford was being placed in the proper perspective. She had no doubt that soon she would be able to go about her business without being haunted by memories of him.

Chapter Two

"I felt that I *should* come," said a narrow-faced woman dowdily attired in dingy silk and drooping black feathers, "not because I expect any pleasure from doing so, naturally, but I am, after all, a cousin of dear Danville's on his mother's side, so it is clearly my duty to call upon his daughter and offer her my support."

The speaker paused for a moment, obviously expecting her listeners to applaud her sacrifice.

Lady Digby, one of the ladies to whom this remark was directed, looked at her with amusement. "A most commendable sentiment, Ophelia. However, Lady Sylvia has been an independent soul from the time she was in leading strings, and I can't imagine her needing anyone's support."

She was kind enough not to add "least of all yours" aloud, but she did so mentally. Mrs. Ophelia Simpkins could claim a distant kinship with three peers of the realm and she could be relied upon to appear in their drawing rooms with painful regularity. It was a tribute to their patience and good breeding that she was treated with civility. Lord Greystone, the most fortunate of them because at the greatest distance from her gloomy attentions, provided her with a generous allowance that allowed her to maintain her small London residence after the demise of her husband.

It was generally felt that Mr. Simpkins had shown excellent judgment in retiring from this vale of tears at the earliest possible moment. "What could be expected after twenty years with Ophelia?" Lord Petridge, a distant cousin of Mrs. Simpkins, had demanded. "Showed damned good sense in cocking up his toes when he did!" And there were many who agreed with him.

"Naturally, she requires guidance, Jane," responded Mrs. Simpkins to Lady Digby in the patient tone of one obliged to explain the obvious. "She may be all of two-and-twenty, which as we all know puts her on the shelf, but she is still a relatively young, unmarried woman, unaccustomed to the ways of the world—"

She was interrupted by a scornful snort from a lady arrayed in a singularly old-fashioned manner, her hair powdered and her beauty patches in place, who had been restlessly tapping her cane in the corner of the drawing room.

"Sylvia Danville has seen more of the world in her two-and-twenty years than you have in your five-and-sixty, Ophelia, and well you know it!" she said irritably. "Besides trotting all over the globe with those parents of hers, she is as used to mixing with people of fashion as you are to taking tea with those prune-faced friends of yours. Why, that chit could wrap men around her little finger before she cut her eye-teeth, and she has done nothing save brew scandal broth since then!"

"Well, really, Augusta!" exclaimed Mrs. Simpkins, her narrow cheeks reddening indignantly at this unwelcome interruption. "It is the outside of enough for *you*, of all people, to speak of scandal broth! Why, everyone knows that—"

She paused abruptly, folding her lips tightly. Anger had almost made her indiscreet, and no matter how infuriating Augusta's behavior, one could not mention the striking similarity of appearance between her two eldest sons and a certain rakish earl, dead now for many years. That scandal belonged to a time long gone by, and it would have been unforgivably ill-bred to fling it at her head now, no matter how irritating her behavior. Nonetheless, she itched to do so, and it was only by a herculean effort that she managed to restrain herself.

Augusta, reading her thoughts correctly, grinned. "What is it that everyone knows, Ophelia?" she inquired wickedly, enjoying few things in life as much as chivying some hapless victim. "I can see that you are longing to tell me."

"Nothing at all," responded Mrs. Simpkins, refusing to rise to the bait. Instead, she sniffed and straightened the feathers in her bonnet, reminding herself that it wasn't worth becoming distressed about anything Augusta Riverton said. She could only sympathize with poor Lord Riverton, who had spinelessly accepted two sons that were clearly not his own.

Everyone in the room turned with considerable relief at the sound of the opening of the door. It was not, however, opening to admit Lady Sylvia. Instead, Gerard and Amelia Mannering were ushered in by the butler, and the rest of the company eyed them with considerable interest.

"He's a fine-looking young man," murmured Augusta audibly to her nearest neighbor. "Doubtless one of Sylvia's conquests."

"You are entirely correct, ma'am," returned Gerard, bowing to her. "I admit happily that I am one of her throngs of admirers. My sister and I met Lady Sylvia several months ago in our travels, and had the pleasure of sailing with her from Alexandria. We have called this morning to see if she has recovered from her journey."

"Lady Sylvia is rather delicate, as I'm sure you know," added Amelia, who found herself quite unable to resist saying something to overset this old-cattish group. Having made her conversational gambit, she smiled seraphically upon them.

There was another barely repressed snort from Lady Riverton, the idea of Sylvia's delicacy obviously having escaped her, and the rest simply looked mystified. If Sylvia were noted for anything other than her beauty and her heedless ways, it was for her boundless—and often troublesome—energy.

Gradually the conversation again became general, and Amelia sat back and smiled upon the group, leaving Gerard to charm the ladies closest to him. She had never, she told Sylvia later, seen such a collection of tabbies in one place. "It was really most amusing. They were so anxious to have something to gossip about that I longed to give it to them."

That turned out to be quite unnecessary, for the morning callers were soon provided with more than enough material for conversation. It all began quite innocently, however.

When Sylvia arrived in the drawing room, having stopped to change to a morning dress after an early ride in the park, she was radiant. The richness of her vivid red hair and blue eyes were accentuated by the paleness of her skin and the cornflower blue of her print muslin gown.

For the moment, the delicacy of her constitution did not appear to be in question.

Her glowing appearance won a murmur of approval from Augusta, although some of the others, impressed though they were by her beauty, felt that her coloring was a little *too* vivid (Lady Riverton was heard to exclaim "No, you ninny! She doesn't need paint!" in a stage whisper to Mrs. Simpkins.) and that her gown clung a little too closely to be in good taste. They exchanged significant glances, eyebrows lifted, as though indicating that this was exactly what one could expect of a Danville, particularly one whose mother was a woman of the theatre.

Cheerfully oblivious to the stir she was creating, Sylvia dutifully embraced Mrs. Simpkins and greeted her other callers, reserving her warmest welcome for the Mannerings.

Touched by the special recognition given her, Mrs. Simpkins rose nobly to defend her young relative from the knowing smiles.

"I would expect that it was quite warm when you left Egypt, was it not, dear child?" she inquired officiously.

Sylvia regarded her with a creased brow, surprised by her sudden interest. "Why, yes, Cousin Ophelia."

"Much warmer than that of London, was it not?" Mrs. Simpkins prodded.

Sylvia nodded, still puzzled by the direction of the conversation. Mrs. Simpkins's remarks were often annoying but seldom so obscure.

"It is, of course, because of the warm climate of Egypt," announced Ophelia triumphantly to the others. "The child is accustomed to a much warmer climate, so naturally she dresses very lightly."

Sylvia, understanding now her unusual interest in the

climate, glanced down at her light muslin gown in amusement. "But at least I have not damped it, Cousin Ophelia," she remarked lightly. "Though I understand that clinging gowns are all the crack now, so I daresay I must do so."

"Indeed you shall not!" said Mrs. Simpkins sharply, forgetting for a moment to whom she was speaking. A glance at Sylvia's expression recalled to herself again, however, and she hurried to correct her indiscretion. "That is to say," she said anxiously, folding her bony hands tightly together, "I am certain that it is most unhealthy to do so. It must surely make one susceptible to chills and you must take care of yourself."

The flash in Sylvia's eyes faded as suddenly as it had come, for she recalled that Ophelia depended upon the Marquess for her bread and butter, and it would be most unhandsome of her to be unkind to one who could not retaliate properly—although she had no doubt that Ophelia would soon forget herself again and order her about as though she were no more than a schoolgirl.

She smiled at the older woman. "I am certain that you are quite right, Cousin. I promise you that I shall take excellent care to avoid a chill."

Reassured by Sylvia's pleasant tone, Mrs. Simpkins was able to devote her acrimonious attention to Augusta, who was showing annoying signs of disagreeing with her about the wisdom of damping one's gown.

"It would have done you no good to damp your gown, had we been wearing such styles when we were girls, Ophelia," Augusta informed her gleefully. "No one would have noticed at all. That is, of course, why you find it so annoying now."

Mrs. Simpkins straightened her narrow shoulders and

pursed her mouth. Augusta had never been anything but the most outrageous of women.

"I am grateful that we wore a decent amount of clothing when we were girls, Augusta," she said stiffly. "It is no wonder that morals are what they are today with the young women wearing virtually nothing."

Augusta, who enjoyed nothing in life as much as an argument, rapped her cane joyfully on the leg of a dainty gilt table, causing the ornaments on it to rattle about like the metal disks in a tambourine.

"Ophelia Simpkins, you cannot have it both ways!" she crowed, scenting the kill and moving in for it. "For years you have cast aspersions upon me for what you have called my 'moral laxity,' and you know quite well that we wore what amounted to a suit of armor when we were girls!"

She sat back and waved the cane at her victim. "Explain that, if you can, Ophelia!"

Mrs. Simpkins looked at her with disgust. "You know quite well, Augusta, that you would have been the same regardless of when you lived and what the fashion was. You have always been guilty of the most wanton behavior imaginable!"

Augusta cackled gleefully. "Such fustian! What you really mean, Ophelia, is that the gentlemen were always where I was to be found. It galled you then and it galls you now!"

Before the argument degenerated into a truly vulgar pulling of caps, Lady Digby tactfully intervened. "I believe that you have another guest, Lady Sylvia," she said pleasantly, pointing to the drawing room door.

In the doorway stood a small child, his dark hair tousled as though he had just awakened, his nightshirt white against his dusky skin. He looked disconsolately around the crowded room, filled with unfamiliar people, and his lips began to tremble.

"Here I am, Robert," said Lady Sylvia, extending her arms to him.

To the amazement of the others, he dropped the woolly lamb he had been clutching to his breast and flew across the room to her, his small bare feet scarcely touching the floor. He threw himself into her arms and hugged her tightly.

"Lost!" he sobbed gustily into her shoulder. "Rob was lost!"

"Hush," she murmured, stroking his head gently. "It's all right now, Rob. You're not lost anymore. You're with me."

This appeared to comfort him and he proceeded to make himself comfortable in her lap, crushing her delicate gown beyond recall. Then he reached up and again threw his arms around her neck, giving her a resounding kiss.

"I love Mama!" he announced loudly.

There was a sudden, shocked silence, and then Lady Digby hurried to fill it.

"What a beautiful child, Lady Sylvia," she said, smiling and putting out her hand to touch his thick dark hair. "His coloring is striking."

"Indeed it is," agreed a thin-lipped lady caller, glancing pointedly at the rich redness of Sylvia's hair.

Sylvia intercepted her gaze, and the lady looked away first, flushing. She glanced at her other guests, but most of them avoided catching her eye. Lady Riverton was watching with avid interest, and Mrs. Simpkins's chin was sagging visibly.

"Do close your mouth, Cousin Ophelia!" she said sharply. "You put me in mind of a fish."

Mrs. Simpkins closed her mouth abruptly, and Sylvia had the grace to look ashamed. There was little point in taking out her anger on Ophelia. The others were just as guilty. Even the Mannerings looked a little taken aback, although they had seen Robert on the voyage.

It was clear to Sylvia that her guests believed that she truly was Robert's mother. For a moment she was shaken by anger, infuriated by their credulous behavior—but then another thought occurred to her.

Her lips curved into a wicked smile. She could, of course, dispel their misapprehension by explaining his presence and the death of his mother, but she had no desire to explain anything to people who were obviously willing to believe the worst of her. They all knew very well that, had she been married, they would have heard of it. Gossip traveled quickly in the *ton*, even when their members were separated by hundreds of miles. She saw Lady Riverton's eyes searching her hands eagerly for any sign of a wedding ring.

Povey appeared in the doorway, with a distracted Sally behind her, wringing her hands. "Oh, my lady, I am so *very* sorry!" she exclaimed. "The baby slept late after our trip, and I was fixing his bath, and when I turned from the fire, he had let himself out of the nursery!"

"That's enough, Sally," said Povey briskly. "Now then, Robert, come along with us!" she said in a tone that brooked no argument.

Sylvia kissed him soundly on the cheek before handing him back to Povey. "Now you go along with Povey and Sally," she said encouragingly, as he started to wail. "And I shall be up to see you in a few minutes." And she

whispered a few words of Arabic to him, promising him
a story and a cup of chocolate.

Comforted by her promise and the restoration of the
lamb, Robert allowed himself to be borne away to the
nether parts of the house.

There was a brief silence after their departure. Even
Lady Riverton held her peace, watching the scene with
hawk-eyed interest.

"Poor little fellow," murmured Lady Digby. "He was
quite distraught until he saw you, Lady Sylvia. I was
touched by the way he clung to you and smiled when you
spoke to him. It bespeaks a closeness that is all too rare
today when mothers are so busy."

She stared at her hostess with a speculative eye, waiting
for Sylvia to clarify their relationship. Sylvia, however,
was anything but forthcoming, for she was by now enjoying hugely the shock displayed by all of them, even the
unshockable Lady Riverton. She saw no reason to resist
the temptation that they offered her.

"Children are so difficult, are they not?" Sylvia sighed,
in the tone of one long accustomed to dealing with the
infant brigade. "One never knows what they will do next,
although Sally *knows* that Robert has always been inquisitive. In our trips along the Nile, we had always to be most
careful, for Robert longed for a closer look at one of the
crocodiles."

She regarded her guests with amusement. She had
anticipated neither Robert's sudden appearance nor his
sense of drama. He had spoken frequently of his mother
since her death, always speaking of her as though she were
still alive. They had not tried to correct him, and he
periodically paused to announce loudly to all nearby that
he did indeed love his mama. Lady Greystone had ob-

served that he merely needed a little security, and he would grow out of the habit once he was safely established at Greystone. None of them had considered the possibility of Robert identifying her to society as his mama, for he was usually with Sally and not in the company of guests.

She could almost see the mental calculations of the others as they tried to determine when this child had been born and how all knowledge of such an event had escaped them.

"I am sorry that Robert could not stay longer," she remarked smoothly. "He is rather shy of new places, as you see, and he has had a good many changes in the past few weeks."

She left them to believe that the changes she referred to were only those caused by the trip, not adding that they had included the loss of his mother and the removal from his family home to the home of the Danvilles.

"Of course," murmured Lady Digby. "Most children find it difficult to travel—and he—Robert—appears very young."

"He is three," Sylvia responded. "And he misses his father, of course. However, he was unable to make the journey with us. We hope that he will join us at Greystone Park a little later in the summer. He has his work and then of course there is the *ezba*, the family estate, to look after."

There was another brief silence while she allowed them to digest this information.

"Robert is a handsome child," ventured Ophelia, searching for confirmation of the child's parentage. "Does he resemble his father?"

"Oh, yes, he has the same hair and eyes and complexion. His father is one of the most handsome men I have ever known," Sylvia assured her, but volunteered nothing more. She could tell by the avid expressions of the others that they were anxious to discuss this delectable bit of news among themselves.

Lady Riverton and Mrs. Simpkins exchanged glances. How very like a Danville to flaunt this child in the face of the *ton,* for whom the one sin was lack of discretion. One might do as one pleased in private, but in public, one maintained appearances. Even the outrageous Lady Riverton had never indicated that her two older sons were not her husband's offspring, nor had Riverton himself renounced them, for doing so would have created a public scandal.

"Her poor mother!" exclaimed Lady Riverton with relish as she was helped into her sedan chair after her call. "It is no wonder that the Marchioness remained in Egypt! How could she have faced all of us with that wretched child in tow? How could she have allowed the chit to be so indiscreet?"

"We may be jumping to conclusions, Augusta," Lady Digby warned her. "Robert may not be Lady Sylvia's child, or she may well have contracted a marriage that we know nothing of."

Lady Riverton snorted, her favorite way of displaying her contempt. "You heard him as clearly as I did, Jane. That child called her Mama, and the chit never blinked an eye, even though she was sitting there with no wedding ring to show for herself. That is the Danvilles for you! My father used to say that they'd spit in the eye of the Devil himself!"

She laughed as she waved to Lady Digby and closed the curtains of her chair. It was good to have one of the Danvilles home. She hadn't enjoyed herself so much in years. Even if it turned out that the girl *had* married, her husband was a foreigner rather than an acceptable member of the *ton*, and there would still be a delightful scandal. Most would say that it served the Marquess right for not having brought her up properly at home in England.

"To Ralston House!" she called sharply, poking her head through the curtains and poking the front carrier with her cane. "And don't be slow about it!"

Then she leaned back against the cushions and cackled. She was certain of encountering other early morning callers at Ralston House, and she could scarcely wait to see their faces when she recounted her story.

Chapter Three

"I will never understand, my lady, indeed I will not, how you can do some of the things that you do. Why would you allow your callers to believe that Robert is your child?" demanded Povey, taking ruthless advantage of the fact that she had known Sylvia from the cradle. "You know very well that everyone in town will hear about that inside of two hours!"

Sylvia shrugged carelessly. "Why should I bother myself with what they think, Povey? They will discover their mistake soon enough."

"Will they indeed?" said Povey, her arms akimbo. "And who's to tell them, I ask you? You, who should have done so, won't!"

Sylvia shrugged again. "What does it matter, Povey?" she asked impatiently. "You know that I don't care what they think, nor do Papa and Mama. I certainly was not going to say to them, 'No, you are mistaken in what you are thinking. Robert is not my child. I have not secretly taken a husband or lover while in Egypt.' If they think I have done so, then they must make of it what they will."

"Oh, there's not a doubt they will do so," said Povey

grimly. "I daresay that they are busy spreading the news right now. It will sweep through the town like wildfire."

And it certainly did, for there was nothing the *ton* loved more than a scandal, and this one promised to be a particularly enjoyable one. It had all of the necessary ingredients: a beautiful and wealthy young woman; a love-child or, at best, the child of an unsanctioned marriage; and a noble family long noted for their dramatic indiscretions.

"I, for one, am not surprised by this turn of events," pronounced Miss Claire Bitfort-Raines gravely, when told the story by Mrs. Simpkins later that same morning. "She has always been heedless and, although I understand that some people admire such behavior, calling it 'liveliness of mind,' I, for one, consider it merely a lack of proper breeding."

Mrs. Simpkins was torn. She longed to agree with Miss Bitfort-Raines, for she felt that she was speaking the truth, but to do so would discredit her own family, no matter how distant the relationship. And Lord Greystone remained her benefactor. She swallowed hard and attempted to respond.

"I fear that her upbringing has not been—" she began, but Miss Bitfort-Raines interrupted her ruthlessly.

"Upbringing! I should scarcely refer to the harum-scarum way she grew up as 'upbringing'! Why, she has no more notion of decorum than any urchin on the streets of London!"

Mrs. Simpkins, a little taken aback by the vehemence of her response, felt that this was overstating the matter, for even though Lady Sylvia was unarguably the daughter of an actress—and everyone knew, of course, what one could expect of people connected with the theatre—she was also the daughter of a peer of the realm. She attempted to say something of the sort, but was again cut off by the single-minded Miss Bitfort-Raines.

"You know as well as I what she is, Mrs. Simpkins! Do you recall the day in the park when she was no more than ten and she set her horse to jump a hedge there? Right in the midst of the thickest of the throng?"

Mrs. Simpkins nodded. She did, in fact, recall the incident very clearly. She had been riding in the carriage with Lady Greystone, who had been kind enough to call for her and take her for an airing, her first time out after a wasting fever. They were accompanied by Lord Greystone and Lady Sylvia on horseback, and had been joined by Miss Bitfort-Raines, whose mama was riding in the carriage just behind theirs.

A thoughtless young gentleman just down from Oxford had ridden close beside their carriage with Lady Sylvia, teasing her about her riding. He had been amused when she announced that she had been practicing her jumps at Greystone and that she had grown quite accomplished. He had gestured to a hedge in the distance and remarked carelessly, "Then I'm sure that such an obstacle as that would present no difficulty for an intrepid horsewoman like yourself."

Sylvia, stung by his mocking tone and unaccustomed to being treated as a child, had gathered the reins and dug her heels into the ribs of her indignant mount. To the dismay of those present, she left the road—and the mocking young man and her groom and her father—and headed directly for the hedge. She had indeed cleared it, with inches to spare, and had returned triumphantly to the carriage.

Mrs. Simpkins, who had nearly fainted with fright, had

been astounded to hear Lady Greystone merely remark mildly to her daughter, "That was well done, my dear, but you really should not risk your horse on an unfamiliar jump, you know. You could not have been certain of what was on the other side."

"But I was, Mama!" Sylvia had protested earnestly. "We drove here several times last May when we visited London, and I recalled quite clearly just how things were there."

Lady Greystone had said no more, nor had her father, and Mrs. Simpkins had been shocked by their casual attitude toward Lady Sylvia's lack of decorum. Indeed, their only real concern seemed to have been for the welfare of her mount.

The affair had been a subject of avid discussion for at least half a dozen days thereafter, and grim had been the predictions of the ladies of the *ton* about the damage being done to Lady Sylvia through her parents' carelessness. The majority of the gentlemen, far less concerned by matters of propriety, had been favorably impressed by her pluck and her skill in handling the ribbons.

"She's a right one," had commented Mr. Arthur Ashby, the young man whose disparaging remark had been the reason for the whole episode. "And she's going to be a beauty, to boot. Give her a few years and she will make all the other girls look no-how." And, inelegant though his remark was, it had proved to be entirely accurate.

"Why, Mrs. Simpkins, had I done such a thing as that, my mama and papa would have dealt with me ruthlessly," Miss Bitfort-Raines continued in a righteous tone. "They expected more elegant behavior of me."

Mrs. Simpkins reflected that if Miss Bitfort-Raines had

forced the plump pony she was riding that day into a trot, it would have expired on the spot. And even had the pony been capable of making the jump, Miss Bitfort-Raines herself was of a cautious nature. She would never have attempted anything so reckless.

"And it was quite disgusting to see the absurd fuss that was made over that child after her jump!" continued that young lady bitterly. "One would have thought that she had done something quite spectacular instead of being guilty of the most distempered of freaks! It is a shocking thing that so many people admire that sort of madcap behavior!"

Her color had mounted as she spoke, and it was clear that the passing of the years had not blunted the indignation she had felt when Lady Sylvia had received the undivided attention of the young men who had witnessed her jump. Miss Bitfort-Raines and her pony had been forced to rejoin her mother at the edge of the crowd, while Sylvia had remained in the limelight. And that incident had quite clearly defined the position of each young lady in society from that time.

When Lord and Lady Greystone had brought Sylvia back to London for her coming out when she was seventeen, Miss Bitfort-Raines had made up her mind to outshine her. Her parents, although not of noble blood, were fully as wealthy as the Danvilles, and they had spared no expense for this important event in the life of their only child. Miss Bitfort-Raines was quite a pretty young girl, although her blonde good looks seemed a little austere and remote. "Like a damned marble statue," said young Arthur Ashby after dancing with her at her first ball. "Only I daresay the statue would make livelier conversation. The only thing to be said in her favor is that she ain't a jaw-me-dead like Ariadne Bates."

With such limited approval she had been forced to be content. Nonetheless, Miss Bitfort-Raines had known herself to be on home ground. The Danvilles appeared in London only erratically, and their daughter, although acquainted with many members of their set, did not have the Bitfort-Raines' advantage of having lived on the spot for a lifetime. Miss Bitfort-Raines had been quite certain that she would bear the palm when the season was fully under way.

To her chagrin, however, the gentlemen, young and old, had again flocked to the side of Lady Sylvia. Although the profile of Miss Bitfort-Raines was aristocratic and her figure flawless, she was once again forced to be an onlooker as the gentlemen crowded around her nemesis. Moreover, she was forced to listen to the encomiums delivered by those about her.

"She has animation," remarked one of the older ladies, coolly examining Lady Sylvia through her pince-nez. "And she has something of the spirited look of her grandmother, although Clementine Danville was a brunette, not a redhead. She will do, I think."

"By Jupiter, I should just think she will!" exclaimed the ebullient young Ashby, who had been attempting to claim Lady Sylvia's hand for one of the country dances. "She is all the go, full of frisk! And to think that she has gone trudging about the deserts of Egypt! Why, did you know that she has even gone to the British Museum? I would never have suspected it," he added in wonder, coupling the trek around the museum with the one across the desert. And in his mind, they were indeed equivalent activities.

He lowered his voice as one who was about to impart a dark secret. "And I have it on good authority that she spends a deal of her time reading, too. Mountjoy said that he saw her in Hatchard's—and when she left, her footman took out a bundle of books so heavy that he could scarcely carry them alone!"

The ladies looked shocked, and Ashby hurried to add, "But I assure you that you would never suspect her of being a bluestocking. She don't give you the megrims by prosing on like your tutor would. She is, I think, one of those who is always merry."

Having bestowed on her his highest accolade, he departed to try his luck at taking her in to supper if there were no more dances available.

Miss Bitfort-Raines had watched it all in disbelief. Being a young woman of little humor, she could not appreciate the enthusiasm of the gentlemen for Lady Sylvia's liveliness, particularly when it was coupled with her very vivid, if somewhat irregular, beauty. And she possessed the additional advantage of being unselfconscious. Miss Bitfort-Raines was forever weighing her effect upon those about her; Lady Sylvia never troubled herself with such a thought.

Despite that—or perhaps because of it—she was the acknowledged belle of the season, and Miss Bitfort-Raines was forced to watch her hold court through ball after ball—even the one held at Raines House in honor of the daughter of the house.

Lady Sylvia's conquests had never ceased to rankle, and as she listened to Mrs. Simpkins's account of this latest *on-dit*, it occurred to Miss Bitfort-Raines that this might be the opportune moment to even the score. After all, Lady Sylvia had begun this London visit by offending the sensibilities of some very important ladies. Already she had scandalized polite society by her behavior. While she was out of favor would be the ideal time to completely discredit her in the eyes of the *ton*. Accordingly, she sought a private interview with her mama that very evening.

"A masquerade ball, Claire?" her mother had responded blankly. "Well, of course, if that is what your heart is set upon—but why a masquerade ball, of all things?"

"Sylvia Danville is in London, Mama, and it occurred to me that it would be amusing to have a ball while she is here."

Mrs. Bitfort-Raines, her plump forehead creased in thought, looked even more puzzled. "Well, that is a lovely thought, of course, my dear. But I had not thought you and Lady Sylvia to be on such terms that you would give a ball in her honor."

"Oh, not in her honor, Mama," Claire hastened to assure her, instantly regretting having linked the two. "It simply happens that this would be a good time for a ball, just an impromptu one, you know, and hearing that Sylvia is in town made me think of masquerades."

"Yes, she has always been remarkably fond of costume affairs," agreed her mother. "I recall how amused everyone was when she came as Anne Boleyn and she induced Lord Merriville to come as Henry VIII. He is such a fine figure of a man that it took yards of batting to make him look like Henry. Someone was laughing about that just the other day."

Just what one would expect of her, added Miss Bitfort-Raines to herself. The posturing and capering about with no regard for dignity occasioned by the wearing of costumes had always suited Lady Sylvia down to the ground.

And the fact that she had induced a dignified man like Lord Merriville to join her in her romp simply indicated the strength of her harmful influence. It was more than time that such an influence was broken for good and all.

Aloud, she merely replied, "And perhaps she will be able to attend before she leaves London for Greystone Park."

"Yes, that would be pleasant, dear," said her mother placidly. "Even though you two have never been bosom companions, it would be agreeable if you could spend a little time with her before she leaves."

As little as possible, her daughter responded silently, shuddering at the thought of spending time with Sylvia. But a masquerade should help to bait the hook to bring her here. And then she would even the score. Miss Bitfort-Raines had waited a long time for this moment to arrive—the darling of the *ton* humiliated publicly.

"When do you plan to give the ball, my dear?" inquired her mother, glancing through the stack of mail in her lap.

"On Friday," was the response.

"On Friday!" shrieked her parent, jerked unexpectedly from her peaceful employment. "Claire, what can you be thinking of? We cannot possibly be ready for a ball in three days! It will be the shabbiest affair imaginable if I must simply toss it together!"

"You needn't worry about a thing," her daughter assured her. "All that you and Papa need do is be present for the evening. Niles and I will take care of everything else. In fact, we have already begun."

And indeed they had. From the moment Mrs. Simpkins left, Miss Bitfort-Raines had been busy laying her plans. The invitations were already made out and posted.

She and Niles, her maid, had spent the afternoon addressing them.

"And if the masquerade doesn't fetch her, Niles, the
knowledge that Sir Charles will be in attendance will do
so," said Miss Bitfort-Raines grimly. "I daresay she will
not be able to resist the temptation to see him again."

Niles had smiled in agreement. "Well, he *is* a handsome gentleman, miss," she said, adding slyly, "and she
has not had the opportunity to see the two of you together. Although I am not sure, miss, that she will enjoy
the striking picture you make."

Miss Bitfort-Raines had smiled in appreciation of this
bit of wit. She had been more envious than ever of Sylvia
when she had returned to London several years ago,
engaged to the very eligible Sir Charles Redford. Miss
Bitfort-Raines herself had been casting out lures to that
gentleman for some time and it had been a severe blow
to discover that Sylvia Danville, of all people, had finally
succeeded in engaging his affections. It had been a moment of glory for her when the engagement had been
broken soon after their arrival.

Miss Bitfort-Raines had done her best to attach Sir
Charles immediately, but he had at first shown little interest in her. Still, during the rare times that he was in
London and not abroad on some mission in the tedious
struggle with the French, she had invited him to dinner
and occasionally to the theatre, and he had done her the
honor of standing up with her at any number of balls.
Finally, however, after years of patient plotting, she had
achieved her goal: an engagement. Their wedding would
take place this autumn when Sir Charles would have time
enough to take his bride on a lengthy wedding trip. The
tiresome Bonaparte had for once cooperated beautifully

with the Peace of Amiens so that there would be some time for Sir Charles to have a life of his own.

She smiled complacently. It was most fortunate that he was in London at this particular time. It would be amusing to see him with Lady Sylvia again—meeting for the first time in public. And if she had no prior knowledge of their engagement, it would be still more amusing to break it to her—also in public.

"And you must find the gypsy, Niles," she said. "I must have her if I am to bring this whole affair about. You must not fail me."

"I promise you that I will not, miss. I will make some inquiries tomorrow."

Miss Bitfort-Raines smiled. It would be a most delightful ball. And it could well be the last one that Lady Sylvia Danville was ever invited to in London.

Chapter Four

Lady Sylvia discovered her invitation to the masquerade in the next morning's post. "From Claire Bitfort-Raines," she murmured to Povey. "How she must be enjoying all of this brouhaha."

"There would *be* no brouhaha, miss, if you had behaved yourself yesterday," Povey reminded her sharply.

Her unrepentant charge chuckled. "The ladies could not quite decide how to treat me at the Melvilles' dinner party last night. The gentlemen were just as they always are—gallant and attentive—but the ladies were a study in contrasts. When we retired to the drawing room to await the gentlemen after dinner, Lady Melville was quite determined to be broad-minded and so was very kind to me, but two or three of the other ladies eyed me as though I belonged in the menagerie at the Tower. Lady Digby was also kind, of course, but several of the others stopped just short of cutting me. Even Augusta Riverton seemed undecided in her treatment of me. It was really quite entertaining."

"And what did *you* do, miss?" demanded Povey suspiciously, who knew her mistress too well to think that she would be able to resist amusing herself in such a situation.

Sylvia looked at her in simulated amazement. "Why, what do you mean, Povey?" she inquired. "I chatted politely with the ladies, of course."

"And what did you chat *about?*" prodded Povey suspiciously, certain that there was more to the story than that.

"Oh, about life in Egypt—and how handsome the men were—and how I missed being there."

Povey raised her eyes to heaven. "I knew that you would never let it rest after you set the cat among the pigeons yesterday. What else did you say, miss?" she asked, preparing herself for the worst.

Sylvia's eyes widened innocently. "Why, Lady Abercrombie had just had an interesting event last month, and now thinks so well of herself that she must think poorly of every unmarried young woman. She told everyone who would listen about the difficulties presented by a baby with colic—although you know of course that it was the nanny who had to struggle with the child. It was extremely fatiguing. I longed to be elsewhere. Even Claire Bitfort-Raines has more conversation than Ariadne Abercrombie."

"And what did you do?" demanded Povey again, certain now that she had been working mischief. Nothing chafed Sylvia more than being patronized, and Povey knew that Lady Abercrombie must have called forth the worst in her. Her troublesome charge smiled at her cherubically.

"Why, I told her that one really had never faced a problem until one had an infant in Egypt, where many do not live through childhood and it requires an act of God to find a doctor, where sandstorms can cause one with weak lungs to become deathly ill, where Robert received a necklet with a blue bead to ward off the Evil Eye, where children——"

Povey closed her eyes. "You would try the patience of a saint, my lady, and there is no denying it! Whatever made you go off on such a wild hare when you knew that would confirm their belief that Robert is your child?"

"I was simply telling her the truth, Povey, as well you know. Lady Abercrombie was going to go prosing on forever about that baby of hers, just as though no one else ever had one. To hear her, one would think that it required remarkable intelligence to bear a child. I merely wanted to provide a little excitement for a perfectly deadly set of bores, Povey."

"You mean that you wanted to continue your hoax, miss! You are going to catch cold at this one, I fear."

"Nonsense! You and Robert and Sally and I shall go on to Greystone next week and this will all be forgotten by the next time I return to London."

"That is if they don't all cut you cold before then, Lady Sylvia. And they very well may—particularly when you insist upon thrusting the matter before them by taking Robert riding with you in the park during the busiest part of the afternoon."

She did not add that when the gossipmongers discovered that Robert had been taken to Greystone and placed with Lady Sylvia's own nanny, their suspicions would indeed be confirmed.

Instead she simply remarked, "And I wouldn't put it past that Miss Bitfort-Raines to do so. She doubtless sent this invitation before you began your May-game."

Sylvia's eyes lighted with amusement. "Do you think she would dare to cut me, Povey? At her own ball?"

She patted her palm absently with the invitation as she considered the matter, then she chuckled. "How delightful that would be. I had not thought to attend the masquerade, but I see that it might be entirely enjoyable."

Povey shook her head, giving up the argument. Once Lady Sylvia had taken the bit between her teeth, there was no more to be said. Their departure for Greystone could not come soon enough to suit her. Indeed, she feared that it would not come soon enough to keep her reckless charge from disaster. Had she foreseen this turn of events, she would have persuaded the Marchioness to return to England with them.

That afternoon Povey set forth with her mistress to attend to some of the shopping Lady Sylvia's parents had wished them to do. As the carriage paused on Bond Street, Sylvia studied the passersby with interest. People fascinated her, and it was delightful to be again in the streets of London.

Suddenly, however, she caught a glimpse of a tall, broad-shouldered gentleman in the distance. There was no mistaking that familiar form and gait; she would have known Charles Redford anywhere. She felt her breathing stop for just a moment as she focused upon him. How curious it was that she could pick him out of a crowd after all this time. For a moment her view was blocked by a tall man following closely behind them, but he stopped abruptly and then walked around Charles and his companion.

Then she saw that Charles had paused in front of a shop and was leaning down to listen carefully to the lovely young woman on his arm. Her hair was as dark as his—a fashionable brunette, Sylvia thought bitterly. How very like Charles to be in style, even in his choice of ladies.

That, she thought, had been the crux of their problem: Charles wished to live his life in a manner acceptable to the members of their society, and she had no desire to acknowledge the right of the *ton*—or anyone else, including Charles—to regulate her actions. He had attributed her feelings to the natural arrogance of one of her station; she had attributed his to the fear of criticism. Their parting had not been an amicable one.

Still, as she watched the handsome couple disappear into a jeweler's shop, she felt a sudden twist of her heart, quite as though someone was squeezing it remorselessly, and she was once again a little short of breath. Povey, who had not noticed them, was looking at her with some concern.

"Are you all right, my lady?" she asked anxiously.

"Yes, of course, Povey. It was nothing." Sylvia took a deep breath, leaned back against the velvet squabs of the upholstery, and closed her eyes for a moment.

When she had first met Redford four years ago in Egypt, he had been sent to check on the activities of her father, although neither she nor her family had been aware of it at the time. It had been reported to Whitehall that Greystone appeared to be working hand-in-glove with the French in Egypt, but, as Redford had later reported to his superiors, it was because of his burning interest in the treasures being removed from Egypt that Greystone had been in communication with the enemy.

Since this coincided with his reputation as an eccentric and a collector of antiquities, the authorities at Whitehall had been satisfied and had commanded Redford's return, but he had dallied beside the Nile, spending his time with her. The dalliance had resulted in their engagement.

She knew that he had later told his friends that he had

been instantly captivated by her, by her red hair and blue eyes and the novelty of her behavior. According to the tidbits of gossip that had floated back to her, his momentary madness had also been attributed by his friends to the exotic setting of their romance.

Who, had inquired the gossips knowingly, could withstand the allure of soft moonlit nights spent drifting down the Nile? Certainly not a full-blooded young man like Sir Charles Redford. And, they had pointed out, when he had returned to the real world, he had shaken off the spell cast over him by Lady Sylvia Danville and the mysterious East. He was a sensible young man, and it was only to be expected that his love affair would grow cold and wither away in the cool English sunlight.

When he had finally returned to London, the Danvilles had accompanied him for a short visit, and it was on that trip that Sylvia had begun to understand the extent of the differences between them. She had been in the habit of arising at dawn and retiring to her garden to meditate quietly as a beginning to the day. There on the ship, she had been forced to make do with the deck rather than the garden. When he discovered this, he had tried to make her see the ineligibility of her behavior: that the crew and the other passengers would wonder at her going out alone, particularly at such an unorthodox time; that her attire, a gauzy, loose-fitting morning robe, was inappropriate; that her singing to herself as she went back to her cabin attracted additional unwanted attention.

She had explained patiently to him that she was accustomed to having such a period of time alone in the morning—and that she was accustomed to having it out-of-doors. She couldn't bear to be cooped up as she was in the confines of the cabin. The loose gown, she had averred, was perfectly respectable, particularly when topped by a cashmere shawl, and it made her movements easier on the deck.

"Because if it is private enough, you know," she had explained, thinking that he would understand once he had heard her side of it, "I do a few leg swings and bends to loosen my muscles for the day. I simply must have this time alone. And if I sing on my way back to the cabin, it is only because I have found the time on the deck so invigorating."

He had looked at her in disbelief. "No lady would deliberately make such a spectacle of herself, Sylvia," he had said firmly. "And so you must give up this type of behavior. What will you do when you return to London? How will you have your morning meditation then?"

She had shrugged, a little impatiently. "There is a garden at Danville House, and my chambers have a small balcony. Too, there is always the park."

He had regarded her with horrified disbelief. "You would not consider this kind of behavior in such a public place!" he had exclaimed.

"Well, of course I go early in the morning so that it is quite private," she said, feeling that she was conceding a great deal to the dictates of society. "And I don't go entirely alone. I take a footman who stays close by," she added, thinking that this would placate him.

It did not. "You would behave in such a manner in the presence of your servants?" he demanded. "What must they think of you?"

She looked surprised. "Why must they think anything? They know that this is my habit. They are quite accustomed to my ways."

"Well, I am not," he had said firmly. "I think that you

must give up such behavior before it causes you problems that you have not anticipated."

She had laughed, not realizing just how serious he was. "I have managed to live until now with any 'problems' it may have created, Charles. I assure you that you need not worry about me."

But it had finally occurred to her that he was not worried about her so much as he was about himself and his own reputation. He did not, he told her, wish for his wife to attract unwelcome attention. He preferred a quieter, more reserved manner of life.

She had been uneasy after this; still, she had thought that they would be able to come to an understanding. So she had curtailed her morning meditations, or at least she had for the most part; and she remembered to carry her parasol and wear her gloves and she took Povey to attend her when she strolled about the deck; and she avoided breaking into song except in the privacy of her own cabin. If she found life a little constricting, she told herself that Charles would become freer in his habits once they had spent more time together.

It was when they arrived in London that the trouble had truly begun, however, for it was then that she had discovered his real reason for coming to Egypt in the first place. At the first ball they attended, one of the gossips had let slip—accidentally of course—the news that Sir Charles had journeyed to Egypt to find out the truth about Lord Greystone's activities there.

"Why did you not confess to me, Charles, that you had been sent to spy upon Papa?" she had demanded later that evening. "Why must I find out such things from strangers?"

He had looked at her in amusement. "And how is it

helpful to the cause if a spy announces his purposes?" he had inquired lightly.

"Don't be nonsensical, Charles!" she had said shortly, impatient with his duplicity. "I don't mean when you first came, of course! I mean after you had determined that Papa had done nothing amiss. Why didn't you confess to us then? Or when you made your offer for me? It was really most deceitful of you, Charles!"

His cheeks had flushed darkly at her accusation. "It scarcely seemed the time to bring up such a manner," he had replied stiffly, "nor, for that matter, does *this* seem the time or the place for discussing it. I had assumed that, at the proper time, I would inform you and your family of that matter."

"Well, it isn't necessary now!" she had snapped, ignoring his oblique suggestion that they discuss the matter at another time. "Someone else has done it for you! We were horrified to discover that you had not been more forthcoming with us, Charles!"

He had glanced about the room, uncomfortably conscious of the interest they were occasioning in other guests. "If what I did was ill-advised, my lady, you must recall that I was laboring under the pressure of some emotion at the time. You see, I had fancied myself in love—"

"Yes, I am quite sure that's all that it was, sir: you merely *fancied* yourself in love!" She had wrenched the amethyst ring from her hand and flung it at him. "But I hereby release you! You may consider yourself free of any embarrassment that my family has caused you."

He had stooped to pick up the ring, pocketed it carefully, and then bowed to her, saying sardonically, "Thank you for your gracious release from my burden, ma'am."

And he had turned on his heel and walked from the room. And that, as they say, had been that. They had left London for Greystone Park immediately afterward, and during her journeys home from Egypt and even more far-flung places she had not encountered him again, for Whitehall had kept him busy during their war years, and they had carefully avoided one another whenever chance brought them to the same city. She had not set eyes upon him now for four years.

Gathering her scattered thoughts, she sat up straight and smiled at Povey. Together they set forth from their carriage and took care of their shopping that afternoon. She carefully walked them in the opposite direction of the jeweler's shop, trying to erase from her mind the picture of Charles and his lady. Povey, knowing that something was amiss but uncertain as to its cause, was grateful to think that her mistress was going to the theatre that evening. It was unlike her to fall into a fit of the dismals, but that appeared to be precisely what she was doing, and Povey welcomed even Lord Wilmington, whom she distrusted, as a distraction.

Wilmington was a very dashing gentleman with a reputation for being a wit and a devil with the ladies. And he looked the part. His dark hair was beginning to grey at the temples, but what would have looked elderly in another man looked distinguished in him. When he had first visited Cairo three years earlier, he and Sylvia had engaged in an agreeable flirtation, each of them secure in the knowledge that the other felt no real romantic interest. He had visited again upon other occasions, and their relationship had remained the same: a trifling but pleasing dalliance.

He had called upon Sylvia that morning, having heard some of the frantic rumors that were circulating.

"How is it, Lady Sylvia," he had inquired, leaning over her hand and kissing it in the continental fashion, "that you have been in London less than two days and you have already set the *ton* in a bustle?"

She had chuckled. "You know how little it takes to set them off, Lord Wilmington. It is scarcely my fault if they choose to believe that I have a child that I have kept a deep, dark secret for three years and am now springing upon the world."

He smiled. "You have taken a great weight off of my mind. I came prepared to find that you are indeed now a married lady, leg-shackled for life."

Sylvia laughed. "You know better than that, Wilmington. And is it my fault that they are so bacon-brained? If I had kept Robert's existence a secret so that no one had learned of it in three years, would I suddenly appear and reveal his presence to the whole world?" she demanded.

Wilmington shook his head. "That would scarcely have been intelligent, ma'am, and you are nothing if not intelligent. The gossips have failed to take that into account."

She shrugged impatiently. "I may not be lacking in intelligence, but I am the one who caused this whole bumble-bath. It never ceases to amaze me that there are people who are so interested in what I do and how I do it. Life must be incredibly dull for them if they must spend their time gossiping about me. Surely there is some more interesting subject for their chatter."

"That is where you are quite out, my lady," replied Wilmington, his dark eyes shining with amusement. "Londoners have been fascinated by what you do from the time you were a child. Many of them may have very dull lives, indeed, but *you* do not. And so they wish to hear about each new scandal that you cause. Most of them would not dare to do so themselves, but they are happy when you do it for them. And so they are always delighted—just as I am—when you return to London each year. And you may be sure," he had said, bending over her hand at his departure, "that your dark secret is safe with me. No one will discover from me that you are *not* the mother of that interesting infant."

Sylvia looked forward to an evening in Wilmington's company because his badinage would be amusing and would keep her mind occupied. Of all things, she did not want the time to think about Sir Charles Redford and his lady love. She would deal with that later.

And so it was most unfortunate that, at the theatre that night, no sooner had Sylvia glanced down from their box than her eyes had alighted upon Sir Charles Redford and his lady. They were deep in conversation, and Sylvia had turned immediately to Lord Wilmington and engaged him in a lively flirtation, watching Redford covertly. In a few moments she had the satisfaction of seeing him stare in their direction. When she allowed herself to glance that way, Redford was still gazing at her, quite as though he had been turned to stone, and the young girl beside him was regarding him with a puzzled expression. When Sylvia nodded to him briefly, with the air of one acknowledging a distant acquaintance, he seemed to come to himself and turned back to his companion.

"Yes, I had quite forgotten," said Wilmington, following her glance. "You and Sir Charles were once well known to one another, were you not?" He raised his glass to his eye and studied the young woman with Redford.

"That was a long time ago," replied Sylvia lightly, hoping to avoid a more searching conversation.

"So it was," agreed Wilmington. "And I applaud your wisdom in breaking with him. You would have found him a tiresome young man."

Sylvia was not anxious to discuss her private affairs with Wilmington, so she attempted to dismiss the matter. "Not everyone can possess your wit, my lord."

"Quite true," he agreed languidly. "Nonetheless, he could make a greater effort to avoid boring others with tales of the war. It really is not a gripping subject for most of us. When I pointed that out to him, he looked at me as though he had discovered a particularly repellent insect, and then he informed me that there were some serious matters in the world and that someone had to take care of them if we were to continue in our present way of life."

He sighed. "Nothing is so fatiguing as the self-righteous. I was quite worn down when he finished addressing me."

"I can well imagine it," responded Sylvia grimly. "Charles has always had the effect on me, too."

Wilmington cocked an eyebrow in her direction. "Charles, is it? I had not realized that you were still on such terms with him."

"No, of course, I'm not," she said hurriedly. "It is merely an old habit. He and I have not actually spoken for years."

At that moment someone entered their box, and Sylvia looked up to see the mother of Claire Bitfort-Raines, her ample figure encased in bottle green satin. She immediately engulfed Sylvia in a perfumed, plump embrace, the green feathers in her headdress wobbling dangerously.

"And I must tell you, dear child," she said brightly,

"that the thing I most want is to see you at our little masquerade on Friday night."

Before Sylvia could respond, she tapped Lord Wilmington on the shoulder with her fan and added coyly, "And tell me that we may depend upon your presence, my lord. It could scarcely be a success without you."

He bowed with a sardonic smile. "You overwhelm me, ma'am. How could I refuse?" Turning to Sylvia, he said more warmly, "Perhaps I might have the pleasure of escorting you there, dear lady."

Keenly aware of Redford's curious gaze, Sylvia smiled brightly and nodded. Even though Mrs. Bitfort-Raines seemed anxious to have her as a guest, she was well aware that others might be equally well prepared to snub her. To be on the arm of such a man as Wilmington tomorrow night would do her no harm.

Pleased with her success, Mrs. Bitfort-Raines smiled graciously upon them and departed. Having assured herself of Wilmington's presence was a feather in her cap, for he was an asset to any gathering, being both charming and eligible—as well as dangerous enough to give him a certain piquant appeal. And to have Lady Sylvia Danville, whose latest escapade was rapidly becoming the talk of the town, would ensure the success of the ball. Everyone invited would come, if only to stare at her. Claire had been quite right—the ball would be an unqualified success.

Chapter Five

"And so you saw Lady Sylvia at the theatre last night, Charles," said Miss-Bitfort Raines in a matter-of-fact tone as she poured a cup of coffee for him during his call the next morning.

He looked at her, startled. He had forgotten that Claire's mother had been at the theatre last night, but he remembered very vividly how much Claire disliked Lady Sylvia. This was not a subject he cared to discuss with her.

He smiled with the polished ease of those who spend much of their time in government circles. "Yes, Diana and I did see her at the theatre last night. She was attended, I noted, by Lord Wilmington."

He did not add that he had recognized her laughter immediately, even after four years, nor that he knew the fire-glow of her hair at a glance.

"So Mother said," remarked Claire. "Quite an appropriate choice, I would say. *His* reputation is scarcely untarnished, either."

Redford decided not to pursue the subject, although he was far from certain that Sylvia deserved the reproaches that he had heard heaped upon her. She was heedless, he

knew, but scarcely the brazen creature that some seemed
determined to make her. He knew, of course, that part of
Claire's resentment was because of him, and, little though
he liked it, he began to feel an uneasy responsibility for
Claire's attitude toward Lady Sylvia's situation.

"Everyone knows that Lady Sylvia does not do anything in an ordinary manner," he began, but he was not
allowed to finish his sentence.

"That is an amazingly casual way to speak of her behavior, Charles!" exclaimed Miss Bitfort-Raines. "I
would have thought that you, of all people, would have
been among the first to condemn such an outrage. Why,
you have told me yourself that she cares nothing for the
rules that the rest of us live by! I recall quite clearly that
you said—"

"Yes, yes," he interrupted hastily, wishing that he had
never confided some of Sylvia's eccentricities to Claire,
"but there is a vast difference between the indiscretions of
her girlhood and those which she is accused of now."

Miss Bitfort-Raines dismissed his interjections with a
brisk wave of her hand. "Nonsense! She never fails to set
everyone talking when she is in town. This is a natural
progression in her flaunting of the conventions. Any sensible person would know that it was only to be expected."

Redford was less certain of this, although he conceded
to himself that it was a possibility. Nonetheless, he had no
desire to discuss it with Claire and was relieved when
Niles entered the room and provided a distraction for her
mistress.

Miss Bitfort-Raines began to question her maid closely
about arrangements for the masquerade, and he was free
to pursue his own uncomfortable thoughts. He had no
idea what game Lady Sylvia was playing at now, but he

wished to heaven that she had stayed away from London while he was in town. He saw clearly that life would be most uncomfortable for him as long as she remained. It was unfortunate indeed that his assignment from Whitehall would confine him primarily to London for the foreseeable future.

Once she was satisfied that matters were well in hand, the orchestra engaged, the cases of champagne delivered, and the elaborate centerpiece of spun sugar ordered from Gunter's, Miss Bitfort-Raines turned to him once again.

"I shall go as Marie Antoinette," she announced, having decided that her thick curls and admirable form would show to advantage in such a costume. Too, the late queen was considered a romantic figure, and she hoped that some of that aura would cling to her.

"And you will make a splendid Louis," she added graciously, thinking complacently of the handsome couple they would make. Miss Bitfort-Raines was always keenly aware of the impression she made upon those about her and lost no opportunity to display herself in the most appealing way possible.

Redford did not respond. He felt no desire either to powder his own dark hair or to wear a wig. Nor did he feel any admiration for the late king. Still less did he like having Claire always making decisions for him.

"Perhaps we could think of something a trifle less ostentatious," he began, but he was once again cut short by his lady, who did not appear to be listening.

"And Pierre said that he would be honored to dress your hair for you, Charles, and to provide you with your costume, so you need not trouble yourself about that." She patted her luxuriant blonde curls complacently. "He said that I would make an admirable queen."

Redford, who always liked to make his own arrangements, frowned slightly. In many ways Claire was fully as imperious in her behavior as Sylvia had been. But at least Claire could always be trusted to stay within the bounds of good taste, while Sylvia was indifferent to any such constrictions. Still, she was fond of ordering him about, and what had been mildly amusing at the beginning of their relationship was now a source of irritation. He had no intention of allowing her to call the tune.

With this in mind, he rose to take leave of her, saying decisively, "I assure you that there will be no need to send Pierre to me, Claire. I am perfectly capable of arranging my own costume."

And, saluting her gravely on the cheek, he departed, promising that he would join them for dinner that evening.

Miss Bitfort-Raines watched his departure with raised eyebrows. Charles was normally very manageable, but her mama had warned her that all gentlemen, even the most agreeable ones, sometimes became very obstinate for no apparent reason. It appeared that even Charles, the most reasonable of men, was not free of such masculine idiosyncrasies. She sighed and rang for Niles, who reappeared almost immediately.

"Did you find her, Niles?" she demanded.

Niles nodded, her small eyes shining. "Her name is Madame Zeena, miss," she said eagerly, "and she is a genuine gypsy. You should see her, miss! She is tall and dark-eyed and wears golden bracelets and earrings and necklaces—and she can read palms and she has a crystal ball!"

"Very well, Niles," replied her mistress in a damping tone. Niles was really becoming too caught up in all of this. She seemed distressingly susceptible to such superstitious nonsense. "Show her in."

"I am in, mistress," said a tall woman standing just inside the door. Her voice was surprisingly strong and assured, and her lack of deference annoyed Miss Bitfort-Raines, who preferred a subservient manner in those about her.

"I understand that you tell fortunes," she said briskly, attempting to establish her authority.

A glimmer of amusement appeared in Madame Zeena's dark eyes, and she inclined her head briefly. "I share what I see, mistress," she returned, her tone dignified. "It is not necessarily the future. It is merely what might be if events follow their course. Sometimes the picture changes."

"Yes, of course," said Miss Bitfort-Raines condescendingly, not listening to a word. "Now, let me explain to you what I wish for you to—"

Before she could continue, Madame Zeena had moved swiftly to her nearly empty teacup, picked it up, and handed it to her. "Swirl the cup so that the tea washes its sides," commanded the gypsy.

Startled, Miss Bitfort-Raines found herself doing exactly that. Madame Zeena then took the cup from her and deftly turned it upside down into its saucer, draining away the last of the liquid. Then she carried it over to the sunny windows of the drawing room and studied its contents carefully, holding the handle of the cup toward her.

"Come here, mistress, and look into the cup with me. Here we see part of your past and part of your present."

In spite of herself, Miss Bitfort-Raines rose and walked to the windows, where she stared intently into the cup.

The gypsy pointed a long, tapered finger to a dark pattern near the bottom.

"What do you see here, mistress?" she asked.

Miss Bitfort-Raines shrugged. "Who can tell?" she replied carelessly.

Madame Zeena traced an outline for her. "It is a wolf," she said gravely.

Her subject laughed indulgently. "A wolf? And does that mean, perhaps, that I should avoid wolves? I shall, I promise you."

"It is but a symbol. It says that there has been jealousy in your past. And here," she continued, pointing to the rim of the cup, "is a hawk. Again, jealousy," she said, staring for a moment at Miss Bitfort-Raines. "This time in your present."

Niles, too, stared at her mistress, whose cheeks reddened unbecomingly.

Madame Zeena continued inexorably. "And here, close together and in your present, are a cat and a door."

Miss Bitfort-Raines' laughter was notably weaker this time, and she inquired with a show of nonchalance, "And what, pray, does that signify?"

"The cat is deceit and the door is a strange event," responded Madame Zeena. "They are connected in some way, mistress—and jealousy seems to be the key."

Miss Bitfort-Raines managed a genuine laugh this time and said, "You will do very well, Madame Zeena. They will love you at the masquerade. And you look magnificent—just like a fortune-teller should look."

The gypsy bowed her head briefly in acknowledgement, her dark eyes searching the face of the other woman. "I will be here, lady," she responded, and turned to go.

"Just a moment," said Miss Bitfort-Raines imperiously. "There is one more thing."

The gypsy turned and waited, and the young woman, accustomed to being in charge, felt oddly ill at ease under her gaze. It was a nonsensical notion, of course, and she forced herself to continue in a businesslike manner.

"There will be a young woman at the masquerade tomorrow night, a young woman for whom I want you to read a special fortune. Either Niles or I will point her out to you."

There was a brief silence as she waited for Madame Zeena to comment, but the gypsy remained silent, awaiting the rest of her instructions.

"We will tell you just what to say and when to make your pronouncement about her future," said Miss Bitfort-Raines.

"You do not wish me to tell her fortune myself?"

"No," replied her employer, "I want you to deliver precisely the message I give to you, and I shall want you to speak in a very dramatic manner."

"You wish for many people to hear it?" inquired Madame Zeena.

Miss Bitfort-Raines, pleased with her quickness, nodded. "Yes, it is all a hoax, of course, and it shall be immensely amusing."

"And what is her fortune to be?" was the next inquiry.

Another brief pause ensued while Miss Bitfort-Raines assumed an appropriately light tone. "You will tell her to beware of a tall, dark stranger, for he has betrayed her and left her alone with a child; he has abandoned her to be ridiculed by others. He has betrayed her once and he will betray her again unless she avoids him."

Even to her own ears, this sounded vindictive, but she forced herself to meet the thoughtful eyes of the gypsy.

"And the young lady will be amused by this?" asked Madame Zeena gravely, looking first at Miss Bitfort-Raines and then at the teacup.

"Naturally!" she snapped. "It will be talked about for months!"

The gypsy woman studied her for a moment, then nodded and silently left the drawing room.

"She will be a great success," said Miss Bitfort-Raines to Niles with a forced smile.

And Niles watched as her mistress walked over to the teacup used by the gypsy and turned it upside down, shaking out the offending tea leaves into a saucer.

Niles stared at the new arrangement in the saucer with a fascinated eye. "What do you suppose those mean, miss?" she asked breathlessly.

In response, Miss Bitfort-Raines firmly turned the teacup upside down over the saucer and swept from the room to attend to her Marie Antoinette costume.

That afternoon Sir Charles was relaxing in the relative peace of his club when Adrian Chambers, a good friend from his younger days, lowered himself comfortably into the chair next to his.

"And so, old fish, I understand that I am to dust off my domino and present myself at the home of the Bitfort-Raines' tomorrow evening," he said, casually crossing his long, buckskin-clad legs.

"I am delighted that you will be able to attend, Adrian," Redford told him gravely. "You will be an asset to the party."

"Wouldn't miss it for the world," Chambers assured him. "Wilmington left just before you arrived and he will be escorting Lady Sylvia Danville. Haven't had a chance to see her yet, but I hear that she has stirred things up properly. Nothing surprising there, of course."

Sir Charles stiffened. He had not sought the seclusion of his club so that he could hear more of this. Why would Sylvia be with a man like Wilmington? And, in view of Claire's feelings about her, he had not considered the possibility of Lady Sylvia attending the masquerade that night. He frowned to himself as he considered the matter. Why would Claire have invited Lady Sylvia when she disliked her so intensely? Under no circumstances would he appear in front of Sylvia Danville as a powdered, mincing Louis.

Happily oblivious to the feelings of his listener, Chambers chattered on. "Wilmington said they were going as Caesar and Cleopatra," he chuckled. "Isn't it just like her to spit in their eye? All of the tabbies think she has a love-child from her time in Egypt, and here she comes as an Egyptian queen to make them all sit up and take notice. It is precisely what you would expect of Lady Sylvia."

Sir Charles did not answer. He was seeing a masquerade four years ago. She had gone as Cleopatra then, he as Antony. It had been, in every way, a delightful evening. And tomorrow night she would be with Wilmington, a notorious rake, trying to destroy what little was left of her reputation. And apparently it meant nothing to her that she was going in the same costume she had worn for him. Doubtless the night that he recalled with such intensity had meant little to her.

Anger, mixed with an emotion he had no wish to name,

washed over him. It was always this way with Sylvia: he prided himself upon his polished self-control, and she seemed always to cause him to lose it. He was determined that she would not do so again.

When he finally escaped Chambers, he made his way wearily home. To his intense annoyance, he discovered Pierre awaiting him in his entrance hall.

The little hairdresser bowed low. "Pierre Lamont, at your service, Sir Charles. Miss Bitfort-Raines has told me that I may be of assistance to you, and I have rushed here to place myself at your disposal."

Sir Charles looked at him with distaste. "I fear that you have wasted your time in coming here, Lamont. I told Miss Bitfort-Raines that I had no need of assistance."

The little Frenchman bowed again and twirled his dark moustache ferociously. "The young lady, she told me that you would feel this way."

Here he smiled ingratiatingly and appeared to study his subject. "So many gentlemen feel that they do not need the services of one like Pierre, but I assure you, m'sieur, that you will not regret it. I will make you look exactly like the sainted Louis."

"You mistake the matter, monsieur," returned Redford, signaling to his butler to show Lamont to the door.

"But the young lady!" protested the Frenchman, correctly interpreting the gesture.

"I will send a note explaining the matter to her and removing all responsibility from your shoulders," returned Sir Charles. And his butler, who had been awaiting just such an opportunity, escorted Pierre briskly to the door and closed it firmly behind him.

"My apologies, sir," said Bates as he turned from his

duties. "I wouldn't have allowed him entrance, but he did say that Miss Bitfort-Raines had sent him."

Sir Charles nodded as he closeted himself in his study. "It is quite all right, Bates." He did not add that it was exactly the behavior he had come to expect of that young lady.

Walking to the window of his study, he stared at the park across the street. It was not the park he saw, however, but a ballroom in Cairo four years earlier. And it was not Claire Bitfort-Raines whose smile he saw. It was that of Sylvia Danville. The years seemed to melt away like snow under a Mediterranean sun.

He rang for his valet, and when that individual appeared, his instructions were brief. "Somewhere I have a toga, Parker. Find it for me. I shall go as Marc Antony tomorrow night."

Chapter Six

Miss Bitfort-Raines stood at the top of the stairs, regarding her handiwork with satisfaction. She could not have hoped for more had she been planning her ball for weeks. The rooms were crowded with guests, all hoping to see the notorious Lady Sylvia do something worthy of further gossip. Thus far she had not appeared, but Miss Bitfort-Raines had no doubt that she would soon arrive. Then her plan could be put into action and the gossips would have their new scandal, and she would have avenged herself once and for all. Niles had Madame Zeena securely placed in a small anteroom, reading fortunes for the curious and awaiting her victim.

She patted the skirt of her elaborate costume complacently, secure in the knowledge that she looked stunning as Marie Antoinette. Charles had sent her a note, saying that he would be delayed by business affairs, but he too should be arriving soon. She certainly had no wish for Madame Zeena to make her dramatic announcement before his arrival. It would be completely satisfying to force him to recognize the enormity of Lady Sylvia's transgressions by publishing them to the world. Charles still insisted upon taking a rather romantic and forgiving view of her escapades, but Miss Bitfort-Raines was quite certain that tonight's events would force him to see her in the proper light.

At that moment she was startled to see him appear in the entrance of the ballroom, attired not in the magnificent costume she had hired for him, but in a simple Roman toga. She watched with mounting fury as he made his way across the room to her.

"Charles! Whatever happened to the costume I sent to you?" she demanded in a low voice as he bowed over her hand. "Was there an accident? Did Pierre fail to deliver it to you?"

He coolly raised his eyes to hers. "No, there was no accident, Claire. I had told you that I had no desire to get myself up in all of those trappings. I am sorry if I have distressed you," he added, feeling that she was entitled to at least the appearance of an apology.

"Distressed me!" she hissed. "Look at me, Charles! Do I look as though I should be escorted by someone in a toga? We will look ridiculous together."

He bowed again. "Then I shall put myself at a greater distance, Claire."

He started to move away, but she caught his hand and forced herself to put on the semblance of a smile for anyone who might be watching.

"Nonsense, Charles," she said, taking his hand and trying to sound teasing. "You must stay with me. I have been waiting for an opportunity to dance with you."

Unwillingly he allowed himself to be led to the dance floor, thinking again that he was weary of having her feel that she could direct things in whatever high-handed manner she chose. At a signal from her, the orchestra began to play, and he was forced to lead her out for the dance.

"Isn't this romantic, Charles?" she asked, peering up at him coyly through carefully darkened lashes. "Doesn't the costume make you think of me in a different way?"

Since he thought that she looked absurd in her top-heavy wig and plumes, he made no response other than a cool nod. She giggled in an affected, girlish manner that he found profoundly annoying and whispered to him from behind her fan. "Lady Royalton is sitting in the corner looking like a stormcloud! She still thinks that you should have offered for her granddaughter—although everyone knows that she is such an antidote that she will still be on the shelf five years from now."

There was still no reaction from her partner, and she was startled to see him looking over her shoulder with a fixed gaze.

"What is it, Charles?" she asked, glancing in that direction as soon as the movement of the dance would allow it.

What she saw there was far from pleasing. With Lord Wilmington at her side, Lady Sylvia stood in the entranceway, dressed simply in a narrow white linen shift, gathered under the bosom and falling in graceful folds. One shoulder was bare and the gown was draped gracefully over the other. She wore a wide beaded necklace and arm bands and bracelets of turquoise and coral. The candlelight caught the flashing gold of her dangling earrings and the fiery glow of her hair, which was dressed simply in the style of Cleopatra, long and turned neatly under at the ends.

And that she *was* Cleopatra, fully as dangerous and alluring as that notorious queen, was all too evident to Miss Bitfort-Raines. A single glance at Charles confirmed it. And she understood now why he was dressed as Marc Antony.

In the wink of an eye all of her tribulations came rushing back to her: Lady Sylvia at the middle of an admiring circle after setting her horse over the forbidden hedge long ago; Lady Sylvia the year of their coming out, when she was surrounded by suitors and the other young ladies were forced to make do with the few gentlemen who did not form a part of her admiring court; Lady Sylvia today, still attracting men who should know better. It was all of a piece, Miss Bitfort-Raines told herself furiously, and there was no doubt that the lady had brought upon herself the punishment that would soon be administered by Madame Zeena.

Before she had time to reflect upon that happy event with satisfaction, Charles excused himself and left her standing at the edge of the dance floor. Chagrined, she managed to cover her discomfiture by turning to talk to a young matron who was not dancing. From the corner of her eye she saw Charles disappear into an adjoining room. She had no dobut that her nemesis was also there.

"Lady Sylvia!" said Redford imperiously as he joined that lady.

She inclined her head politely, giving her attention to smoothing her skirt as though that were a far more important activity than greeting him. "Sir Charles Redford," she murmured. "What a pleasure to see you again."

"I know very well that you do not mean a word of that," he returned, "but that is neither here nor there. I must speak with you privately!"

Sylvia's eyebrows arched at that remark, but she said nothing, merely following him onto the terrace. It was time to exorcise her demons. She needed to rid herself of dreams of Charles Redford. Once in the relative privacy of the shadows, she turned to him questioningly.

"And what is so urgent, Sir Charles?" she inquired in a frosty voice.

Redford had promised himself that he would be calm and speak to her with a composure that would impress upon her the importance of his words. That should surely be no difficulty, he thought, since he was always a calm and rational man. Instead, he once again felt his patience slipping away. She had the most infuriating habits of any human being he had ever known.

"Why must you tear your reputation to ribbons?" he demanded, his voice sounding petulant even to himself. "Will you never grow up?"

"Probably not," she responded, her voice indicating a complete lack of interest in the conversation. "But what possible difference could that make to you?"

Since this was a reasonable question, he was all the more annoyed. "Do you know what is said of Lord Wilmington?" he asked, answering a question with a question.

"What is there to know?" she inquired carelessly.

"That he has had countless liasons, that he rarely is honorable in his dealings with women, that he is, in short, a dangerous man!" he replied, irritated beyond the telling and determined to keep her from seeing him. "How could you think so poorly of yourself as to have dealings with such a man?"

"*He* has been every inch a gentleman, Sir Charles," she said coldly. "In fact, unlike some men that I could mention, Lord Wilmington has treated me with great respect."

She saw no need to add that she had not the slightest

interest in the man. She wondered fleetingly too how she could feel any interest in Redford, when he cared for nothing save criticizing her every move.

Redford forced himself to ignore her jibe. "His very particular attentions can only harm you in the eyes of the world," he insisted. "For once, Sylvia, can you not consider appearances and keep yourself from his company?" She noted that he was distressed enough to become less formal in his address.

She shrugged and started to step past him to re-enter the drawing room, but Redford caught her by the arm.

"You must listen to me," he said. "If you will not consider your own well-being, at least consider that of your family. Will you not take my word that he is a man to be avoided at all costs?"

Sylvia looked at him coolly. "Why ever would I do so?" she inquired.

Angered by her response and her evident lack of emotion, he looked down at her narrow white gown before he continued. "And why must you be so shameless in your choice of attire? Is it not enough that you have already scandalized the majority of polite society without again attracting the attention of gossips like Augusta Riverton because of your choice of dress?"

Sylvia smiled up at him, annoyingly unperturbed. "I don't recall your criticizing this dress before, Charles," she pointed out. "And it is precisely the same dress that I wore to the ball in Cairo when you told me that not even Cleopatra had ever looked so lovely."

She glanced at his toga significantly. "And I believe that costume is what you wore that night as well. You must have suspected that I might wear this gown tonight."

"I knew that you have so little regard for gossip that

you might very likely do exactly this," he said through gritted teeth. "You have no more sense of propriety than an infant!"

"I have been told that is one of my more endearing characteristics," Sylvia returned with a beatific smile.

"Only a besotted fool would say such a thing!" snapped Redford.

"Indeed?" she inquired gently. "I believe that you said that yourself, Charles, soon after you met me."

He stared at her for a moment as she slipped from his grasp and started toward the open window. She was not allowed to escape so easily, however. Catching her arm again, he pulled her to him roughly. Sylvia felt the hem of her skirt catch and tear on the rough surface of the brick lining a flower bed. There was no time to think of it, however, for she was once again closer to Charles Redford than she cared to be and it took all of her will power to maintain her cool composure.

"Never fear that it is happening again," he said defiantly. "I might have been besotted then, but I am anything other than that now!"

For a moment his closeness almost worked its old magic on Sylvia, and she could feel herself giving way. Then she forced herself to think of the young woman she had seen him with on Bond Street and again at the theatre. There had been no mistaking his proprietary air with her. It would be madness to allow him to suspect that she had any feelings left for him under the circumstances. The Danvilles might be eccentric, but they were proud as well. She would never give him the satisfaction of knowing that she still thought of him.

"Shall we go in?" she murmured absently, ignoring the tightening of his arm about her waist. "I believe that I am

engaged for the next dance. Lord Wilmington will be
waiting and it would be ill-bred to leave him standing
there."

"Sylvia!" Redford exclaimed impatiently. "Have you
attended to anything that I have said?"

"How could I have failed to hear you, Charles?" she
inquired pleasantly. "You have found fault with my appearance, my behavior, and my judgment. You have
made it exceedingly clear that you think me ill-dressed,
rude, and foolish."

His grip on her tightened, and she glanced down at his
arm and then up at him once more, again smiling gently.
"I can think of only one reason for your behavior, sir."

"And what is that?" he demanded.

Her eyes widened innocently, showing not a trace of
emotion. "Why, jealousy of course, Charles. What other
sensible reason could there be?"

She slipped from his grasp as he stared at her, and
turned toward the door again. However, he recovered
immediately and took her arm in his as they re-entered
the ballroom.

"You must know that you are absolutely incorrect in
your assumption," he murmured angrily, keeping his
voice low so that he would not be overheard and forcing
himself to smile at Lady Riverton, who waved to him
eagerly, anxious to know precisely what was happening
between them.

"Look at that!" he continued. "Augusta Riverton can't
wait to get her talons into me—and it is all because of
your outrageous behavior! How could you have brought
that child to London with you?"

It was her turn to stare at him, and she could feel the
anger rising white-hot within her. So Charles was of a

piece with the others! He had believed the story about Robert, not even bothering to ask her about it.

She wrenched away from him, caring little whether she were seen by Augusta Riverton or the whole of the *ton*. Before she had a chance to respond as she wished to, however, a tall woman in a full scarlet skirt and glittering with gold jewelry appeared beside her, looking into her face with great intensity. She caught both of Sylvia's hands in her own and turned them palm up in the candle-light. The nearby guests were startled by this bit of drama and paused in their dancing to see what was taking place. Lady Pendicott, who had been watching Sylvia and awaiting the opportunity to say something critical about her to Mrs. Vincent Payne, who was standing beside her, saw both Sylvia's angry expression and the movement of the gypsy and immediately drew closer.

Miss Bitfort-Raines edged forward eagerly, too. It had infuriated her to see Charles seek out Lady Sylvia, and she looked forward to this moment of humiliation with all of the intensity of one whose whole life has been lived in the shadow of another. She was determined now that there would be no more shadow. No longer would anyone regard Lady Sylvia as a dashing figure; instead, she would be an object of pity, mentioned with knowing smiles and laughter. She gestured to the orchestra to cease playing, and the music and the conversation of the masqueraders faded as they stared at the strange tableau before them.

Sylvia's words to Charles had died away in surprise. She wished to reclaim her hands, but before she could, the gypsy—for she realized suddenly that this *was* indeed another fortune-teller—had begun to speak in a deep voice that vibrated through the startled throng.

"I was asked to read your fortune, my lady—a fortune

given to me by another—but I must read what I see. There is great danger, my lady," Madame Zeena said, her voice carrying clearly through the crowded room. "It is a danger that encircles all of us here tonight."

A startled murmuring rippled through the crowd and Miss Bitford-Raines flushed. The idiot! Whatever did she think she was doing! She had not been hired to frighten the guests at the party—only to humiliate Lady Sylvia Danville. She felt her hands begin to clench.

When the murmuring had died away, Madame Zeena continued. "You will save all of us from this particular trouble, my lady—but it is not the only one that stands close to you."

There was a brief silence as she again studied Sylvia's face. "You and a child are in grave danger, my lady. Beware of those you think you know."

And with those words she was gone as suddenly as she had appeared, vanishing into the crowd. Sylvia found herself looking dozens of speculative, startled bystanders, Miss Bitfort-Raines among them, her face dark with fury, and she understood instantly who had hired the gypsy to read a special fortune for her, the fortune given to her "by another." She wondered briefly what that fortune might have been.

Always at her best in a crisis, Sylvia ignored her own reaction to this unnerving repetition of the warning she had heard in Cairo, complete now with a reference to Robert, and turned to Sir Charles, saying in a clear, sweet voice, "How like dear Claire to plan surprises for us. I don't wish to miss any of the other delights she may have arranged for the evening, Sir Charles, so I shall be as quick as I can in mending this rent in my gown."

Here she gestured to the small tear in the hem of her

skirt. "I shall rejoin you shortly." And so saying, she too disappeared into the crowd.

Miss Bitfort-Raines looked down at her hands, now clenched into fists. What had possessed Madame Zeena? She had paid the woman to deliver a specific message, not to conjure up one of her own, and certainly not to announce that she had been employed to deliver a prepared message. Hurrying to the anteroom where she was to meet the gypsy, she rehearsed what she would say to the woman.

"What can I say, lady?" shrugged Madame Zeena indifferently when she faced her angry employer moments later. "I must say what I see. And that is what I saw."

"Then I shall certainly not pay you!" replied Miss Bitfort-Raines angrily. "I wanted attention drawn to Lady Sylvia, but not in the way you did so. You have merely made everyone more fascinated by her than before."

"Remember the wolf and the hawk, lady," cautioned Madame Zeena. "Jealousy is something that will eat its owner. You must be very careful."

"You must be mad!" exclaimed Miss Bitfort-Raines. "I am not jealous of Sylvia Danville. Why, I—"

Here the gypsy held up her hand. "You will not pay me?" she asked.

"Under no circumstances!" exclaimed Miss Bitfort-Raines hotly. "Why, it is—"

"Then I must leave this place," returned Madame Zeena, ignoring the angry words of her former employer as she walked majestically from the room.

Miss Bitfort-Raines was left to her own thoughts, and they were not pretty ones. Once again her plan to put Lady Sylvia in her place had been scotched. Niles, arriving quietly at the door to the anteroom a few moments later, took one look at the expression of her mistress and returned to her room in the attic. There were times when it was best to leave Miss Bitfort-Raines alone and this clearly was one of them.

Chapter Seven

It was most strange, thought Sylvia as she made her way upstairs to find a quiet place to mend her gown, that two gypsies, hundreds of miles apart, would deliver essentially the same message to her. She stared down at the palms of her hands. What had they seen there? Why had they looked so closely into her face? She was beginning to feel more and more uneasy.

What was the danger that threatened them? Why would Robert—the only child connected with her—be in danger? And whatever—or whoever—was she to beware of? Who did she know that was not what he—or she—seemed to be? Still turning these questions over in her mind, she opened the door to a quiet chamber, took out her reticule and began the business of repairing her skirt. As she worked, she suddenly became aware of voices in the adjoining room, those of a young woman and a man. She could not distinguish what they were saying until the young woman's voice rose sharply.

"Let go of me!" she exclaimed, her voice growing hysterical. The sound of a scream was cut off abruptly.

Sylvia arose quickly and stole silently to the door connecting the two chambers. She opened it soundlessly and saw the dark young woman who had been with Charles struggling in the hold of a tall man in a black domino. One of the girl's hands was clutching her throat and she appeared to be choking.

"Let go of her!" exclaimed Sylvia sharply.

The man's head jerked up, his face still securely covered by his mask, but he did not release his hold. Instead, one hand fumbled at the clasp of the young woman's necklace. Seeing this, Sylvia, still gripping the sharp, dainty scissors she had been using, marched over to them and jabbed their full length into the man's hand.

Cursing, he dropped the girl to the floor and fled the way Sylvia had come, slamming shut the door to that chamber. Sylvia helped the sobbing girl to her feet and settled her comfortably in a chair, taking a handkerchief from her reticule.

"Just wipe your eyes, my dear," she said reassuringly. "You are quite all right now."

"I don't know who he was," the girl sobbed. "I came up here to pin up my costume where I had torn it. I looked up and suddenly he was there—and he wouldn't let me go."

"Well, he did let you go," replied Sylvia comfortably. "He was probably not even an invited guest—just someone who had gotten himself in for the evening. Perhaps even a footman hired for the occasion. In any event, you need not worry about him any longer."

"Yes, I do thank you!" exclaimed the girl, wiping her eyes with a handkerchief from Sylvia's reticule. "However did you make him release me?"

Sylvia smiled and held up a dainty sewing kit. "I have discovered that I seem always to catch my gown upon something when I am dancing, so I carry this in my reticule. He seemed to have an aversion to scissors." She patted the young girl's arm comfortingly and repeated her reassurance. "At any rate, he has gone and we need not worry that he will put in another appearance."

And to be certain of the truth of her words, she opened the door to the adjoining chamber, her scissors poised for another attack should it prove necessary. What she saw there caused her to forget the needle, however.

In his dash through the room, the intruder had apparently overset the candelabra on the dressing table, and hungry flames were even now licking at the base of the heavy velvet draperies. It would not be long before they spread. Sylvia looked quickly about the room, seeing only a pitcher of water that was certainly not adequate to extinguish the flames. Grateful for the narrowness of her skirt that kept it from swinging into the flames, she jerked as hard as she could at the draperies, finally managing to bring down one panel.

It collapsed onto the carpet and she dropped its heavy folds as nearly as she could over the flames, using a fireplace poker to press down the fabric. She paused long enough to pull down a curtain from the bed and throw it on top of the other drapery. When the tester came cascading down, too, Sylvia added it to the stack, hoping to smother the flames completely.

Closing the door firmly behind her, she rushed back into the other bedchamber and pulled the young woman from her chair.

"There is a fire," Sylvia explained, guiding her firmly toward the door. "We must alert the others before it spreads!"

And together they ran down the stairs, Sylvia moving

as quickly as her narrow shift would allow. At the bottom of the stairway stood two footmen, watching their head-long descent with wide eyes. Sylvia explained the situation rapidly, sending one to the servants' hall for help to fight the fire and the other ahead to alert the butler that the house must be vacated immediately. Then she hurried to the ballroom to begin the process, trying not to think of what would happen if there were a panic and everyone tried to crowd through the narrow entranceway to the street.

She looked about quickly for one of the Bitfort-Raines family. When she could find no one, she hurried through the crowd to the orchestra, motioning for the conductor to stop the music. Startled, he broke off in the midst of another waltz, and the dancers stopped where they were, staring at Lady Sylvia standing in front of the orchestra.

"Please make your way very quickly to the entrance hall and out the front doors," she announced in a clear, strong voice. "The butler has opened those doors and will help you to your carriages."

"Lady Sylvia, why are you giving orders in my father's home?" demanded Miss Bitfort-Raines from a corner of the room. "What new game are you playing at now?"

There was no movement in the audience as they looked from one young woman to the other, and Sylvia, fearful that the fire was spreading and that they would all be caught inside, turned to the crowd and cried, "There is a fire upstairs and we must move quickly before it spreads."

That warning served to galvanize the group, and it was a matter of only a few minutes before the house was cleared entirely. The majority of the party gathered at a safe distance from the house, watching the flickering of the flames in the second-floor windows and speculating about the extent of the damage. The story of the attack of the unknown masked intruder and Lady's Sylvia's rescue spread through the group.

Miss Bitfort-Raines watched bitterly as a crowd assembled around Lady Sylvia, demanding details of her story and congratulating her upon her quick actions.

"We could have been burnt to a cinder if that Danville girl hadn't acted as she did!" exclaimed Lady Riverton, surveying the scene from the comfort and security of her sedan chair.

"Nonsense!" replied Miss Bitfort-Raines sharply, overhearing her. "One of the servants would have told us soon enough."

Lady Riverton snorted inelegantly. "We would have been toasted, Claire, if we had waited for one of the servants to rescue us, and well you know it. And don't go pinching at me merely because Sylvia Danville has put your nose out of joint again!"

Before she was forced to reply to this facer, Miss Bitfort-Raines was rescued by the appearance of her father, mopping his brow.

"What has happened, Harold? You may tell me the worst!" exclaimed Miss Bitfort-Raines's tearful mama, clinging to his arm. "Have we lost everything?"

"No, indeed, my dear," he responded. "Thanks to the young lady's quick thinking, the fire was contained in one area. In fact," he added in a hearty voice, "I see no reason that those of us still here may not go back in and have the rest of our masquerade."

A murmur of approbation ran through the crowd, and soon everyone was once again inside, listening to the orchestra and sipping champagne as they crowded around the refreshment tables. Miss Bitfort-Raines could not have been more chagrined. Everywhere she turned, she heard new accounts of Lady Sylvia's quickness and bravery. Nor was that to be her only burden.

As she approached Diana Redford, that young lady seized her hand and pulled her eagerly over to Lady Sylvia's side.

"And this, Claire, is the young lady who saved me from the attack of the stranger just before the fire." She turned to smile at Sylvia. "And I am afraid that I don't even know your name to thank you properly."

Sir Charles Redford, who had been inside with Mr. Bitfort-Raines, raised his eyebrows. "What are you talking about, Diana?" he demanded. "Are you telling me that *you* were the subject of the attack? You mentioned nothing of this to me."

"I didn't have the opportunity, Charles," she responded contritely, "or I would have. Everything happened much too quickly for me."

She turned again to Sylvia and extended her hand. "I didn't even have a chance to thank you, miss. Nor to introduce myself. I am Diana Redford."

Sylvia's throat tightened. So this was Charles's young sister. She had not met Diana during the time of their engagement because she had not been in London when they arrived and their engagement had been broken very quickly thereafter.

Taking herself in hand, she smiled at the young girl. If she had been more alert, she would have noticed Diana's resemblance to Charles sooner. Both were dark and tall, with the same striking profile and the same easy grace.

She smiled at Diana. "I am delighted to meet you, Miss Redford. I hope that you have quite recovered from your fright."

Diana laughed. "I would like to have seen the man's face under that mask when you stabbed him with your scissors."

Charles stared at Sylvia. "Have you now taken to assaulting people, Lady Sylvia?" he inquired. "Not that I am surprised, of course," he added dryly.

Diana looked at her brother, surprised by his tone. "Do you know one other, Charles?" she asked.

"Permit me to introduce you, Diana. This is Lady Sylvia Danville. We met some years ago in Egypt."

He turned to Sylvia and bowed. "I am, of course, not surprised, Lady Sylvia, to discover that you had a part in this evening's madness."

His sister's eyebrows drew together. "Whatever is the matter with you, Charles?" she demanded. "Lady Sylvia saved me from a man who was choking me for the diamond necklace you just chose for me, and she saved all of us from a fire that could have destroyed the house and us with it."

Redford bowed more deeply. "My profound apologies, Lady Sylvia," he said dryly. "You appear to have found a champion—and a new way of making a spectacle of yourself."

Diana cleared her throat, obviously displeased with him.

"I had cautioned you, Charles, that it was most unsuitable to give diamonds to a girl just coming out," said Miss Bitfort-Raines. "And you see now that I was quite correct."

"Claire, you know that he would have gotten me pearls had we not seen the necklace so much like dear Mama's. It was her favorite, you see, Lady Sylvia," said Diana in explanation, "and it was lost just before her death. So

Charles gave way when I begged him for it. He must not be blamed when he was merely being kind."

Miss Bitfort-Raines dismissed her explanation with a sniff, but Lady Sylvia, interested in this new view of Redford as an indulgent brother, looked at him appraisingly.

Keenly aware that she had once again betrayed him into an unforgivable rudeness, Redford added in a politer voice, "My sister is having her first season in London, so all of this is quite new to her. I would like to thank you for rescuing her from what must have been a most unpleasant experience."

Sylvia returned his bow coolly. "I was delighted to be of assistance. I only wish that he had not been so careless in his making his exit; then we might have been spared the fire."

"I am certain that you wish it no more than I, Lady Sylvia," said Miss Bitfort-Raines dryly. "Had it not been for your rashness, we might have had the bedchamber and draperies intact."

"Why, Claire!" exclaimed Diana in surprise. "What a ridiculous thing to say! The fire was not Lady Sylvia's fault! What if it had been allowed to go unchecked? We should all have died right here where we stand!"

"You are too kind," returned Lady Sylvia. "I am certain that someone else would have stopped it." She started to move away to rejoin Lord Wilmington, when the voice of Miss Bitfort-Raines stopped her.

"Will you not wish us happy, Lady Sylvia?" she inquired archly, slipping her arm through Redford's and holding her hand where the candlelight sparkled upon the same amethyst ring that Sylvia had worn. It had been, he had told her long ago in Egypt, his mother's engagement ring.

Sylvia looked up quickly and saw the flush that colored Redford's cheeks and the triumphant light in the eyes of Miss Bitfort-Raines. She forced herself to smile absently and murmur, "But, of course, Miss Bitfort-Raines. How very lovely for both of you. You seem made for one another."

Inside, however, her stomach was churning. There would be no question now of whether or not she should re-establish the relationship with Charles. There was nothing left to establish. He had planned his future and there was no room left in it for her. For a blinding moment she was certain that she had wanted him, no matter how stuffy he was, but her pride quickly asserted itself and she reminded herself that he had believed the rumors about Robert.

She carefully avoided catching his eye and turned instead to Wilmington, who was waiting for her patiently. The lilting melody of another dance filled the evening air as she smiled at him.

"Shall we, my lord?" she inquired brightly.

"I have waited a lifetime, dear lady," he replied gallantly, bowing to the others and then sweeping her onto the dance floor.

And Miss Bitfort-Raines was left with the somewhat limited satisfaction of watching her fiancé stare gloomily after them. Determined not to be outdone again by Lady Sylvia, she held out her hand to him.

"And shall *we*, Charles?" she asked coyly.

"Shall we what?" he demanded, still not looking at her.

"Dance, of course, Charles! Wherever is your mind?" she returned, her voice becoming sharp.

Redford did not reply, nor did he seem to be attending to her at all. She held out her hand to him and together Marie Antoinette and her Marc Antony joined the other masqueraders on the dance floor.

Chapter Eight

On the following morning, Sylvia found her drawing room filled to overflowing with callers, flowers, and invitations. She might have done herself significant damage by the affair with Robert, but acting with such presence of mind at the Bitfort-Raines' home had reminded the *ton* of their reasons for delighting in Lady Sylvia: not only had she provided them with food for conversation, but she had also done it with style.

"Nothing of the commoner about *her*," said Augusta Riverton significantly for the fifth time that morning. Lady Riverton had carried the story from house to house in the first wave of callers, arriving finally at Danville House. Miss Bitfort-Raines had fared less well in her tale.

And so, although the matter of Robert was not forgotten, it was, for the moment at least, forgiven. It was a triumph for Lady Sylvia and a resounding defeat for Claire Bitfort-Raines. Those standing nearest to Madame Zeena last night had heard her words quite clearly and had had no difficulty in working out just what Miss Bitfort-Raines had planned.

"It was only to be expected," said Lady Riverton knowingly as they awaited the arrival of Lady Sylvia. "Claire Bitfort-Raines has always been a spiteful little cat. It must have weighed heavily upon her that Sylvia Danville had Charles Redford before she did. She never could abide the attention Sylvia got and having her cast-off wares for a husband must have been the final straw."

"I don't believe that I would refer to Sir Charles as 'cast-off wares,' Augusta," said Lady Digby reprovingly. "He is quite a fine young man, you know. Claire has nothing to be ashamed of there."

"Yes, but that may be just the trouble, Jane," cackled Lady Riverton. "Does she *have* him to be ashamed of or not ashamed of? *I* saw him looking at Lady Sylvia last night even if you did not. It is the same old story—the men gather around her like moths around a candle flame."

Mrs. Ophelia Simpkins, basking with satisfaction in the reflected glow of the limelight, felt obligated to comment upon this remark. "And that is no fault of her own, Augusta. She doesn't set out to allure them."

Lady Riverton stabbed her cane impatiently at the floor. "Lord, no, Ophelia! Who said that she did? She didn't do so any more than the candle sets out to gather the moths, but it happens all the same!" She paused for a moment, then added smugly, "There are some of us who simply attract the men and that's all there is to it."

Since her young relative was being praised, Mrs. Simpkins allowed this provocative comment to pass unchallenged, merely reflecting that Augusta Riverton grew more odiously puffed-up with each passing year. It was ridiculous that a woman with one foot in the grave was still as vain as a seventeen-year-old. One would think that a single glance in her dressing table glass would prevent her making such outrageous remarks.

Fortunately, the appearance of Lady Sylvia herself in the drawing room gave the conversation another turn, and her callers bombarded her with questions, anxious to have her version of the episode. Even Lady Pendicott, who had watched her every possible moment at the Bitfort-Raines' ball, fully prepared to tear her reputation to shreds, was one of the group, hoping even now that Sylvia would disgrace herself.

"And weren't you afraid for your life, Lady Sylvia?" asked Annabelle Pendicott in a breathless voice after Lady Riverton had given a dramatic account of the encounter with the intruder.

Sylvia, who was growing weary of the whole business, shook her head and laughed. "I daresay I would have been if I had had time to consider the matter—but you must remember, Miss Pendicott, that I was armed. It might have been quite otherwise if I had not had my weapon."

"I suppose that all the young ladies will take to carrying scissors in their reticules now," remarked Lady Pendicott dourly.

"They could do far worse than imitate Lady Sylvia!" said Arthur Ashby, taking exception to Lady Pendicott's tone of voice. "I don't know of another young lady in London who could have managed to do what she did last night."

There was a murmur of agreement and Lady Pendicott retired from the lists, defeated.

Sylvia was relieved when the last of her callers departed, and was about to retire to the nursery to see

Robert, when another late caller was announced. It was Miss Diana Redford.

"I am sorry to be so late, Lady Sylvia," she announced cheerfully, smoothing her dark curls as she sat down. "I had intended to be among the first of your callers today, but I slept far longer than I normally do and my maid didn't awaken me."

"Nor should she have," said Sylvia. "You must have been exhausted after your experience last night. You needed your rest."

"No more than you," she replied. "I have come, of course, to thank you again for rescuing me—and to apologize."

Sylvia looked at her blankly. "Whatever for? You have done nothing that requires an apology."

Miss Redford's cheeks grew pink. "I did not realize that there was once a—an attachment between you and my brother, Lady Sylvia. I am afraid that I made a fearful mull of everything last night, introducing you to Charles in the presence of Miss Bitfort-Raines."

"Not at all," responded Sylvia cheerfully, determined to set her at her ease. Charles had undoubtedly taken his sister to task last night, and she longed to tell him what she thought of his officious ways. The child had endured enough turmoil for one evening without having him set upon her about an affair long dead. "It was long ago and very brief, so there was no reason for you to give it a thought. I assure you that *I* did not blame you in the least."

"I must confess that I did not think that you would have," said Miss Redford, brightening. "In fact, I told Claire that you seemed to me most unconcerned about seeing Charles and hearing of their engagement." She did not add that her brother had not appeared particularly pleased by that bit of information.

"And so I was," agreed Sylvia. "I'm afraid that I had other things on my mind just then. I hope that I did not give offense to your brother."

"I don't think that you did," she responded, a little doubtfully, "although he did poker up when I tried to ask him a little about your relationship. But then Charles is always very formal, and I daresay he felt that I was being too inquisitive."

Sylvia, liking her frankness and innocence, answered warmly. "That is very much his way, I fear. He follows a strict code of behavior himself, and he demands that those about him do the same."

"Yes, he sets a very high standard, does he not?" agreed Miss Redford, relieved to see that she understood. "But he is, of course, usually correct," she added, unwilling to be disloyal.

Sylvia, who certainly did not agree with this comment, nonetheless admired her for defending him, and turned the conversation into more agreeable avenues. As a result, when the two ladies parted company thirty minutes later, they were very pleased with one another, and each was determined to pursue the relationship.

"I cannot imagine why your engagement with Lady Sylvia did not prosper," Miss Redford remarked to her brother later that evening in the privacy of their own dining room. "She seems a lovely person—and her time in Egypt has been so interesting."

He looked up, startled. "What would you know about that? Did you see her today?" he demanded.

Miss Redford looked indignant. "Naturally I did, Charles! Do you think that I am so rag-mannered that I would not call upon her after what she did for me last night? Whatever would she think of me?"

Sir Charles sighed. Their parents had died five years ago, within days of one another, and the care of Diana had fallen upon his shoulders. It had not been a heavy burden, for she had been an agreeable, manageable child, but if she cultivated the relationship with Sylvia Danville, he saw deep waters ahead.

"Of course you must do the proper thing, Diana," he responded. "It simply did not occur to me that you would call upon her. This has been a busy day for me."

And most certainly it had been. Just calming Claire had taken the better portion of the morning. Nor was he looking forward to calling upon her after dinner and listening to more of her recriminations. She was normally a rather reserved and quiet person, but she had been outspokenly bitter about his appearance in the guise of Marc Antony, attributing his defection to the unwholesome influence of Lady Sylvia.

In fact, to hear her tell it, Sylvia was at the root of all of the trouble stemming from the masquerade. The fire would never have occurred if she had not attacked the intruder, causing him to overturn the candelabra in his mad dash from the chamber. He had patiently pointed out that the intruder had been attacking his sister, whose throat bore the bruises of the assault, and that the consequences for Diana might have been even more dire had Lady Sylvia not intervened.

"I might have known that you would take her part, Charles!" she had exclaimed angrily. "But it is because of her rashness that our home was damaged and my ball ruined!"

"She had no way of knowing that the man would begin

a fire, Claire," he had returned, beginning to lose patience, "and I for one am most grateful that nothing more happened to Diana." He attempted to steer the conversation into safer channels. "Have you any idea how the man gained entrance to your home?"

This did not prove to be a happy choice of comment, for his lady bristled defensively.

"I might have known, Charles, that somehow this whole fiasco would be blamed upon me! You put me out of all patience with you! At the very least, you should feel some decent amount of sympathy for what *I* have undergone!"

It was at this point that he had given up all hope of making her regard the situation rationally. Since he had been accustomed to thinking of her as a sensible woman, he was displeased at this new view of her. However, upon reflection, he was inclined to agree with her at least partially: none of this would have occurred if Lady Sylvia Danville had not arrived upon the scene. He knew Lady Sylvia's comment about his jealousy of her new relationship to be nonsensical, but that her behavior was troublesome to him was undeniable. She was always the proverbial thorn in his flesh.

Claire had made no allusion to Madame Zeena's words, but he was aware from what had passed that evening that she had been planning something for Sylvia and that the exposure of her plan was what had overset her so severely. Although he knew that Claire had been wrong, he felt that Lady Sylvia was actually to blame for her poor behavior. She seemed to bring out the worst in those about her. And he had no desire to see his young sister further her acquaintance with one so obviously dangerous.

It was with that it mind that he called upon Sylvia the Monday after the masquerade. She was with Robert when he was shown into the drawing room, and, giving the child a kiss on the top of the head, she relinquished him to the butler to be taken back to the nursery and Sally. She was less than pleased to see her guest, but she forced herself to retain her composure and extend her hand to him.

"How kind of you to call, Sir Charles," she said pleasantly, being careful to show no reaction to his touch. His hand was still as warm and firm, his eyes as dark and bright as she remembered them, but she allowed herself no response.

He looked at her quizzically, knowing how little she meant her words, but responded in the same cool and distant manner, grateful that she was trying for a little conduct. He bowed briefly over her hand.

"I wished to thank you again for your actions on behalf of my sister," he said stiffly.

"I did not realize at the time, of course, that she was your sister, Sir Charles, but I would have acted in the same manner for anyone," she responded, her manner equally as stiff. "It was no great affair, at any rate, and it has been made far too much of. I hope that your sister has recovered from the shock of the attack."

"She is quite well, thanks to you, although it will take some time for the bruises to fade, of course. I am grateful that it was not more serious than that."

"Do they have any idea of the man's identity?" asked Sylvia. "Have there been such problems at other large parties?"

"Not that I am aware of," acknowledged Redford reluctantly. "And the Bitfort-Raines are at a loss to explain why he put in an appearance at their party."

"He was not one of the guests, I am quite certain," said Sylvia. "His hands were rather coarse and rough, the hands of a working man, I would say."

Redford looked interested. "One of the servants, perhaps," he commented. "There were several brought in for the occasion. Although the butler thought he could account for the presence of all of them at the time of the fire, it is certainly possible that one of them escaped his notice."

He was anxious to pursue the matter, but it occurred to him suddenly that he had not come merely to conduct an investigation. He had come about a far more serious matter: his sister. Redford forced himself to bring the conversation back to her.

"My sister, as I am sure you know, Lady Sylvia, is most grateful to you for your help."

She nodded briefly and waited for him to continue, her eyes beginning to gleam. He looked distinctly uncomfortable and she was going to do nothing to relieve that discomfort.

"And naturally we are all grateful for you taking the quick action that saved the house from any further damage."

If Sylvia thought it unusual that neither Miss Bitfort-Raines nor her parents had called to express their appreciation, she did not say so. Mr. Bitfort-Raines had written a hurried note and sent flowers the day before, saying that his wife was remaining in bed to recover from the shock to her nerves. There had been no mention, however, of his daughter. Sylvia found it difficult to imagine that Miss Bitfort-Raines had taken to her bed with a nervous condition; she thought it far more likely that the young lady had taken a pet and was sulking in her room.

There was another lengthy pause while he tried to determine the best way to handle the situation. Lady Sylvia merely sat quietly, her hands folded in her silken lap, her amusement at his predicament showing in her bright eyes and the upward curve of her lips. One glance at her told him that there would be no help from that quarter, and his irritation with her began to grow.

"The difficulty, my lady, lies in Diana's impressionable nature. She is very young, and you have caught her imagination through your courage."

There was another long pause as he struggled with the problem. "I understand that she called upon you yesterday morning," he said finally.

Sylvia nodded.

"And you expect her to call again this morning?"

Again Sylvia nodded.

"What I would like, my lady, is for you to be elsewhere when she comes to call. It would be a simple matter to have your butler inform Diana that you are engaged."

"And why would I do such an unmannerly thing, Sir Charles?" she asked coldly, knowing precisely why he was asking this of her.

"Because you know full well, Lady Sylvia, that you are not a person whose company will be beneficial to her. You are intimate with such people as Lord Wilmington, whose reputation is questionable at best, and the Mannerings, who are not people of our station. You are also, as always, the talk of the town, a magnet for the attention of others. A young girl spending time in your company would inevitably draw the same sort of notoriety to herself. I do not wish that for Diana."

"Then why do you not tell Diana this, Sir Charles?" Sylvia demanded, certain of his reply.

There was another pause. "She would not be inclined to accept my reasons," he acknowledged reluctantly. "She is, after all, very young and inexperienced, and for the moment she looks upon you as a heroine. She would think me most unkind to forbid her to see you."

"And so, Sir Charles, you would like for me to be the one who appears unkind?" she asked coldly.

A little discomposed to hear it phrased in just this bald a manner, Sir Charles hesitated, then nodded his head. "Yes," he responded simply.

"And if I do not feel that I can oblige you?" she asked.

He shrugged. "Then I shall have to try to handle it my own way," he replied.

"And so you should," said Sylvia briefly. "I can think of no reason that I should undertake this for you. I find your sister a very agreeable young woman, and I shall not be so mannerless as to refuse her entrance to my home. If you wish it otherwise, you shall have to arrange it, Sir Charles."

"I might have known that you would take this attitude," he said, rising as he spoke.

"Yes, I think you might have," returned Sylvia frankly. "I have never been less than honest with you, sir. You are the one whose tastes run to deception. You appear to have a happy relationship with your sister. If you wish to keep it, I would suggest that you be more straightforward in your dealings with her than you were with me."

Redford, rigid with anger, bowed to her and took his leave. As the door opened to let him out, Diana's carriage pulled up at the curb. For a moment he paused, thinking that he might enter it and tell her his wishes directly.

Then, unhappy at the thought of the confrontation and uncertain of the best approach, he simply bid her good morning and departed.

Sylvia watched him from her drawing room window. She had felt a brief rising of hope when he hesitated on the doorstep, but when he had turned and walked away, she had allowed the curtain to fall back into place and resumed her place on the sofa.

Charles Redford would never be able to fight his natural inclinations, she reflected. He would have preferred that she do his dirty work for him, allowing Diana to think that she felt no interest in her while he maintained his status as the loving brother.

She was astounded to think that she had once been in love with the man. Then, unable to be less than honest with herself, she acknowledged that she was still astounded. Whether or not she liked it, she knew that he still had a place in her heart. Even with the gypsies' warnings, she could not dismiss him completely. And she had not a doubt that he was the dark man they referred to—though she could see no possible reason for fearing him.

Well, she had had a taste of the reality of Sir Charles Redford, she told herself. Enough to remember precisely what he was like. Surely if she continued to observe him, she would grow disenchanted and be able to dismiss the memories of him.

And clinging to that hope, she turned to smile and greet Miss Diana Redford. She was a charming young woman, and by no means deserved the sort of Turkish treatment her brother had recommended. Charles was absolutely incorrect in his thinking: Diana Redford would come to no harm through their friendship.

Chapter Nine

During Diana's call that morning, the Mannerings put in an appearance. They had been absent for a few days, having gone to call upon their grandmother in the country. Upon their return, they had heard the story of the fire and had called immediately to receive a full account of it.

"And this is the young lady that you saved!" exclaimed Amelia upon being presented to Miss Redford. "You must tell me exactly what happened, my dear!" she said, turning to Diana. "I'm sure that if I had been in your place, I should have fainted dead away. There would not have been enough smelling salts in London to revive me!"

Diana laughed, and Gerard Mannering rebuked her with a twinkle in his eye. "She speaks only the truth, Miss Redford. Why, I have seen her go to pieces when she merely *hears* a frightening tale. To play a part in one would be entirely beyond her. But *you*, I understand, actually struggled with the fellow."

"Indeed she did," said Sylvia. "I was afraid for her because she *was* struggling. Had she gone limp in his arms, he might have caused her less pain."

"Were you injured, Miss Redford?" asked Amelia, her tone becoming concerned. "I had not realized that."

"She has a ring of bruises around her throat," replied Sylvia. "The man tried to rip the necklace away and fairly choked her in doing so."

"How dreadful!" exclaimed Amelia, her hand going to her own smooth throat.

"She was most fortunate to have Lady Sylvia close by," said Lord Wilmington smoothly. He had entered the room unannounced and stood quietly just inside the doors.

"Why did Pelton not announce you, my lord?" asked Sylvia, rising to give him both her hands. "I shall have to scold him for being so remiss."

"I pray that you will do nothing of the sort, dear lady," replied Wilmington. "He wished to do so, but I told him that I know my way quite well and do not stand on ceremony."

Gerard Mannering frowned a little at his words. It seemed to him that Wilmington was a rather dangerous customer to have running tame in the household. Particularly when Lady Sylvia's parents were so very far away. Nonetheless, he made his bow and smiled in a perfunctory way at Wilmington.

The ladies welcomed him, for he had the pleasing manners and easy grace that must always make a gentleman acceptable in any company. He leaned toward Amelia, saying, "I understand, Miss Mannering, that it was you and your brother that made Lady Sylvia's journey to London such a pleasant one. I am obliged to you for that."

Amelia dimpled and responded lightly, but Gerard frowned more deeply. Whatever did the fellow mean by saying that he was obliged to them for making Lady Sylvia's journey pleasant? What had that to do with him? He seemed to be taking entirely too much upon himself, and Gerard resolved to watch him closely.

He had heard some of the conversations about Wilmington, and he remembered the words of Adrian Chambers about the man. "If he ain't a dirty dish," Chambers had announced to a group of his cronies one evening at a very discreet gambling establishment, "he's so close to being one that it makes no odds. Why, I ain't even sure that I would play cards with the fellow." And Adrian Chambers was scarcely the most particular of men, having spent his own fair share of time drinking blue ruin at Mother Tucker's and gambling in some of the more questionable hells. Mannering, who was present in the room although not a member of Chambers's party, had thought that if a man like Chambers so distrusted Wilmington, he was undoubtedly an individual to avoid.

The Mannerings had heard the gossip about Robert, but they had chosen not to mention the matter to Sylvia. They had seen the child on their journey to London of course, but Sylvia had never explained the relationship and, although they had been curious, they were much too well-bred to ask prying questions. Despite Sir Charles's rather slighting reference to their station, their manners were impeccable.

As Gerard watched Wilmington's behavior now, he became increasingly uneasy. He knew that the man had been a visitor with the Danvilles several times during their past few years in Egypt. And what he knew, the *ton* must know as well. He had heard the rumors of Robert's parentage, and he noted Wilmington's dark good looks. If he were frequently seen in Lady Sylvia's company, it would be only a matter of days before speculation arose about *his* relationship to Robert.

Both sister and brother had grown very fond of the lively Sylvia, and they had no desire to see her reputation abused. Mannering determined that they would spend as much time as possible with her; it was conceivable that their presence would help to protect her. At the very least, it might help to keep Wilmington at a safe distance.

"Is there something amiss, Mr. Mannering?" inquired Lord Wilmington, lifting his glass and studying that young man carefully. When he discovered that the Mannerings had become a part of Lady Sylvia's life, he had set out to discover what he could about them. He knew that they were moderately well-to-do, the grandchildren of a wealthy cit. They were well educated and agreeable and they traveled on the fringes of the *ton*, their birth precluding a firmer footing in that exclusive portion of society.

Flushing a little under his appraising eye, Gerard smiled and replied, "Not at all, my lord. I was simply lost in admiration for these two courageous young ladies."

Diana and Sylvia laughingly disclaimed their right to such a compliment, and the conversation turned to more pleasant topics. Nonetheless, Mannering determined that he would be watchful. He had no doubt that Wilmington was a dangerous man.

By the time the callers took their leave, arrangements had been made to ride together in the park later that same afternoon, and to attend the theatre that evening. Miss Redford was included in their plans, and Mr. Mannering had engaged to bring a friend of his along to provide even numbers for the group.

"I would be delighted to have you come, my dear," Sylvia had said to Diana, pulling her quietly to one side before her departure, "but perhaps your brother would not wish for you to accompany us."

Her conscience had troubled her a little, for after hearing Redford's comments on Lord Wilmington, it seemed the outside of enough to take his own young sister into that gentleman's orbit of influence. Even though she had dismissed his accusations as the workings of a jealous mind, she did not wish to take the risk of hurting Diana by exposing her to such a hardened flirt.

"Nonsense!" that young lady had replied, however. "Charles wouldn't mind at all—and besides, he is out of town for the next two evenings. So there will be no problem at all."

Sylvia allowed herself to be satisfied with that, for she planned to be certain that Wilmington had little chance of conversation with Diana alone. She was relieved that they were merely going riding and to the theatre, rather than to Vauxhall for the evening as Lord Wilmington had originally suggested. She and Gerard Mannering had overridden that idea immediately. She had no wish to make Diana's brother an enemy for life through her own negligence. And if it had occurred to her that Wilmington was also a dark gentleman, she did not allow the thought to linger.

The afternoon and evening passed most pleasantly. Gerard Mannering's friend, an amiable—and obviously harmless—young gentleman named Nelson Harriston, was the cousin of a family known to Sylvia, and so she felt that she could enjoy their outing with some peace of mind.

Despite Redford's comments about the Mannerings, she had no qualms about Gerard Mannering and Diana. Gerard would always conduct himself as a gentleman.

Lord Wilmington was the only one that would bear watching. Well-bred though he was, he could not refrain from indulging in flirtations, and a young woman new to the *ton* could easily be susceptible to such attentions. Sylvia found his attentions amusing, but she had no intention of allowing Diana to suffer a broken heart, and so she intended to watch Wilmington like a hawk.

When they entered their box in the theatre that evening, Sylvia was careful to see that Diana was seated between young Mr. Harriston and Gerard. Lord Wilmington smiled as he watched her machinations.

"One would almost believe that you don't consider me a proper influence on the young, Lady Sylvia," he murmured as he took his place. "Or dare I hope that you are jealous?"

Sylvia laughed. Whatever his faults, Wilmington was unfailingly entertaining.

"But of course, my lord, how could I be anything other than jealous? Do you not leave broken hearts strewn behind you like leaves on an autumn wind?"

He looked pensive. "I sense, my lady, that you are not taking me seriously. And the fact that you have mentioned an autumn wind makes me fear that you think of me as an older man."

"Indeed not, Lord Wilmington," she responded briskly. "Other than your graying hair and your occasional shortness of breath when we have been walking vigorously in the park, I do not think that you have many of the failings of an older man."

Wilmington was a vain man who prided himself upon his fitness and fairly youthful appearance, but he was a man of humor as well. His laugh rang out through the theatre, causing several people to turn and stare at them.

"You show no mercy, my dear—that is one of the reasons I delight in you. You are absolutely truthful, even when I least wish to hear the truth."

Lady Sylvia smiled at him. "Then you will not be distressed, my lord, if I make a request of you." Here she lowered her voice so that no one else in the box could overhear her words. "You noted that I do not wish you to devote yourself to Miss Redford—and you were entirely correct. She has not had time to become accustomed to flirtations, and I would not wish to see her made unhappy."

"And is your concern because she is the sister of your Sir Charles?" he inquired, his eyebrows lifted.

"Not at all," she responded, her manner a little chilly. "I would feel the same about any young girl who was in your company because of me."

"I believe, dear lady, that your concern for Miss Redford is shared by other of her friends," he remarked dryly, his eyes on the seats below them.

Sylvia glanced down and stifled a groan. Below them sat Miss Bitfort-Raines and her mother, both of them staring at their box. It was clear from their expressions that they were not pleased to see Miss Redford in company with them. Diana had caught sight of them, too, and waved to them blithely. She received in return the briefest and most unsmiling of nods. Doubtless they were as horrified to see Miss Redford in her company as to see her with Lord Wilmington. Their manner informed Sylvia clearly that the unpleasant news of their outing would be shared as soon as possible with Sir Charles.

She sighed and promised herself that she would be more careful of Miss Redford in the future. At least for the moment she need only keep her eye on Lord Wilmington.

Once they had made it safely through the evening, she could find a way to keep this kind of situation from occurring again. Under no circumstances would she allow herself to be placed in the position of chaperone for Diana Redford. Delightful though she was, there were too many disadvantages to develop the relationship into a more intimate friendship. Having reached this decision, a sense of well-being filled her, and she prepared to enjoy the play.

Since her mind had been occupied with the problems at hand, Sylvia had not had the leisure to examine their situation more closely. Feeling that most of the problems had been elminated, she had just begun to relax and enjoy the evening when she saw a familiar figure below her. There was no mistaking him. It was Sir Charles Redford.

"How delightful to see him here tonight. Do you suppose he will join his sister or Miss Bitfort-Raines?" inquired Wilmington, following her startled gaze.

"I thought that he was out of town," murmured Sylvia to herself.

Wilmington smiled. "Now that does explain a great deal, my dear. But he doesn't appear to be, you know—he looks to be very much *here*."

His words proved to be prophetic. In a matter of minutes, the door to their box opened and Sir Charles Redford stood at their side.

"Charles!" gasped Miss Redford, looking up as he entered the box. "I did not think that you would be back from Lansing until Wednesday!"

"So it would seem," replied her brother pleasantly. "It appears that it was fortunate that I was compelled to change my plans. I do hate to overset your plans, but I am indeed here."

That was not an arguable statement, and the gentle-man did not appear approachable, so most of the group in the box wisely kept silence.

Lord Wilmington did not. He adjusted his glass and stared at Sir Charles. "Why so you are, Sir Charles," he responded with interest. "And I see that you are still the most fascinating of conversationalists."

"Diana," Redford continued quietly, ignoring the inter-ruption, "you will be leaving with me in just one moment. First, Lady Sylvia, I would like to speak to you alone."

And he opened the door leading to the hallway, waiting for her to precede him. She went quickly, anxious to have this unpleasant business over with. She heard the door click shut behind her, and she turned to face him.

"I can think of no reason that would adequately ex-plain your actions," he said in a low voice, his eyes on hers. "I must believe that it stems from a desire for ven-geance, however. I had not thought you capable of strik-ing at me through my sister, but I see that I did not read your character correctly."

He moved back to the door. "I will take her with me, Lady Sylvia. You and Lord Wilmington need not bother yourselves with escorting her home tonight. Nor need you bother on any other occasion, I assure you."

Sylvia made no attempt to stop him as he re-entered the box to claim his sister. After all, he was essentially correct, although she hadn't used Diana as a means of striking at him—or at least she had not been aware of any such intention.

Diana waved to her briefly, her face crimson with em-barrassment and anger, as Redford hurried her from the box, and the two of them disappeared into the crowd pouring down the stairs.

Chapter Ten

Sylvia was distressed by the incident with Diana Redford and her brother, but she was not unduly troubled. She knew that she had been indiscreet, but she knew also that she had been doing her best to protect Diana. If Charles Redford wished to think otherwise, then he was quite welcome to do so. And she had no doubt that he would. Had he not handled matters in his usual high-handed manner, thinking that he knew better than anyone else what should be done, they might have made less of a scene.

She chuckled as she thought of that. Making a scene did not perturb her in the least, but it was entirely out of character for Charles. Forcing a confrontation of any sort was alien to one of his temperament. He must have been mortified when his anger cooled and he considered what he had done, enacting a public spectacle simply because he had given way to his temper. And she was quite certain where he would lay the blame for that.

The second morning after their contretemps dawned bright and beautiful, and Sylvia determined that she would take Robert out with her to the park when she went

for her morning meditation and exercise. Thus far his few
walks had been with Sally and Povey, while she had
merely taken him on carriage rides to flaunt his presence
to the *ton*. He was accustomed to having the freedom of
the gardens at home in Egypt, and being kept so much in
the house was beginning to tell upon him. He was an
active, vigorous child, and exercise was a necessity for
him.

Sylvia was well aware of the reason she had not taken
him out more often: she had been too caught up in her
own affairs and she had merely used him to irritate those
who were criticizing her. She was impatient with herself
for her own selfishness and resolved that she would make
it up to him. They would go to the park. And they would
go early, long before most of the *ton* was abroad, so that
she knew she was doing this for Robert and not for her
own purposes.

Accordingly, they set out in the barouche after breakfast, much to Robert's delight. Once in the precincts of
the park, Sylvia had the driver stop and the two of them
alighted. She had managed to slip out without Povey's
knowledge, and Sally had been given leave to take the
morning for herself. A footman waited discreetly by the
carriage, for Sylvia had informed him that there would be
no need of his presence during their walk today.

Together the two of them ambled happily along the
country walks, Robert pointing eagerly at each linnet
pecking in the grass and each butterfly fluttering through
the flowers. When they emerged finally at the margin of
the lake, Robert amused himself by tossing tiny pebbles
into the water and watching the ever widening circles they
caused, and Sylvia seated herself upon a small bench in a
patch of sunlight to watch him. She reflected that their

choice of time had been excellent; they had encountered only a few people along the way and the peacefulness had done much to restore her sense of well-being.

It was not only Robert who felt confined in the city, she thought, laying plans for their immediate removal to Greystone. It did not seem to her that her dose of reality had done much toward dispelling the memories of Charles Redford. It had, however, clearly shown her once more how incompatible they were—and of course with his engagement, the whole question of whether or not she should change her mind about him was a moot point.

It seemed unlikely that he was the dark man in the gypsy's warning, but she found that she could not dismiss the matter lightly. Now that she had twice heard the same warning, her mind wandered frequently to the questions it raised. Who was the dark man? Was it Charles, as she had thought, the closer connection to her because of their long-ago engagement—or could it perhaps be Lord Wilmington, who had become so very attentive? Wilmington certainly seemed the likelier candidate. Charles was altogether too stodgy to be a villain. And what in her life was other than it seemed to be? And why would Robert be in danger, as the last gypsy had indicated?

As she turned that matter over in her mind, able to reach no conclusion, the warmth of the sun began to do its work, and she drowsed gently in its buttery rays. She was recalled to the present when she heard a cry from Robert. Sylvia jerked upright and stared about her, but she could see no sign of the child. Terrified, she glanced first at the lake, but she had heard no splash and she could see no sign of his having waded in.

Leaping from her bench, she ran back down the path the way they had come, pausing for a moment to listen for any sound that would indicate the direction Robert had taken. Seeing two gentlemen tooling along in a natty curricle, she ran toward them, quite unconscious that the ribbons of her bonnet had come loose and her shawl, brought to protect her from the coolness of the early morning, was trailing behind her.

"Have you seen a small boy?" she cried. "About so high?" And she indicated his height with her hand.

They shook their heads, startled by her manner and the disarray of her dress, but one of them, Arthur Ashby, had recognized her, and said swiftly, "How may we be of service to you, Lady Sylvia? Where is your carriage? Is the boy with a servant?"

She shook her head to his last question. "No, we were all alone. And the carriage and the servants are a full half-mile from here." And she cursed herself for her foolishness in leaving the footman behind.

In the distance, back toward the lake, they heard another cry, unmistakably the voice of a child, and she turned and raced in that direction, ignoring her bonnet as it fell to the grass. Arthur Ashby hastily handed the reins to his companion, then leaped lightly from his vehicle to follow her. Tall and long-limbed, he managed to cover the ground more swiftly than Sylvia and when he reached the edge of the lake he saw a child thrashing about in water just over his head. Without regard for his elegant buckskins or his finely starched linen, he waded into the water. It took only a few strides to reach Robert, who clung to him like a limpet, completing the soggy destruction of his beautifully arranged neckcloth.

As he waded back to shore with Robert in his arms, Mr. Chambers's companion, who had followed them as quickly as he could, bearing the discarded bonnet, regarded him with horror. "You might at least have removed your boots, Adrian," Boots Symington, so-called because of the tender attention bestowed upon his own flawless footwear, reproached him. "Just look at the ruin you have caused. Those Hessians will never be the same!"

"Boots, give me your jacket and don't talk us into a stupor! The boy will take a chill if you don't hurry!"

Mr. Symington looked at him in shocked disbelief. "You're going to use my new jacket, just made by Weston, to cover that soaking child? And I am to walk about in public in my shirt sleeves?"

"Here, sir, we will cover him with this!" said Sylvia, taking her shawl and wrapping it about the shivering boy.

Recalled by her gesture to a sense of duty as a gentleman, young Mr. Symington hastily removed his coat and laid it across the boy, tucking him in as well as he could and then turning his head from the wreckage of his wardrobe. Together they set off to make the trek to the abandoned curricle. They could see it in the distance, farther away than it should be now because, as Mr. Ashby pointed out crossly, his companion had failed to tether the horses properly.

The park was now beginning to be a little busier, and several riders passed them, regarding them with interest. Sylvia gave no thought to the appearance they must present, thinking only of Robert and what had happened to him, but the two young men accompanying her were painfully aware of the spectacle they were creating. Mr. Symington in particular was acutely conscious of his coatless state as he trotted in the wake of the other two.

One of the riders drew up sharply as he came even with them. "What has happened, Ashby?" he demanded abruptly. And Sylvia looked up to see Sir Charles Redford, seated on a magnificent chestnut. She was silent as Mr. Ashby gave a brief account of the accident. Commanding them to wait where they were, he turned back to find Lady Sylvia's carriage and send it to them.

The four of them waited, at least three of them grateful for the reprieve. Chambers in particular, carrying the soaking Robert, who had not relinquished his hold on his rescuer's neck, was happy for the opportunity to catch his breath. "Being a hero ain't all it's cracked up to be," he told a few of his cronies later, as the story made the rounds.

Mr. Symington, aware that he had cut a rather inglorious figure in the whole affair, spent the time wishing devoutly that he had stayed in bed that morning. Never again would he give way to Adrian's persuasive pictures of the joys of an early morning ramble.

"Dangerous, that's what it is!" he said later. "Damned dangerous! A fellow could be set upon by footpads or thrown into the lake! Or," he added darkly, alluding to his particular grievance, "you could have your wardrobe ripped from your back without so much as a by-your-leave!"

Sir Charles accompanied the barouche to pick them up, and he remained at Danville House after Ashby and Symington had departed. They had insisted upon escorting Lady Sylvia safely home, following the barouche in their curricle, Ashby's dripping figure the object of interest to the passing crowd.

The two rescuers were thanked profusely, but Symington had taken little comfort in that. He did, in fact, spend the remainder of the day in front of a fire with his valet constantly re-filling a steaming footbath. "Could have caught my death!" he was heard to mutter several times, in between sips of brandy taken to ward off any potentially life-threatening chills that might have been brought about by exposure to taking the early morning air without his jacket.

It did not appear that Robert had suffered any actual hurt, but he was thoroughly wet and just as thoroughly frightened. When questioned by Sylvia and Sir Charles, he could tell them very little. Someone had snatched him from behind while he was throwing his pebbles in the water, and had clapped a hand over his mouth. It was only a minute or two later, as they were hurrying down one of the paths, that the man's hand had slipped and Robert had been able to cry out. That had been what had awakened Sylvia.

Apparently Robert had never seen the man's face, nor did he know why he had been thrown in the lake. He told them that they had come to the road, and the man had stood there a minute of two, apparently looking for someone. Then they had seen riders in the distance, and the man holding him had cursed and turned back toward the lake. It was only moments later that Robert had felt himself flying through the air into the water.

"Do you know anything about this?" Redford asked Sylvia when they were alone. Povey and Sally had given Robert a warm bath and tucked him into bed with warming pans at his feet to ward off chills. Now Sally sat quietly sewing beside his bed as he drowsed.

"What should I know, Sir Charles?" she demanded angrily. "I know that I was unforgivably careless, taking Robert out by myself and then going to sleep instead of watching him! Why, he could have drowned, even if no one had snatched him up!"

And she turned away from him to the drawing room

windows, her shoulders shaking. She knew that the fault was hers and that it was not because of her that he was now safely in bed.

Sir Charles watched her, troubled by her tears, silent though they were. Lady Sylvia might give way to anger in front of others, but never to tears. The child was dearer to her than he would have expected. While he did not approve of her connection to Robert, he could honor her for her affection for him.

"The gypsy said this, you know," she said grimly, straightening her shoulders as she regained her composure. "She said that Robert was in danger and I did not really believe her."

"Nor should you have!" he answered sharply. "I cannot believe that you would credit such nonsense!"

"Normally I would not," she replied, turning to face him. "But think about it, Sir Charles. How can I not treat it seriously? And how do I know that this is the last attempt that will be made to kidnap Robert? Perhaps it wasn't just a random act of cruelty."

He started to remark that there was no reason to suspect that another attempt would be made, but the words stuck in his throat. If the kidnapping was not a random one, if someone wished to hurt Lady Sylvia, it might well occur again. Then a sudden thought struck him. It was indeed odd that this had occurred so soon after the gypsy's warning. It could be, perhaps, that the gypsies themselves had a hand in this. It would bear looking into. He knew full well that Claire had arranged for the presence of the fortune-teller, and he could find out from her how to contact the woman.

"Danville House is well secured, is it not?" he asked abruptly. "And your servants are trustworthy?"

She looked at him in some surprise. "Yes, of course it is," she replied. "And our butler and housekeeper have been here for years. My father maintains only a skeleton staff during the time that we are away, but those have been with us forever."

"And new people are hired when you are in residence?"

She nodded. "Since we are here for so short a time, just the cook and an extra maid, and a footman or two have been hired."

"And your butler made those arrangements?"

"Yes, of course."

He nodded thoughtfully, saying, "I shall talk to him before I leave to be certain that all of the locks are secure and that they are checked carefully each night."

Sylvia stared at him, surprised. "That is very kind of you, Sir Charles. But I am quite certain that we shall be all right. Surely you cannot believe that we would be bothered at home."

"We will simply take precautions, Lady Sylvia. There is no sense in taking a chance. With your permission, I will make make this known to the local magistrate."

She nodded. "Thank you, Sir Charles. You have been far kinder than I would have—" She broke off here, realizing how ungracious she would sound, but he finished it for her.

"Than you would have expected me to be," he said. "That is a comment that I deserve, for no matter what my state of mind last night, I should have handled the matter more circumspectly."

Sylvia raised her eyebrows. "Is that an apology, Sir Charles?" she inquired, disbelief clear in her tone.

"My apology is for the manner in which I handled

things, madam. I still feel precisely as I did," Redford replied stiffly.

"You relieve my mind, Sir Charles," Sylvia responded lightly. "I had begun to fear that you were not yourself. Regret for the appearance of the deed, rather than the deed itself, fits more closely with my understanding of your character."

"I am sorry that I have offended you, madam," he returned, his face devoid of expression.

"Nor is that what you mean either, Sir Charles," she chided him gently. "You are not sorry at all. Rather, you wonder that I was so ill-bred as to say such a thing to you. I do wish, sir, that you would learn to be more forthcoming in your conversation. You are forever playing at appearances. You would have made a fine actor."

"You do me too much honor," Redford said dryly. "I believe that you are the one more capable of presenting a dramatic spectacle that an audience would appreciate. You have both the temperament and the experience."

"Now that is much better, Charles," said Sylvia approvingly, dropping formality for the moment. "You said precisely what you meant. For a moment you were entirely natural."

Redford simply bowed in response and removed himself from the room, feeling that saying anything else was pointless. Sylvia could twist any conversation to suit her own purposes. He would not allow himself to become ruffled by any of this, however. He had other matters to attend to: laying the information about the suspected kidnapping with the magistrate, and discovering the gypsy's whereabouts from Claire.

He decided to attend to the magistrate first; not only was that the more pressing matter, but it was also the more agreeable task. Claire, he was certain, would not wish to do anything helpful for Lady Sylvia, and she would suspect his motives in doing so. He could scarcely tell her that he felt some responsibility for this unpleasant situation, which had developed, he feared, out of Claire's jealousy.

Chapter Eleven

The interview with Claire was every bit as unpleasant as he had feared it would be. She had welcomed him with reservations, for her attitude had been cool since his choice of costume at the masquerade. Claire and her mother were having a late breakfast before shopping, and Mrs. Bitfort-Raines excused herself hastily soon after his arrival, saying that she had dozens of things to do before they left.

"Not that I mean to rush you, Charles," she said apologetically, because of course Claire would prefer to spend time with you. Nonetheless, we have a multitude of things to accomplish today. I shall just run along now and attend to some of them right now! Why don't the two of you retire to the morning room for your coffee? I will tell Briggs to serve you there." And she went bustling from the room.

"I didn't expect you, Charles," said Miss Bitfort-Raines, her voice as frosty as her eyes as she led him from the dining room. "You did not call yesterday morning as you normally do."

"No, I had some things to attend to, Claire. I escorted Diana to Lansing yesterday."

"To Lansing?" she asked in surprise. "Why did you take her there? I was under the impression that she had several engagements this week."

"She was obliged to break them. I felt that she had become too exhausted by the round of parties, and I thought that a little time in the country would help her to recover."

Claire stared at him blankly. "Diana—exhausted? Whatever are you talking about, Charles?"

He moved a little uncomfortably in his chair. "That is the story that we are telling others, Claire. I simply decided that she would be better off—in view of the recent developments—to spend some time away from London."

Miss Bitfort-Raines smiled widely. This was more than she had hoped for. "How very wise of you, Charles, to have removed her from the sphere of Lady Sylvia's influence. I am more glad than I can tell you that you listened to my advice. Of course, I had not thought of sending her to Lansing, since it is too accessible to London. I felt that sending her to her great-aunt's in Yorkshire would have been wiser."

Redford grew more uncomfortable. She was showing entirely too much pleasure in a situation that was painful both to him and to his sister. He was also annoyed that she was assuming that he had taken Diana to Lansing because of her advice. And he had told her at the time that sending Diana to their great-aunt's home was out of the question, not only because it was too far away, but also because the two ladies in question could spend no more than an afternoon together without wearing upon one another's nerves. No matter what her offense, he could not serve his sister such a trick.

"I appreciate your interest in my sister's welfare, Claire, but I assure you that I had made up my mind as to the best course of action before your advice," he replied, stirring his coffee with more vigor than was absolutely necessary.

Claire smiled and remarked in what he thought of as her most patronizing tone, "Of course you had, Charles dear. And it was very wise of you. The farther away she is from Lady Sylvia's sphere, the more peacefully we will all breathe. It would be criminal to allow the corruption of your own sister when merely exerting yourself a trifle would solve the problem."

"I don't think that 'corruption' is actually the word that is needed here," he demurred. Their conversation was going to be as difficult as he had imagined it might be.

"That is where we differ, Charles!" Miss Bitfort-Raines said shortly, showing more animation than was her wont. "There is no other word that so suits the activities of that person—I cannot bring myself to say 'that lady'! She is entirely wanting in morals!"

He had decided to skirt some of the most inflammatory issues, so he chose not to reply to this outburst. Instead, he used a tack that he hoped would throw her off balance for long enough to accomplish his purpose.

"Do you think, Claire, that your gypsy would be willing to tell my fortune?" he asked blandly.

If he had suddenly announced that he was moving to the South Seas to take up residence with a cannibal king there, she could not have looked more astonished. "You, Charles?" she asked blankly. "Why?"

"Oh, I don't believe her, of course, but I found her

manner rather fascinating," he said offhandedly. "And then, when one of her warnings seemed almost immediately to be accurate, I knew that she must be hand-in glove with the intruder. Had he not been interrupted, he might well have robbed the house before setting the fire. I would like to expose her, if possible, so the credulous do not give her and her ilk more business because of what happened here."

"You are absolutely correct, Charles!" exclaimed Miss Bitfort-Raines eagerly. "It is quite unbelievable how many of my callers have wished to know where they might find Madame Zeena. I did not tell them, of course. I merely said that she was undoubtedly miles away by now. I could not have them placing themselves in her hands because of what happened here!"

"Very sensible of you, my dear," he said admiringly, although he was certain that her actual motive for refusing them the information was quite different from the one she professed. "But you do, of course, know where to find the woman?"

"Naturally. Niles made the arrangements for me, so she knows. Would you like for me to go with you, Charles?"

"I think that seeing you would strike fear into her heart," he said diplomatically, determined that he would see the fortune-teller alone.

The memory of her last interview with Madame Zeena brought an angry flush to her cheeks. "And so it should! Her behavior toward me was unforgivable!"

"And so you see why I should go alone," he continued tactfully. "She will be far more likely to give herself away if she is not made fearful by your presence."

Miss Bitfort-Raines conceded reluctantly. She had

thought of several things that she would like to say to Madame Zeena, and the only reason she could forego that pleasure was in the hope of seeing that woman dragged before the authorities.

She summoned Niles, who willingly disclosed to Sir Charles her location. "Although you must hurry, sir," she said anxiously, "because they are footloose folk, and there is no knowing when they might suddenly take a notion to move along."

"I shall be quick," he promised her gravely, and it had looked as though he would indeed be able to depart without disclosing to Claire any of Lady Sylvia's problems. Unfortunately, however, that was not to be.

Briggs appeared at the door. "Lady Riverton to see you, madam," he said gravely, but before Miss Bitfort-Raines could respond, Briggs received a sharp poke in the back of one knee.

"You are blocking my passage!" said Lady Riverton in annoyance, raising her cane again. Briggs, however, anticipated her and moved briskly to one side, opening the door wide for her.

She settled herself in a chair close to the entrance and stared with bright-eyed satisfaction at Miss Bitfort-Raines and Sir Charles. "I hear that you were on the scene of the excitement this morning, sir! Very amusing it must have been. I never thought to see the day when Arthur Ashby and Boots Symington would be looked upon as heroes. And you did your part, too, by all accounts."

Claire stared at him, puzzled by Lady Riverton's words, and he felt his heart sink. He had no doubt that she would be angry that he had not told her of the attempted kidnapping and that, once again, she would suspect that he was involved with Lady Sylvia.

Lady Riverton caught his glance and understood its significance immediately. Her smile grew wider and she rattled her cane in anticipation. She had hurried here in order to enjoy Miss Bitfort-Raines's discomfiture at her fiancé's involvement in Lady Sylvia's latest scandal, but she had not expected to be the one to tell her the news— and in the presence of Sir Charles, to boot. Her cup was full.

"Hadn't heard about it, had you, my dear?" she demanded happily. "Well, I don't know but that you were right, Sir Charles, in not telling her. Everything that Lady Sylvia has a finger in turns to scandal."

"Lady Sylvia?" said Miss Bitfort-Raines in an ominous voice, turning to stare at Sir Charles.

He wished himself at the other side of the globe. It would be unpleasant enough to be subjected in private to the scene that was sure to follow, but to undergo it in the presence of the gimlet-eyed Lady Riverton was unthinkable.

He made a push to save the situation. "I hadn't mentioned it, Claire, because I knew how distressing you would find it," he said, attempting an ease of manner that he was far from feeling. He chose his next words carefully. "Early this morning in the park someone attempted to kidnap the young boy in Lady Sylvia's charge, but before he could make his escape Arthur Ashby and Boots Symington came upon the scene, and he threw the child into the lake. Fortunately, Ashby managed to pull the boy out before he suffered any real harm."

"The young boy in Lady Sylvia's charge!" exclaimed Miss Bitfort-Raines, focusing precisely on the point that he feared she would. "You mean Lady Sylvia's—"

Before she could complete the thought and give Lady

Riverton still more food for gossip, Sir Charles interrupted smoothly. "Yes, my dear. Lady Sylvia's young charge was almost drowned, and we must be grateful that Ashby was as quick as he was."

Furiously angry and jealous though she was, Miss Bitfort-Raines realized that he had saved her from an indiscretion that Lady Riverton would have used gleefully against her. Swallowing her angry comments about Lady Sylvia's relationship to the child, she turned her attention to the other point he wished her to avoid.

"And what had you to do with all of this, Charles?" she asked, trying to regain a reasonable amount of composure. "I collect that it was Mr. Ashby who snatched the child from the jaws of death."

Redford nodded his head encouragingly, pleased with her efforts. Unfortunately, her self-control again crumbled and she added cuttingly, "Were you comforting Lady Sylvia, Charles, while all of this was going forward?"

Lady Riverton rattled her cane joyfully. With any luck, this squall would develop into a full-blown storm.

"I encountered them as they were returning to Lady Sylvia's barouche," he replied calmly. "I merely rode back and sent the driver to fetch them."

Miss Bitfort-Raines was silent as she considered his response, but Lady Riverton was not to be deprived of her pleasures. "And then you rode back to Danville House and were closeted privately with Lady Sylvia for the next hour, sir!" she exclaimed. "Boots Symington sent his valet round with a note to Lady Sylvia to reclaim his coat. Just like that popinjay to think of his wardrobe before anything else! At any rate, the valet had to cool his heels for almost an hour and then he saw you leaving the drawing room."

She stared at him challengingly, as though expecting him to deny her words.

"That is quite true," he conceded, somewhat to her surprise and discomfiture. "I wished to find out as much as I could about the crime so that it could be properly reported. Also," he added reluctantly, "I wished to be sure that everything at Danville House was secure."

Both of his listeners looked startled. "And were you thinking there could be more trouble, Sir Charles?" demanded Lady Riverton, scenting the development of a new story.

"It is best to be prepared," he replied. "I cannot imagine that there could be any difficulty, but it seemed wise to take precautions."

"Nonsense!" snapped Miss Bitfort-Raines. "You are making a great piece of work about nothing! It is always the same with Sylvia Danville! Everything must become theatrical! I have never found it suprising that she is the child of an actress! It is ludicrous to think that she or the child could truly be in danger."

"The gypsy!" said Lady Riverton suddenly. "That's why you thought it, Sir Charles. You were remembering what the fortune-teller said: something about both Lady Sylvia and the boy being in danger—and that someone close to them wasn't what he seemed. *That's* what you were thinking of, sir!"

Redford was unable to deny it, and Miss Bitfort-Raines glared at him. "So that is why you wished her direction. Not merely to bring her to book for her misdeeds, but to protect Sylvia Danville. Well, Sir Charles, I wish you the joy of Lady Sylvia's company. I can think of no more dire malediction than that!"

And so saying, she rose and left the morning room without another word for either of her guests.

"I can't think what you see in that girl, Charles Redford," said Lady Riverton frankly, when the door had closed after Miss Bitfort-Raines, "but if you want to keep her, you'd best stay far away from Sylvia Danville."

He bowed stiffly. "Thank you for your advice, ma'am. I'm sure that it is well meant."

She cackled. "Very niffy-naffy, aren't you, my boy? You'd like to give me the rough side of your tongue, but you won't do it because you might set up my back. You'd be better served if you spoke your mind. And it would be better still if you *knew* your mind. Which is it that you want—Claire Bitfort-Raines or Sylvia Danville?"

He bowed before leaving the room. "I am, of course, grateful for your wise counsel, Lady Riverton. You must forgive me for leaving you now. I will have Briggs step in immediately."

Her laughter rang in his ears as he left the room. She was, he feared, all too correct in her assessment of him. Sylvia had accused him again and again of a lack of candor. He had told himself that she simply did not recognize the need for tact in dealing with others, but he acknowledged to himself now that perhaps he had not been honest even with himself. Perhaps he was diplomatic simply because he did not wish to risk a confrontation of any sort. And perhaps he *was* still undecided about his feelings for Sylvia Danville.

He straightened his shoulders as he left the house. There would be at least one confrontation now. And he turned his steps in the direction of Madame Zeena's encampment.

Chapter Twelve

Following the instructions given him by Niles, Sir Charles had no difficulty in finding the gypsy camp in a small grove beyond the perimeter of the city. Faded eiderdowns, once brightly flowered, were airing in the morning sun beside wagons drawn close together. He dismounted and approached the camp, preceded by a group of curious children. A tall man looked up from shoeing a horse and nodded at him. Sir Charles, taking that to mean that he would be with him in a moment, leaned back against a tree and took stock of what he saw.

Like everyone else, he had heard tales of the gypsies since he was a small boy. When he wandered too far from home, his nanny had told him that he would be stolen by them and he would never see his dear family again. Too, he had heard that they were frequently guilty of petty theft and that, although they were remarkable with horses, it was wiser never to buy one from them. Watching the deft movements of the blacksmith before him, he decided that at least a portion of the stories were true: some of them were gifted in working with horses.

The children were subjecting him to their own assessment, studying him from a secure distance. They had no difficulty in agreeing that he was a wealthy *gorgio,* for his horse and his clothes and his manner all proclaimed that. Too, they regretfully decided among themselves that he was not here to purchase any of their horses, for at the moment they had only those noted for their looks. Any knowing buyer would give them the go-by.

Unfortunately, they concluded, judging by the appearance of the chestnut belonging to the gentleman, he was a fine judge of blood and bone, and could not be gulled into purchasing an animal that was made to appear spirited by shaking a pail of pebbles under his nose until the very appearance of the pail was enough to make the horse prance. Sometimes too the judicious application of a hedgehog to a horse's flanks just before showing him made him appear—for the moment—lively. Nor were they hopeful that he would be taken in by the fresh breath of an old horse fed henbane mixed with elderberries to cover the odor of the decaying teeth of an old horse. They sighed. It was regrettable that such a prize would slip through their fingers.

After a brief wait, the gypsy blacksmith finished with his horse and turned him over to one of the waiting boys. He approached Redford warily, his dark eyes hooded. Inclining his head briefly in what Redford correctly interpreted as a greeting, he waited for the caller to speak. The arrival of a *gorgio* was frequently a precursor of disaster, for very often he was a representative of the authorities, there to inform them that they were to move along or to accuse them of some petty crime. Redford did not appear to be such a man, but one never knew. The gypsy waited silently to be informed of the purpose of Redford's call.

"I believe that a Madame Zeena is a part of your

group," he said pleasantly, suddenly conscious that eyes were watching him from the shadowy interiors of several of the closely drawn wagons. He could see no one, but he was aware of movement within them.

The gypsy nodded, and waited again.

"I would like to speak with her," explained Redford patiently, beginning to think that it might take hours before it would be possible even to begin his interview with that lady.

"May I ask what your business is?" inquired the gypsy, studying his guest closely.

"I would like to have my fortune told," replied Redford, feeling very much the fool. "I saw her at the masquerade ball the other evening and was very impressed by her." That much at least was true.

The gypsy studied him for a moment or two more and then nodded. "She has the gift," he said. "I am her son, and I have frequently known her fortunes to be true."

And how much do you help with making those fortunes become reality? Redford wondered. Aloud he merely said, "Perhaps you have heard that there was a fire at the ball that very night, and that a young lady was responsible for warning everyone else of it."

The gypsy nodded warily. He was no fool, and all too often matters that were mere whims of fate were attributed to his people. He waited to see what this *gorgio* would say next.

Redford was watching him quite as carefully. The gypsy had given no indication that he knew anything of the attempted kidnapping, but then if they were connected in any way, he would of course give no sign. He had admitted to knowledge of the fire only after being questioned. It angered him to think that the man who had attacked his sister might very well be in one of these wagons—or for that matter might be the very man before him.

In his most persuasive voice, Redford said, "I had hoped to have Madame Zeena tell my fortune that evening before all of the excitement of the fire. This is the first opportunity I have had since then to seek her out. I was pleased to find that you're still here."

The gypsy nodded thoughtfully. "We are preparing for our departure even now," he said, indicating the remnants of a fire that several women were carefully putting out, scattering the ashes and raking fresh dirt over the place where it had been.

"Where will you go next?" inquired Redford nonchalantly, not wishing to disturb the man by showing too much interest.

The gypsy shrugged. "Who can say? Perhaps to the south, where we have relatives, perhaps to the West country. We shall see."

"May I see your mother before your departure?" Redford asked, taking two gold sovereigns from his pocket and fingering them absently.

The man gave the merest wisp of a smile and nodded. "I will get her," he replied. "There will not be much time, but enough to know what your future holds—if you are sure you wish it."

He left Redford feeling slightly uneasy. Had there been a veiled threat behind his words? Or were they just the stock-in-trade of a Romany?

Very soon he had no further time to reflect upon the matter, for Madame Zeena appeared before him. He had not thought she would appear so striking in the cold light of day, for costume and candlelight do much toward creating the illusion of romance. Even in the unsparing brightness of this late spring morning, however, she was a compelling figure.

She was indeed tall, almost his equal in height, and, although she was obviously an older woman, her back was straight and her step firm. Her dark hair, only slightly streaked with grey, was pulled back and partially covered by a bright scarf.

"So you have come for dukkerin'?" she inquired, her eyes bright with curiosity. There must be some matter pressing indeed for a wealthy *gorgio* to come to her so privately instead of sending for her. She wondered what trouble was weighing upon him that he felt that he must come to her. Her son Angelo was inclined to believe that he brought trouble, but in studying his face for a moment, it seemed clear to her that the trouble—whatever it was— was gnawing at the *gorgio* himself.

"Dukkerin'?" he asked, puzzled by the word.

Madame Zeena nodded, pointing in the direction of a small brook beyond the encampment. "Telling your fortune. Let us go away from the others so that we will not be disturbed."

Redford followed her obligingly, grateful to note that the gaggle of children followed them only to the last wagon. He had no desire to speak with her in the presence of so many prying eyes.

"And now, sir, what is it that troubles you?"

He was slightly taken aback by her question, but recollected that she must have some information about him so that she could manufacture a suitable fortune. Asking him such a question was merely part of the process.

"I wish to know something of my future," he returned politely. "Particularly I would like to know—" He paused a moment, grabbing at straws. What would one ask a gypsy? He did not want her to become unduly suspicious, as her son undoubtedly was.

"I wish to know if my marriage will prosper," he finished glibly, hoping that this would satisfy her.

Madame Zeena nodded. She had remembered him now. She had seen him with that proud young woman who had hired her and refused to pay her—and she had also seen him come in from the terrace with the young red-haired woman whom she had warned of danger. The proud young lady that was giving the ball had glared at the two of them, showing her jealousy as vividly as she had when she had hired Madame Zeena and given her instructions.

The gypsy smiled. That young woman had much to learn. She took Redford's left hand in both of hers and studied the back of it, pressing it between her fingers, then did the same with his right hand. "You are a man of great strength and determination," she murmured.

Finally, she turned over the right palm and stared into it. "I see two women," she began, having decided to arrest his attention at the outset. "One is tall and fair, the other has hair the color of an evening sunset before a fine day."

Redford started at this, and the gypsy felt his hand move convulsively in hers. She smiled more deeply and continued.

"You are a man of good character, but you are not always truthful," she continued. "A very careful, intelligent man." She stopped and stared more closely at his hand, turning it in her own and then studying his face again.

"But I know that what you just said is not true," he said, growing impatient. "I do not lie to people. I—" He suddenly remembered what Sylvia had reproached him with when she had broken their engagement.

"You can never be honest, Charles," she had told him in the heat of her anger when she had discovered his mission as a spy. "Not even with yourself," she had added after he had carefully explained the reasons for his apparent lack of truthfulness.

And he recalled his thoughts this very morning after the unpleasant conversation with Lady Riverton. And now, only an hour or two later, he was hearing those thoughts echoed by this presumptuous gypsy fortune-teller, who behaved as though she had read the information in his palm. He wondered for a moment just how she *had* done it, but then assumed that he must have given himself away in some manner.

Madame Zeena watched him struggle with himself. And so it was true, she thought. This *gorgio* could not even tell himself the truth. He would be no great bargain for any woman as he was, even the spiteful proud one.

"Shall I go on?" she asked, holding forth her hand for his.

"Of course," said Redford, although his reply was reluctant. He had no desire to hear anything more about himself, but he held some hope of learning something of value about the fire and the kidnapping from this woman after he had undergone the entire procedure. Surely after listening patiently to her nonsense and paying her the sovereigns he would have an opportunity of asking her some questions.

"You will have one long love, and this is a woman you already know," she said, carefully avoiding any mention of a particular woman.

The proud young woman wanted him, but so did the

other one, the one circled about by dangers. Madame Zeena had instinctively liked the second young woman, and had wished to warn her, for she was very vulnerable. She had seen, too, the anger in her eyes when she looked at this man. It had been, however, the anger that springs from a deep attachment. The second young woman was also in love with this man, no matter how unworthy he might be.

Madame Zeena sighed. Women were often unfortunate in the choice of their lovers, she reflected, but the palm of this feckless young man showed more promise that she would have thought, even with the matter of lying. Her own people set no great store by the truth, reserving it primarily for their dealings with those closest to them. The red-haired young woman wanted this man and, if Madame Zeena could assist her, she would have him. It would be gratifying, too, to thrust a spoke into the plans of the proud young woman who treated others with such a high hand.

Peering more closely into his palm, she muttered, "What is this?"

"What do you see there?" demanded Redford, caught once again.

"It is a break," she said, thinking of what the maid had told her about her mistress and her engagement to this man before her. "I see that you will almost marry, but you will realize your mistake and correct it. The one that you marry will be your companion through a long and happy life. There will be many problems, but you will overcome them."

Redford considered the matter. Certainly that had happened with Sylvia, an engagement *had* been broken— but he had not done the breaking. It had been Sylvia who had decided she had made a mistake and cried off. Surely the woman could not be referring to his engagement to Claire. Then he caught himself, irritated that he was behaving in the same credulous manner of any know-nothing off the streets. He knew, of course, that the gypsy merely played a sort of game, putting together bits of information and making guesses that she thought her customer would find interesting. And she was remarkably good at it.

"You have relieved my mind, Madame Zeena," he said dryly.

She heard the sardonic note in his voice and raised her eyes to his. "I would not feel relieved, sir," she said gently. "I merely tell you how things *may* happen. You still determine the outcome yourself. And I have pointed out to you one of the problems that you face—and it is a great one."

Redford frowned at this reminder of his lack of honesty, but dropped the sovereigns into her hand and decided that it was time to pursue his real reason for coming here.

"When you came to the home of Miss Bitfort-Raines on Friday night," he began, "did you come alone?"

Madame Zeena nodded, her eyes hooded. The *gorgio* had something particular in his thoughts, and she would give him information sparingly. One never knew what such a one had on his mind, and it was best to move carefully.

"No one even escorted you to the door?" he persisted. "It was late when you were leaving the house. Were you to come back here all alone?"

Madame Zeena looked at him with some amusement. "Are you thinking that I would be afraid of the dark, young *rye?*" she asked. "That is very kind of you, but I travel everywhere, you know, and think nothing of going about by myself when I wish to do so. I am not afraid."

"I thought perhaps your son might have escorted you. London is not the country, and, if you will forgive my saying so, you are no longer a young woman," he responded.

"If I were a young woman, Angelo might have felt it necessary to go with me for protection, for the *gorgios* regard our young women with no respect. For an old woman, though, it is different. No one even notices me."

Looking again at her impressive figure, Redford thought that it was extremely unlikely that she would go unnoticed, but he did not argue the point. It was clear that she would not change her story.

He tried another tack. "When you left their home that evening, did you notice anyone unusual—anyone who looked out of place?"

Again she looked amused. "It was a masquerade ball, young *rye*. *Everyone* looked strange. You yourself were wearing a short skirt and sandals."

Redford was beginning to grow annoyed, but he concealed it with an effort. "How did you leave the house?" he asked. "By the servants' entrance?"

Madame Zeena tossed her head. "That is the way the young lady of the house would have wished me to leave. But I am *not* a servant! I left by the *front* door. The young lady did not choose to pay me, and so I did not choose to obey her wishes."

Redford frowned. "Miss Bitfort-Raines did not pay you for your services? What was her reason?"

This was the opening the gypsy had hoped for, but she merely said, "The young lady wished for me to tell the fortune of another young *rawnie*."

"Well, that is precisely why you were employed, was it not? To tell fortunes?"

Madame Zeena nodded. "Of course. But the dukkerin' is mine. *I* tell the fortunes, not the young lady."

"What do you mean, Madame Zeena?" he asked, his frown growing deeper. "The young lady was not telling fortunes."

"She told me what to say to the other *rawnie*, the red-haired one in the long white gown."

"And what were you to say to her?" he demanded. He had known, of course, that Claire had been up to something, but he had not been certain exactly what her plan was.

"I was to tell the young lady to beware of a tall, dark stranger, for he had betrayed her and left her with one child. And then I was to add that if she did not listen to my warning, the mistake would be repeated. And I was told to say it very loudly, in front of everyone."

Redford had closed his eyes in disbelief. That Claire, always so proper and so critical of the careless ways of others, should stoop to such a trick as this, was unbelievable. But he knew why she had done it.

He opened his eyes and stared very hard at Madame Zeena. "And why did you not do so?" he asked.

The gypsy was pleased with his obvious distress. It showed that his heart was a little warmer than she had thought at first.

"Because I do not like to be told what to do," she responded. "And, also," she added, a little reluctantly, "because I liked the look of the other *rawnie*—and I feared for her when I looked into her palm."

"Nonsense!" exclaimed Redford impatiently. "You

know that you could not see the danger there that you spoke of. How *did* you know of it? Did you plan it?"

He regretted the words the instant that he had spoken them. He normally had no trouble in handling difficult situations, even when dealing with delicate affairs for Whitehall, but he was too nearly involved in this to remain objective. He knew that there had been no "danger" present in Sylvia's palm, and the only other possibility that he could think of was that this group of gypsies worked at making their fortunes come true. But now that he had betrayed his thoughts, he would more than likely never discover the truth.

Madame Zeena had drawn herself up to her full height. Without a word to him, she had turned away and started back to the camp, her full skirts rustling through the grass.

Redford sighed. He had made a mull of it, but he was certain that his suspicions were correct. Angelo, or perhaps one of the other men, had followed Madame Zeena into the house that night, prepared to start the fire in a place where it would most certainly be discovered quickly and to rifle whatever jewelry and silver he could while in the house. Unfortunately, Diana had been the first available prospect.

Perhaps his call had done some good, however. They would know that he had called their hand, and that should be the end of any further problems for Lady Sylvia. Doubtless they would be gone from the environs of London within the next hour, vanishing like a wisp of smoke.

But as he rode slowly home, his mind turned back to the problem of Claire. If it had been jealousy that had provoked such behavior on her part, he was the one at fault. He shuddered to think that he had renounced the costume of Louis for that of Caesar on that very night.

Then he thought of Sylvia in her Cleopatra costume. Had she not come back to London, flaunting herself and that child under the noses of the *ton* in her usual incorrigible manner, none of this would have happened. She was unquestionably the most annoying and irresponsible person of his acquaintance and he was devoutly grateful that he would soon take a solid individual like Claire to wife. Once Sylvia Danville was safely out of the way, their lives would return to normal.

Chapter Thirteen

Lady Sylvia had every intention of removing herself and her party as soon as possible to the security and freedom of Greystone, but that soon proved to be impossible. Sally and Povey had given Robert a warm bath and put him to bed as soon as they had arrived home. She had also sent for a doctor, not because she thought Robert had suffered any hurt, but because she had felt it would be a wise precaution. That gentleman had arrived very soon after the departure of Sir Charles and examined the youngster carefully. His report had been an optimistic one and had made her feel much better.

"Keep him in bed for the day, my lady," he had said briskly. "He has a slight temperature, but nothing that need distress you. I will come around the first thing in the morning to have another look at him and be certain that everything is all right and tight before he gets up and about."

"Thank you, Dr. Clayton," Sylvia had said gratefully. "We have been looking forward to going to Greystone. I should hate to have to postpone it."

"No need, my lady. But we'll be certain of that tomorrow."

That night Sylvia, conscious of the fears expressed by Sir Charles, called in Pelton. "I will check every window and door myself, my lady," he assured her. "You may go to sleep fully confident that all is well."

Reassured, she did precisely that. And when she awakened in the morning, it was to the news that Robert's fever had risen during the night and that he was tossing fitfully in his bed. Povey had already sent for Dr. Clayton. That good man soon arrived, very confident that all would be well, but he shook his head at the suggestion that Robert might be better off at Greystone.

"I would not move him, Lady Sylvia," he said. "It is not a long journey, but it would not do to jostle him about in the carriage when he is quite weak. And if there were a sudden change of temperature, it could be most unhealthy for him."

Sylvia accepted his ruling and crept about the house, conscience-stricken, for the next several days, accepting no callers and going nowhere herself. Lord Wilmington called daily, but had to content himself with sending her impossibly large bouquets and small gifts for Robert, who was too ill to appreciate them. The Mannerings had left London again the morning after their evening at the theatre, and were not expected back for at least a week.

"You must go out and get some air," said Povey reproachfully. "It will do the child no good if you grow ill as well."

"You know very well, Povey, that he would not be lying in there if I had taken better care of him," she replied, walking to the bedside of the sleeping child and straightening his covers. "How can I go out and enjoy myself while he is in this state?"

"There is no saying, miss, that his dip in the lake caused all of this. It could just as well have been something else, something that he brought with him from Egypt. Dr. Clayton isn't certain just what it is, and well you know it."

Before Sylvia could reply, the butler entered quietly, closing the door softly behind him.

"You have callers, Lady Sylvia," he announced gravely, suiting his tone of voice to the atmosphere.

Sylvia waved a hand at him in dismissal. "I have told you, Pelton, that I will see no one."

"If I may make so bold, ma'am, I thought that since the callers were Mr. Arthur Ashby and Mr. Boots Symington you might make an exception."

Sylvia had arisen at the mention of their names. "Yes, you are quite right, Pelton. Of course, I must see them after what they did for Robert."

When she entered the drawing room, the two gentlemen rose quickly to greet her. Both of them had taken special pains in attiring themselves for the occasion, Mr. Symington even sporting an impossibly large nosegay in the buttonhole of his carefully tailored jacket, a new one fresh from the hands of Weston to replace his ravaged one. He bowed as Lady Sylvia entered and offered her a nosegay that matched his own, but several times its size.

"How kind of you, Mr. Symington," she replied, smiling and handing it to Pelton.

"It is you who are kind, Lady Sylvia," he responded with great sincerity. "I was overwhelmed to receive this coat by special messenger this morning."

"It is the least that I could do, sir, after you so gallantly sacrificed yours in Robert's behalf."

Recalling that his behavior at the time had been anything but gallant, he blushed and hurried into speech again. "Speaking of the little fellow, can you tell us how he is faring, Lady Sylvia? We have heard that he is a little under the weather."

"I am afraid that he has fallen ill with a fever," she replied bleakly. "Dr. Clayton is hopeful that it will soon break, but in the meantime he is quite weak and listless and sleeps most of the time."

"Well, that's the ticket, ma'am," said Mr. Ashby heartily, eager to dispel her troubled look. "Rest is what he needs to put him on his feet again."

She smiled at him gratefully. "Yes, I'm sure that's true, Mr. Ashby. He does need his rest. It's just that I am accustomed to seeing him be so active that watching him lie perfectly still for so many days frightens me a little."

"No need to fear, Lady Sylvia," chimed in Mr. Symington, eager to do his part in cheering her up. "I have a little nephew, and whenever he is ill, my sister has him in bed on the instant and there he stays until he is well. It is all she and her nanny can do to keep him there, though; he is so full of fun and gig that he can't stay still."

"That's just it, Mr. Symington," she responded, her smile fading. "Robert is always just that way, too, very hard to keep still. But now he is so quiet that I can't help being a little frightened."

Mr. Ashby glared at his companion. "I daresay that it has to do with the change of climate, too," he said, determined to restore her spirits. "It is bound to make a difference to the boy. I have heard people who have gone to India say that they have a terrible time adjusting to the weather there. Doubtless it is the same in reverse."

Sylvia, appreciating their efforts to cheer her, made an

effort to respond in a positive way, but the simple truth was that she was growing more fearful as each hour passed. She had had no experience with children, and she was acutely aware that she was the only person responsible for Robert's well-being. She had removed him from Egypt and his father and, in so doing, had assumed the duties of his parent. For the first time she was beginning to question the wisdom of what she had done.

There was little to take her mind off of the situation, for there were few people she knew well and she had had no desire to entertain those who were merely curious. She had absolutely refused admittance to Mrs. Simpkins and Lady Riverton, and even to Lady Digby. Nor had she felt equal to seeing Lord Wilmington alone, amusing though he was, and since the Mannerings had left again for the country immediately after their unfortunate evening at the theatre, they had not even heard of the kidnapping incident before their departure. A note from them had been delivered the morning that they left, making light of the incident with Sir Charles. Gerard had offered in the note to call him out, while Amelia had added that her heart went out to Diana. It was unfortunate, she wrote, that so amiable a young woman had such a disagreeable brother.

Sylvia felt precisely the same way. Therefore, when Pelton entered her private sitting room later that day, bearing a card for her, she was pleased to see that Diana Redford had come to call. She knew that Miss Redford had been banished to the country because of her unsavory associations—Mrs. Simpkins had kindly imparted this in a note to Sylvia when she had been refused admission to the house—and so she was surprised that the young lady had returned to town so soon.

"I took the liberty of bringing this to you, Lady Sylvia," said Pelton, "because I knew the young lady to be a particular friend of yours and she was most insistent that I present this to you personally."

Gratefully, Sylvia went down to the drawing room, eager to take her mind from her troubles for at least a little while.

"It is good to see you, Miss Redford," she said with a smile as she entered the room.

"I cannot tell you how distressed I was to hear of your trouble, Lady Sylvia," responded her guest, sincerity ringing in every word. "Your experience the other morning in the park was shocking, and I understand that the little boy has not yet recovered."

Sylvia sighed and shook her head. "I was very fortunate that Mr. Ashby and Mr. Symington were close at hand to help us," she said. "But Robert, who is always so lively and cheerful, cannot seem to recover from the experience."

Miss Redford reached over and impulsively patted her hand, troubled by the pallor and lethargic manner of her friend. "I am sure that he will soon be well," she said encouragingly. "He looks to be a very healthy little boy, and children are very resilient, you know."

"Well, I suppose that that is just the problem. I *don't* know," admitted Sylvia. "I simply was never around children very much, and I am not certain what to expect— but this is beginning to look very serious to me."

"Will you not come with me for a short drive in the park, Lady Sylvia? My carriage is waiting, and I think it would do you good. It *is* a lovely morning, and I know that you are accustomed to getting more fresh air than you have been."

Admitting the truth of this, and succumbing at last to the argument that it would be of no benefit to Robert if she grew ill herself, Sylvia hurried off to change her attire. She reappeared very quickly, adjusting the green ribbons of her dashing bonnet and looking much more herself.

The ride was a brief but pleasant one, the ladies thoroughly enjoying one another's company. Miss Redford seemed to have recovered from her shocking experience with the intruder, although she still carefully chose gowns that would cover the bruises. By tacit agreement, neither of the ladies made mention of the unfortunate incident at the theatre.

It was not until the carriage arrived at the door of Danville House that Miss Redford said in a slightly constrained voice and with heightened color, "I am certain, Lady Sylvia, that you heard that I was called suddenly into the country."

Sylvia nodded and tried to ease the situation for her. "It seemed a very reasonable idea to me. After what you had undergone, a little rest was an excellent idea."

Miss Redford shook her head abruptly. "You are very kind, Lady Sylvia, but you know that that wasn't the reason for my departure. I would like to apologize for my brother's unforgivable behavior at the theatre. Charles has never put me to the blush before, and I cannot imagine why he behaved in such an unforgivable manner."

"You need not feel, Miss Redford, that you are in any way to blame for your brother's actions," replied Sylvia firmly. "I certainly do not hold you responsible, so please do not give it another thought."

"But it is so unlike him, Lady Sylvia," replied Miss Redford, her smooth brow creased in puzzlement. "He is always the soul of discretion and his manners are unfailingly courteous. I thought he had run mad that evening."

"I fear that I have that effect on him," Lady Sylvia admitted, feeling like smiling for the first time in four days. "He has quite often behaved that way with me."

Miss Redford stared at her open-mouthed. "That is his *customary* manner when with you, Lady Sylvia? I can scarcely credit it!"

"Well, perhaps not precisely customary, my dear," amended Sylvia, "but it happens with astonishing frequency. I seem to have the happy faculty of bringing out the worst in him."

Miss Redford shook her head in disbelief. "I had no idea that Charles behaved in anything other than an exemplary manner. Why, Claire always says that he is the perfect gentleman."

"Perhaps she means that he has the *appearance* of the perfect gentleman," replied Sylvia a little grimly. Then, seeing Miss Redford's startled expression, she added hastily, "Never mind what I say, Miss Redford. I am merely suffering from the megrims. But do not trouble yourself about your brother's behavior toward me. I assure you that if Robert were well, I would be getting along famously."

And she patted the young woman's hand before stepping down from the carriage. "And thank you, my dear, for coming to see me. It has done me a great deal of good."

"I shall call again tomorrow afternoon," said Miss Redford firmly, "and we will take the air together once more. Perhaps the Mannerings will return soon, and they will certainly be able to brighten your days."

"You have already done that, Miss Redford. You are

better than any tonic a doctor could offer me. I should turn Robert over to you."

Miss Redford dimpled. "I should be glad to take charge of him," she laughed. "As soon as he is well enough, we will take him out with us."

Pelton stood at the door of Danville House, holding it open for her, but Lady Sylvia stood on the walk and watched the carriage pull away. She wondered what Charles would have to say when he discovered that his sister had come to call. For Miss Redford's sake, she hoped that he would be able to conduct himself with a little dignity.

Her hope was not a vain one. Sir Charles himself was aware that he needed to have a little more self-control in his dealings with Diana. However, when he discovered that not only had his sister disobeyed him by returning to London but that she had also flouted his express wishes by going immediately to call upon Lady Sylvia, he was furious. He was not accustomed to losing his temper with anyone save Lady Sylvia, particularly not his young sister, who had always looked up to him, and he closeted himself in his library until he could manage to govern it sufficiently to speak with her. He was determined that he would handle the problem with Diana in a more competent manner than he had when he took her to Lansing.

She knew that the butler had told him of her arrival, and she came down to dinner in a defiant mood, prepared to face any show of anger he might be able to muster. She had been shocked by his outburst at the theatre and his subsequent high-handed treatment of her, for it was unlike anything that he had done before. Their relationship had always been an easy, agreeable one, but then, Diana had reasoned during her time at Lansing, she had always done precisely as he had wished.

When he had left her there, he had still been angry, and their parting had not been a happy one. Sir Charles had told her that she might remain at Lansing until Christmas if necessary, but that she would stay there until she felt that she was able to conduct herself in a seemly manner. Also, he had added angrily, she was not to cultivate unacceptable relationships, such as that with Lady Sylvia Danville. When she had ventured to ask what was wrong with Lady Sylvia, he had snapped, "She has no more idea of propriety than a Hottentot, and she will teach you to be precisely the same, if only to irritate me beyond the telling!"

A letter from a young friend of Miss Redford had reached her soon after his departure from London, telling her of the dramatic attempted kidnapping. The child involved—and here the writer was discreet, for she mentioned none of the stories circulating about Robert—was said to have fallen ill immediately after the incident, and Lady Sylvia was remaining at his bedside. The writer had known, she said, that Diana would be interested in the story since Lady Sylvia had so recently rescued her.

Unfortunately for those most nearly concerned, Miss Redford was more than interested: she was determined to return to London to be of service to Lady Sylvia. Miss Bitfort-Raines had been quite correct when she had observed that Diana had made a heroine of her rescuer. It seemed to her that Lady Sylvia was everything that she would like to be: quick-thinking, courageous, lovely, and amusing; and she had said as much to her brother when he had dragged her away to Lansing.

His response to her comment had been to march from

the drawing room, where they were having their argument, and slam the door behind him. When he had appeared again, it had been to bid her farewell and tell her that he would come to Lansing to see her in a week and they would discuss the matter in a rational manner then.

So it was with some misgiving that Miss Redford went down to dinner that evening. She had decided, however, that the best approach to take was a calm and collected one. She intended to behave as though nothing at all had happened. She would not allude to Lansing unless Charles brought it up; instead, she would behave as though she had never left London.

Since Sir Charles had regretted his handling of the situation, he allowed her to do precisely that. He still did not wish her to associate with Lady Sylvia, but he had decided that he would not make that a key issue. He would have to find other, more subtle, ways of taking her from Lady Sylvia's side. If she would defy him like this, he must walk carefully or he would lose her all together, and he was extremely attached to Diana. Too, he knew that making more of an issue of Lady Sylvia would simply serve to make his sister more loyal to that lady. He would try another approach.

Her color was a little high when she entered the dining room, but otherwise she appeared perfectly natural.

"Good evening, Charles," she said, dropping a kiss on the top of his head as was her habit.

"Good evening, Diana," he responded pleasantly. "Fenton told me that you had arrived. Did you have an enjoyable trip?"

Relieved by his sensible attitude and feeling that her brother was himself again, she replied in an easy manner, and the conversation prospered, both of them dwelling on uncontroversial topics.

Finally, feeling that the groundwork had been laid, Diana threw caution to the winds and said diffidently, "I have been to see Lady Sylvia today, Charles."

His fork stopped briefly on its journey to his mouth, but otherwise he maintained his composure. He was able to finish his bite, chew thoughtfully, and wipe his mouth carefully before replying simply, "Indeed? I hope you found her well."

Relieved by his reaction, Diana continued earnestly, "That's just it, Charles. I did not."

He looked at her questioningly and she added, "Did not find her well, that is. In fact, it seemed to me that she was looking quite hagged."

"Because of the child?" inquired her brother, his eyebrows lifted. He had heard some of the stories circulating, but he had not credited them. He simply could not imagine Sylvia giving up her round of activities and staying at the bedside of a child. She was too active—and too thoughtless, he had added to himself.

Miss Redford nodded earnestly. "I took her out in our carriage, Charles. I felt that if I could induce her to get some fresh air, she might begin to regain a little of her normal cheerful look, for I must tell you, Charles, that I was a little frightened by her appearance."

Sir Charles frowned, passing over the fact that they had been out in public together and focusing on the mention of Lady Sylvia's health. "It has only been a matter of a few days that the child has been ill. How could she be in such bad loaf so quickly?"

"I don't know the answer to that, Charles, but I do know that it is so. I was very distressed." Here she eyed her brother from the corner of her eye and added cautiously, "I told her that I intended to call upon her regularly and see to it that at least she took some fresh air each day." She prepared herself for another outburst.

Charles merely folded his napkin thoughtfully and placed it beside his plate. "Yes, I daresay that would be the best thing to do if she is not stirring from the house. She is accustomed to being out of doors."

"That is exactly what I told her!" exclaimed Diana, encouraged by his quiet response. "I am so pleased that you see it that way, Charles!"

"How else could I see it?" he asked absently, remarking to himself that indeed was the truth. It seemed to him that his choices in handling this situation were very limited. He still felt an uneasy responsibility for the whole matter of Sylvia's misfortune. Although he was certain that none of this would have happened had it not been for her headstrong way, he also still suspected that Claire might have caused some of it through her dealings with the gypsies.

He did not care to have Diana seen in public with Lady Sylvia, but at least these would be relatively sedate meetings. He would speak to the coachman about where he should drive the ladies on their outings.

Before Sir Charles went to bed that night, he stood a long time at his window, staring out in the direction of Danville House. It seemed to him that this was very unusual behavior for Lady Sylvia. He had not credited her with such depth of feeling. And he wondered, too, if Dr. Clayton were doing everything possible for Robert. It might be necessary for him to look into the matter himself.

Chapter Fourteen

Sir Charles did not bring up the subject of Lady Sylvia with either his sister or his fiancée, but each lady seemed disposed to speak of her with regularity. From Diana he had the latest medical reports about Robert and the current status of Lady Sylvia's health and spirits; from Miss Bitfort-Raines he had the most recent and most succulent bits of gossip. The ladies seemed disinclined to chat about her with one another, however, since they held very different views of her. Too, Miss Bitfort-Raines had tried to speak with Diana about the propriety of her calls upon a woman like Lady Sylvia. Sir Charles had tried to discourage her from doing so, but Miss Bitfort-Raines was persuaded that it was her duty and that dear Diana would listen to the woman about to become her sister-in-law. Dear Diana did not listen, however, and a rupture occurred between the two ladies.

"They say that she is losing weight," said Miss Bitfort-Raines during the second week of Lady Sylvia's self-imposed confinement. Sir Charles and Diana had dined with her and were taking their coffee in the drawing room.

"No doubt her looks will fade rapidly," she added with satisfaction. "Those pale beauties never hold up well in the long run. It requires sturdier qualities to maintain one's appearance under such a strain. I doubt that she has ever given two thoughts to anyone else's well-being before. She is not a person accustomed to sacrifice."

Since Sir Charles had thought much the same thing about sacrifice being unfamiliar to Sylvia, he ventured no comment. Diana, however, fired up in defense of her idol.

"And I suppose that you *have*, Claire!" she exclaimed, carrying the war into the enemy's territory. "I don't recall your ever sacrificing a fig for anyone else! Your parents do everything you wish them to, as does Charles, and you have never had to give way to anyone—except of course to Lady Sylvia in the matter of beaux!"

Miss Bitfort-Raines turned scarlet to the roots of her pale blonde hair. "I suppose you had that from Sylvia Danville!" she said, her voice razor-sharp. "I should imagine that she has been filling your head full of stories about all of her conquests! Lies, most of them, I am certain!"

Here she turned to Sir Charles, who was thinking seriously of having the carriage brought round at once. "And you!" she exclaimed. "Are you just going to allow her to speak to me in such a manner, Charles?" she demanded. "It is more than time that you took charge and forbade her to see that woman! She will soon be dragging our name into another scandal!"

"Our name!" returned Diana in clipped tones. "I should like to remind you, Claire, that as yet 'our name' *is* our name alone—mine and Charles's! *Yours* is still Bitfort-Raines! And Lady Sylvia would not do such a vulgar thing as tell me stories about her conquests. All of those stories I had from other people, Claire, and I have *never* heard Lady Sylvia utter a disparaging word about *you!* She is far too well-bred to do such a thing!"

That, naturally, brought the evening to an end. Miss Bitfort-Raines accepted coldly Sir Charles's excuses for his sister's behavior; Miss Redford offered none on her own behalf. The ladies bowed stiffly to one another, and Sir Charles retreated to the safety of the carriage, accompanied by his angry sister.

"How mean-spirited Claire is!" exclaimed Diana as the carriage door closed behind them. "I am sorry, Charles, for spoiling your evening, but she really should curb her tongue! She would not say such things if she were not so hideously jealous of Lady Sylvia."

Since Sir Charles was painfully aware of the truth of this, he maintained a diplomatic silence. He had not determined to his own satisfaction whether or not Lady Sylvia was responsible for this change in his usually sweet-natured sister. He had no doubt that Claire had been as shocked as he by this transformation, for in the past Diana had listened to Claire's opinions in respectful silence. He had not informed his fiancée of the fact that Diana had come back to town without permission, not wishing to hear her opinions on that subject.

"And as for Lady Sylvia telling me about her conquests, nothing could be farther from the truth!" continued Diana vehemently. "Indeed, I must do most of the talking because her spirits are so low that she simply does not feel like saying anything. Frequently I am reduced to telling her stories about my childhood at Lansing. Nothing could be more boring, I am certain, but she listens to them and makes me feel that I am quite a fascinating person!"

"Is the boy not getting any better, then?" inquired Sir Charles absently, still thinking about his own problems.

Miss Redford's voice trembled a little as he spoke. "No, his fever has become very high, Charles, and the doctor is no longer very hopeful. Lady Sylvia sent a letter to Robert's father in Egypt, begging him to come at once, but she knows that he may not reach London in time. I cannot tell you how distressed she is by that. She does not weep, but she was very close to it today."

"The boy's father is coming?" asked Sir Charles in surprise.

"His name is Robert Blackwell, Charles. You need not keep referring to him as 'the boy,' as though he were 'the dog,' or 'the table'!" returned his sister sharply.

"Blackwell!" he exclaimed. "That is his name?"

Miss Redford spoke in a tone of exaggerated patience, as though she were speaking to a backward three-year-old. "Yes, Charles. As I said, his name is Robert Blackwell. And you should call him Robert instead of 'the boy' or 'the child' in that tiresome way."

Sir Charles was thinking rapidly. Blackwell was the name of a family well-known in the *ton,* although there were of course other Blackwells, too. And if Sylvia had given the boy's last name as Blackwell, it might well be that she had married him without telling anyone and then left the *ton* to brew its own scandal broth. His anger rose instantly. How like her to make a scandal when there was absolutely no need to do so! That she might actually be married—and married to someone of their own set—was a thought that had not occurred to him. And he wished that it had not, for he discovered that it was not an idea that he found acceptable.

He would most certainly make it his business to meet

Robert's father when he arrived. He had developed an insatiable curiosity about the man. He decided, too, that he should call upon Lady Sylvia the next day. And upon Dr. Clayton as well, to be certain that everything possible was being done for the child. If things were developing in the manner that Diana described, it well might be that she was in need of assistance, and she certainly seemed to have no one to turn to. According to Diana, Lady Sylvia had no other callers than herself—except, she had added, Robert's rescuers, young Ashby and Symington, who called faithfully to hear the latest account of his health.

He allowed himself a brief smile of satisfaction. At least she was no longer seeing Lord Wilmington or the Mannerings. Perhaps she had listened to him after all.

When he called upon her the next day, Pelton at first informed him that she was unable to see him. He engaged the butler in a little informal conversation about the safety precautions taken at Danville House, and Pelton, aware that Lady Sylvia had reposed her confidence in Sir Charles in the matter of checking the household, assured him gravely that, thanks to their careful securing of the premises, no one had broken into the house, although the first morning after taking their precautions they had discovered marks on the servants' entrance, which indicated that someone might have attempted to enter there, but had become discouraged. And, he said proudly, since that time there had been no further attempts.

There had been, he added diffidently, one unpleasantness that had arisen. One of Lady Sylvia's necklaces had been stolen from her room, but it had not been taken by an intruder. Pelton had suspected one of the footmen that he had employed, and a careful search of the man's room had turned up the necklace, and he had been sent packing since Lady Sylvia had not wanted to pursue the matter any further.

Upon hearing this, Sir Charles hinted that there were one or two other matters of security that should be discussed with Pelton's mistress. The butler nodded and showed him into the drawing room, asking him to wait while he checked with Lady Sylvia once more to see if she might be able to leave Robert for a few minutes.

"I am sorry to hear that the child is so ill, Pelton," said Sir Charles, looking suitably grave.

"I will tell her ladyship," said Pelton, bowing as he withdrew.

Sir Charles walked restlessly to the window and stared down. To his intense displeasure, he saw Lord Wilmington's high-perch phaeton pull up in front and that gentleman came to the front door bearing a huge bouquet. His eyebrows drew together with a snap. Just the behavior he could expect of Sylvia Danville! Undoubtedly secretly married, caring for a sick and perhaps dying child, refusing the attention of older ladies of quality and receiving instead those of a notorious rake, she was maddening beyond permission!

A minute or two later Lady Sylvia entered, carrying the bouquet. Sir Charles had intended to begin their interview by offering his sympathy and his services. Instead, he heard himself snap, "I thought that you were not seeing Lord Wilmington any longer!"

Sylvia looked at him in surprise. "Whatever would have made you think that, Sir Charles?" she inquired. "And more to the point," she continued, warming to her subject, *"how* did you know it and why do you think that it has anything to do with *you,* sir?"

Sir Charles, angry because he had betrayed himself at

the outset, retorted, "If you recall, ma'am, I did not wish for my sister to be in private company with that gentleman!"

"And she has not been!" snapped Lady Sylvia, her color mounting. "Lord Wilmington has had the great kindness to call upon me every day during Robert's illness and bring me flowers and books, but he has not forced his company upon me, knowing how despondent I have been. He has once again conducted himself in every way like the gentleman that he is."

Her meaning was quite clear. In her eyes he had once again fallen far short of the conduct she expected of a gentleman. He found himself flushing quite as angrily as she was. It was ironic that he, considered by many the quintessential gentleman, was scorned as a poor representative of that species by this woman, considered by many to be the most complete hoyden of the *ton*. Before he retorted in kind, however, he recalled her trouble with Robert and forced himself to say the proper thing.

"I have heard from my sister that the child—" Here he paused a moment and then amended his words. "That Robert has not improved."

The angry pink faded from her cheeks as suddenly as it had risen, and he could see that she was indeed paler than usual, and that purple shadows had appeared under her eyes. She shook her head and turned away from him, still holding the bouquet.

"Dr. Clayton does not hold much hope for him, Charles," she said in a low voice. "And he looks so frail, lying there under the sheet. It seems to be not just a chill from the lake—it may be malaria. He is wasting away before our eyes—and there seems to be little that we can do."

To his distress, he could see that her shoulders were beginning to shake. The bouquet dropped unheeded to the floor and she put her hands to her face. "And I simply don't think that I can face his father, Charles. What am I going to say to him if he arrives and Robert has already—"

Unable to bring herself to say the words, she began to sob. Sir Charles, who had stiffened at the allusion to Robert's father, could not bear to see her so distraught. Suddenly he remembered the words of young Ashby about Sylvia, that she seemed always to be merry. That was how he always thought of her—light-hearted and laughing, making sport of everyone and everything. Seeing her now so defenseless caught at his heart more readily than anything else could have.

In a moment he had crossed the room and taken her in his arms, stroking comfortingly the silken hair he recalled so well as she sobbed into his shoulder. He didn't know how long they stood that way, but finally her tears subsided and she was perfectly still. His cheek was resting against the top of her head, his lips brushing it from time to time, and he continued to stroke the smooth, bright length of her hair. When she looked up at him, he traced the shadows under her eyes, his own eyes dark with concern.

"You must get some rest, Sylvia," he said gently. "It is clear that you haven't been taking care of yourself." And when the shadows did not disappear with the touch of his finger, he kissed her eyelids softly, as though willing away the troubles that had etched themselves there.

When she opened her eyes again and stared at him for a long moment, it seemed the most natural thing in the world to pull her closer and kiss her gently. Time melted away for both of them, and for a brief and happy while they were again in Egypt—still in love and happy with one another.

Sylvia rubbed her cheek against the reassuring firmness of his chest. "Thank you, Charles," she murmured. "For a moment I felt safe again. Quite as though none of this had happened."

"Safe?" he asked sharply, his brows drawing together. "Has something else happened? Why should you not feel safe?"

She laughed a little and pushed him gently away. "I don't mean safe in the literal way you are taking it, Charles. I mean that I was happy before I had brought this trouble down upon us. Have you never had something terrible happen to you, and then thought that if only it were yesterday at this time, or a month ago at this time—before the terrible thing happened, you know— that then perhaps you could feel safe and good again, and keep the thing from happening?"

He frowned. "But you did not bring this particular trouble upon yourself, Sylvia," he persisted. "You have, of course, done a good many foolish things in your life," he added honestly, "but this was not something that you should feel responsible for. Even if you had had a servant close by, the footpad might still have set upon you."

"But I don't mean only that, Charles," she said sadly, "although that was bad enough. If only I had not taken Robert away from home without his father's permission, I would feel so much better! But, as it is, I know that I am entirely responsible for anything that happens to him."

"Without his father's permission?" asked Sir Charles incredulously, for a moment identifying with the unknown Blackwell. "Do you mean that you just left with no word?"

"Well, of course, I left word for him, Charles," she responded impatiently. "And in a general sort of way he had indicated that I could take Robert to Greystone Park. We simply hadn't decided when I would do so."

She paused for a moment, twisting her handkerchief in her hands, a nervous mannerism that he had never seen her use before. "I just grew restless and impatient—you know that I become that way from time to time, Charles—and I decided that I must go immediately. And so I did. And now all of this has happened."

Her voice had grown flat as she had spoken, and she sank down onto one of the sofas as she finished, staring at nothing and twisting her handkerchief absently.

Sir Charles watched her, troubled by her lack of spirit. He was all too familiar with her impatient nature and her hasty actions, and he could feel some sympathy for the father who might come too late to say goodbye to his son. Still, it was a fleeting sympathy, for his concern was not for the father or the child, but for the young woman seated before him. Reluctantly he acknowledged to himself that he was still dangerously attracted to her, although he was certain that Claire Bitfort-Raines would make the more suitable wife. He could, however, resist the attraction and do what he could to help Sylvia. He owed her that much, still feeling responsible for some of the troubles that had fallen upon her.

Hoping to divert her attention to other matters for at least a brief time, he said abruptly, "I understand that you had to let one of your footmen go without a character."

She nodded listlessly. "He had been rummaging through my luggage and had taken one of my necklaces."

"Was it a valuable piece?" he inquired.

She shrugged. "I don't actually know. It was an Egyptian piece, like one of the very old ones. It looks a great deal like one that father found in his excavations, but I purchased it in a market in Cairo. I should imagine it is just a mock-up because it wasn't particularly expensive. The poor fellow who took it probably just thought it was interesting."

Sir Charles was not disposed to take the same view of "the poor fellow," but before he could pursue the conversation, the door opened and Pelton announced the arrival of the Mannerings.

He was unpleasantly surprised by the welcome that Lady Sylvia accorded them. She rose immediately from her sofa and hurried to Miss Mannering, who hugged her tightly. Her brother contented himself with merely shaking her hand heartily, saying, "We came as soon as we heard what had happened, Lady Sylvia. We are sorrier than we can say that we have not been here to support you during this time."

Amelia had been scrutinizing Sylvia's face. "You have not been taking care of yourself," she said accusingly. "I daresay you are up all night."

Sylvia nodded, her face weary. "Povey and Sally are very good, but Robert is not their responsibility as he is mine. I must feel that I am doing everything possible for him. In fact," she said smiling faintly, "I need to return to him now if you will forgive my leaving you."

"Of course we will forgive you, my poor dear!" exclaimed Amelia. "But you must allow me to come to stay with you and help you, Lady Sylvia. I know that you have no family here, and perhaps it would be a comfort to have someone close by that you could talk to during the long hours. A little company might lift your spirits."

Lady Sylvia looked at her for a moment, her eyes brightening a little. "That is very kind of you, Miss Mannering, but I am afraid that it would be too much of an imposition—"

"Not at all!" insisted Amelia. "I should be delighted to be of service. And Gerard—"

"And I hereby place myself at your service at any time of the day or night," said her brother, bowing low. "Consider me your servant."

As the indignant Sir Charles watched, the three of them made their plans. He could not believe what he was seeing! She was actually going to have these people—the sister at least—into her home! She had really gotten to know them only on her journey from Egypt, for he discounted their earlier acquaintance, and now she was allowing them into her home on extremely intimate terms. He felt that a little advice from someone who had known her for a long time was in order.

He cleared his throat as he stood to take his departure. Lady Sylvia scarcely seemed to notice, but as he came to her side and stood there waiting, she finally looked up from her conversation with Amelia Mannering.

"It was good of you to come, Sir Charles," she said absently, quite as though she were speaking to someone she had met just yesterday.

"Lady Sylvia," he said, assuming his most authoritative tone, "before I leave, would you do me the honor of speaking with me in private for a moment?"

As he saw the other three exchange a startled glance, he realized with an inward groan that his choice of words was decidedly unfortunate. It sounded precisely like the request he had made of her during that disastrous evening at the theatre. He did not allow his expression to change, however, and Lady Sylvia rose gracefully from the sofa.

"Of course," she murmured. "If you will excuse me for a moment," she said, turning to the Mannerings with a glimmer of her old humor, "I trust that I shall be able to rejoin you in just a moment."

Sir Charles saw with irritation the mixture of amusement and indignation in Gerard Mannering's eyes as he favored that gentleman and his sister with the briefest of bows.

By the time they reached the morning room and closed the door behind them, Sir Charles was again at the boiling point.

"How could you invite them into your home like this, Sylvia?" he demanded hotly. "You know next to nothing of them and she, at least, will have the run of the household. And I am certain that her brother might as well move in, too, for he will most certainly be here at all hours, presuming upon your good nature."

"It is you, Charles, who are presuming upon my good nature!" she retorted, her eyes kindling. "Why must you always try to take charge of my affairs? The Mannerings have been very kind to me, and, what's more, they amuse me."

"You have my sister," he pointed out stiffly, thinking of the considerable sacrifice he had made to allow Diana the freedom to see her.

"Yes, I do," she responded, "and your sister is the only one who has been able to make me feel happy at all during this dreadful time, and I have looked forward to our short outings more than you will ever know. But the nights are terrible, Charles! I sit by Robert's side and

imagine the most horrible things in the stillness of the
nights. And now Amelia Mannering has offered to make
herself most uncomfortable by coming here and keeping
me company, and all that you can find to do is criticize
her! You do make me feel decidedly unwell, Charles Redford! I cannot imagine how Diana came to be so amiable
when her brother is such a wretched care-for-nobody!"

And she turned and walked angrily from the room,
leaving Sir Charles to see himself out. He had dismissed
his coachman, and so he made his way home on foot,
thinking matters over carefully. He was no longer particularly angry with Lady Sylvia; she was as volatile as ever.
And it might be that the Mannerings were disinterested in
their kindness and that they really had no ulterior motives. Lady Sylvia was, however, a wealthy young
woman—and at the moment, a particularly vulnerable
young woman. He would, he decided, encourage Diana
to spend more time with her. Perhaps that would lessen
the influence of the Mannerings—and he would be kept
abreast of events.

He was not precisely certain what was bothering him
most: the intimate footing that the Mannerings were gain-
ing in Lady Sylvia's household, the continued presence of
Lord Wilmington lingering on the sidelines, the involvement of his own sister in all of this, or perhaps the attempted break-in and the disappearance of the necklace.
He knew that the gypsies had removed themselves from
the area, and although it was possible they had merely
moved to a different nearby location, he considered it
more likely that they had moved themselves well beyond
his reach.

No matter what the reason, his uneasiness was most definitely increasing. And knowing that Diana would be spending even more time in this situation did nothing to abate it.

Chapter 15

The next few days were difficult ones, for Robert's condition grew steadily worse. Amelia Mannering moved in and remained at Lady Sylvia's side, and Diana Redford came twice a day to do what she could to comfort her friend, although they no longer went out to take the air. Gerard Mannering, as Sir Charles had foreseen, practically took up residence at Danville House, doing what he could to distract Lady Sylvia from her trouble, and Lord Wilmington paid his regular calls, although the object of his attention was still closeted with Robert. Mannering, aware of his calls, made certain that he was always present when Wilmington appeared. He had no intention of allowing either his sister or Lady Sylvia, weary as she was, to be private with Wilmington.

Try as he might, however, Gerard Mannering could not induce Sylvia to step out for any fresh air, and he was forced to content himself with seeing to it that she at least came down to the dining room for her meals, leaving Amelia and Povey or Sally to keep watch over Robert. Nor could his sister convince her that she should sleep in her own bed during the night, leaving two of the others with the child. Sylvia insisted upon remaining at his side.

From time to time she walked to the window that looked out upon the soft greenness of the park across the way, and fancied herself at home at Greystone Park, a child again with none of the responsibility and guilt that she now felt weighing so heavily upon her. She had promised Laura that she would see that Robert was taken care of, and she had failed abysmally. Carter had been absent from the deathbed of his wife, something that she had resented secretly for years, and now, through her own heedlessness, he would be absent from the deathbed of his son.

On the second evening after Miss Mannering's arrival, Sylvia sat again by Robert's side. She had insisted that the others go to bed, although Povey had informed her that she would return in an hour or two to sit with her mistress. Robert had been shaken by chills earlier in the evening, but he was quiet now.

Despite her best efforts, Sylvia found herself drifting off to sleep. She arose from her chair on two such occasions and walked briskly up and down the hall outside his chamber. Finally, however, sleep overcame her. She was not certain how long she had been dozing when she became aware that she was cold. She sat bolt upright in her chair, her shawl slipping to the floor.

The window beside Robert's bed, so carefully closed against the unseasonably cool night air, stood open, and the draperies had been pulled back. Robert himself lay uncovered and, to her horror, she saw that someone had used the pitcher of water at his bedside to wet his sheets and nightshirt so that he was shivering in the chill night air.

Feverishly, she jerked the window shut and locked it, pulling the draperies firmly into place. She called Povey and together they rapidly dried Robert and changed his clothes, pulling the mattress from his bed and replacing it with another. When he was once again dry and covered, they stared at one another in horror.

"Who could have done this, Povey?" she asked in a whisper, and her maid shook her head silently. Neither of them could think of anyone in the household who would wish harm to the child.

"Do you remember what the gypsy said at the masquerade, Povey?" Sylvia asked in a low voice.

"Now, there will be none of that foolishness, my lady," Povey said firmly. "You know that the gypsies tell tales for children."

Sylvia shook her head. "That woman said that there was another fortune that she was supposed to tell me— prepared by someone else—but that she had to warn me. She said that a child and I were both in danger—and that I should beware of those that I think I know. And the first warning said that I should beware of a dark man."

She turned to her ashen-faced maid. "How can I not regard them seriously, Povey? Look at what has happened to Robert—first the kidnapping and now this! How can I risk having something like this happen again?"

They stared at one another. "And who could have done it?" she whispered. There seemed to be no reasonable answer, and thereafter either she or Povey was in constant attendance in the sickroom. If one of them had to leave for even a minute, the other one took her place. Together they provided what protection they could for

Robert, and they confided in no one—having no one that they felt they could trust absolutely.

On the third morning after Miss Mannering's arrival, Pelton appeared in the sickroom with a card. He hesitated beside his mistress and then said, "Forgive me for disturbing you, Lady Sylvia, but Miss Bitfort-Raines is waiting in the morning room. I told her that you were not available for callers this morning, but she said that it was an emergency."

Sylvia stared at him for a moment. "I wonder if something has happened to Diana," she murmured to herself. "She did not call or send a note yesterday and that is most unlike her."

Then she said in a louder voice, "Yes, Pelton, tell her that I will join her in just a moment."

Miss Mannering, who was seated beside her, protested, "I will go down, Lady Sylvia. You are too exhausted to see callers."

Sylvia paused in front of a glass and took stock of herself. "I do look that way, don't I?" she said smiling faintly as she looked at her drawn face and the dark circles under her eyes. "That should improve Claire Bitfort-Raines's spirits."

"Why go down to see her?" insisted Miss Mannering. "She will only distress you."

"She may be here about Diana," said Sylvia absently. "If there is something wrong, I would wish to know it. I shan't be more than a few minutes."

Sylvia was quite correct: Miss Bitfort-Raines had indeed come about Diana Redford, and she presented her purpose briskly, paying no heed to the weariness of her hostess.

"I am sure that you must see, Lady Sylvia," said Miss

Bitfort-Raines in a self-assured voice, "that allowing a young woman like Diana Redford to be in your home on such an intimate footing is scarcely going to increase her credit with the world. It will be quite otherwise. The world will have much to say about her that is unfavorable."

She paused in her flow of conversation for a moment to stare at Sylvia, who merely sat silently, watching her. When there was no response, Miss Bitfort-Raines flowed on.

"I know that you entertain a fondness for Miss Redford—as do I, of course—and I am certain that you do not wish to damage her reputation."

"You are too kind, ma'am," returned Sylvia dryly. "I did not know that you thought so highly of me that you would credit me with such feelings."

Miss Bitfort-Raines turned slightly pink at her remark, but did not allow this to slow her. "I know that I speak for her brother as well as all of her well-wishers when I tell you that you must not continue to see Miss Redford."

"And does Sir Charles know that you are here on his behalf, ma'am?" inquired Sylvia crisply, feeling her anger rising.

Miss Bitfort-Raines did not hesitate. "Yes, of course, he does," she returned in a matter-of-fact tone. "Sir Charles knows that I must regard all of his family matters as my own now that we are so nearly wed."

"How fortunate he must count himself," returned Sylvia dryly, "but I fear that I must distress both of you. I plan to see Miss Redford as long as she cares to call upon me. As I have told Sir Charles before, if he wishes her not to see me, he must forbid her himself. He must not look to me."

Miss Bitfort-Raines rose abruptly. "Then that, of course, is what we will do, Lady Sylvia," she said, her tone curt. "If you have so little concern for the well-being of others, I will simply tell Miss Redford that seeing you is not a suitable activity for a young woman of breeding."

Sylvia inclined her head, not bothering to rise. "I am certain that you will do as you think best, Miss Bitfort-Raines."

And Miss Bitfort-Raines had made her departure, directing her driver to take her immediately to the Redford home. She was balked of her quarry, however, for she learned there that Miss Redford had already departed to pay her calls and that Sir Charles was closeted in his study with his man of business. Thwarted, Miss Bitfort-Raines had retired to her own home, determined to take this matter into her own hands at the first possible moment.

Her quarry, in the meantime, pursued their respective interests, blissfully unaware of the plans of Miss Bitfort-Raines. Sir Charles completed his business affairs, and Miss Redford paid another call to Danville House, returning to her own home in a state of depression.

"I fear that he will die soon, Charles," Diana told her brother that afternoon after her return from Lady Sylvia's home. "I was not able to see Lady Sylvia at all yesterday because Claire called and pressed me into going with her to select wedding clothes. I simply could not escape her, so I sent a note round to Danville House with one of her footmen."

She paused for a moment and added, "And that is the strangest thing, Charles. Lady Sylvia did not receive the note. I cannot imagine that Pelton forgot to take it up to her, but perhaps he might have."

Considering the fact that Diana had used one of

Claire's footmen to send the note, Sir Charles thought that he could imagine why Sylvia had not received the note, but he remained discreetly silent.

She reverted to her sad subject. "Of course, with things there as bad as can be, it is possible. Robert has become still weaker and the fever is very high. The doctor has packed him in ice to try to break it, but nothing had happened when I took my leave."

She sank down onto the sofa beside her brother and covered her eyes. "And it is so very sad, Charles. Lady Sylvia simply sits by his bedside and watches his every move. Miss Mannering forced her to come out to have breakfast, but she would not eat anything. She simply sat and poked at her food, then looked up at me and said, 'What shall I tell his father when he arrives too late?' "

She looked up at her brother. "It was so affecting, Charles—and yet there was nothing that any of us could do to comfort her."

He patted her hand comfortingly. "She is a very strong woman, Diana. She will manage to come through this. And perhaps the child—"Here he caught himself again. "Perhaps Robert will be all right, after all. Sometimes a child is strong enough to withstand such an illness. It is not impossible that the fever might yet break."

He did not tell her that he had asked Dr. Clayton to keep him informed of developments in Robert's illness. The doctor, who had known Sir Charles for a long time, had felt no compunction in doing so, feeling that Lady Sylvia might stand in need of his help if things did not go well.

Sir Charles could not help resenting the fact that Robert's father was far away, leaving Sylvia to bear the burden alone. Even if she had been responsible for bringing the boy away, Blackwell could have followed them sooner. And he was afraid, judging by Dr. Clayton's most recent report, that the burden might prove to be a greater one than he had at first thought.

It had occurred to him earlier that he should risk paying another call and offering his support, but he had known that she would not welcome him. Now he wondered again if he should go.

The two of them sat quietly for a few moments, Sir Charles stroking his sister's dark hair gently, but the relative peace of their afternoon was disturbed by the butler's announcement of Miss Bitfort-Raines's arrival. Sir Charles frowned a little at this unexpected call, for he had no particular wish to engage in conversation with Claire at the moment, but he forced himself to smile pleasantly as she was shown into the room and he rose to greet her.

"This is an unexpected pleasure, Claire," he said smoothly, taking her hand and glancing down at his sister, as though to remind her that she too should greet their visitor.

Miss Redford smiled faintly at their guest and murmured even more faintly, "Yes indeed . . . quite unexpected."

If Miss Bitfort-Raines took note of the tepidness of her greeting, she gave no sign of it. Instead, she turned immediately to business.

"How very fortunate to find both of you together," she said briskly, drawing her chair closer to them as though to get down to business. "I have a matter to discuss that concerns us all."

"Indeed?" inquired Sir Charles, his eyebrows raised. "And what might that be, Claire?"

She smiled a little. "I know, of course, your feelings

about Lady Sylvia, Sir Charles. What I wished to speak to both of you about is the time that Diana is spending with her."

Both of her listeners looked disagreeably surprised.

"And what affair is that of yours, Claire?" asked Miss Redford indignantly. "I believe that we had this discussion earlier and I asked you the same question then."

Miss Bitfort-Raines attempted to look coyly self-conscious at her comment. "After all, Diana, since I will stand in place of your mama after Sir Charles and I marry—"

"In place of my mother?" repeated Miss Redford incredulously. "Indeed, you shall do no such thing, Claire! While I grant you that Charles has cared for me as my father would have, I am now a grown woman and I assure you that I do not stand in need of you as a mother!"

"That statement alone indicates your need of me, Diana," responded Miss Bitfort-Raines with a smugness that made Miss Redford long to disarrange her carefully coiffed curls. "If you were as aware upon every suit as you think yourself to be, you would not be spending so much time with Lady Sylvia Danville and thereby calling unfavorable attention to yourself. People will think that your behavior is as light-minded as hers is."

"I appreciate your interest, Claire," said Sir Charles smoothly, before his outraged sister could respond, "but I assure you that I am quite capable of handling Diana's affairs. You need not trouble yourself."

"It is no trouble at all, Charles," returned that lady, quite oblivious to the mild irritation in his voice. "I could see that you had not been able to make Diana recognize the enormity of Lady Sylvia's transgressions, and I naturally feel an interest in anything that pertains to the welfare of your family."

"Naturally," responded Sir Charles, restraining himself with difficulty as he watched Diana's growing anger. Claire was undoing his careful handling of the situation with one meddling conversation. "But I assure you, Claire, that Diana and I are fully capable of taking care of this matter between us."

At this clear indication that she was neither needed nor wanted, Miss Bitfort-Raines rose haughtily from her chair and gathered her belongings. "I thought that you would wish to do the proper thing, Charles," she said stiffly. "I am sure that I had only your welfare at heart, but if you wish to allow Diana to behave in this careless manner with a woman of Sylvia Danville's ilk, I wash my hands of the entire matter. I did not expect for *her* to listen to me when I asked her to not to see Diana, but I certainly did believe that the two of you would be more attentive to my words."

Sir Charles's face grew dark. "Am I to understand, Claire, that you have visited Lady Sylvia and asked her not to see my sister?" he asked grimly, quite as though he had not done the same thing himself.

Miss Bitfort-Raines nodded with satisfaction. "I have at least done what *I* thought was proper, Charles," she replied smugly. "I can ask no more of myself. One must always do one's duty."

"I can only say, Claire, that I wish you had not taken so much upon yourself—and that you had not done so without first speaking with me," said Sir Charles, his annoyance plain.

Miss Bitfort-Raines looked astonished. "Well, I should hope that I know your feelings upon this subject, Charles. And I felt that I could certainly speak for you."

"I am perfectly capable of speaking for myself, Claire,"

he responded. "In fact, I prefer to do so. How did Lady Sylvia respond to your request?"

Miss Bitfort-Raines reddened slightly. "She informed me that if she had not refused to see Diana when you had asked her to do so, she would scarcely do so now. I informed her that Diana would most certainly listen to me, considering the relationship which we are about to have with one another."

Sir Charles was uncomfortably aware of his sister's startled gaze. "*You* tried to convince Lady Sylvia not to see me, Charles? *When* did you do so—and why did you not tell me?"

"It was some time ago, Diana," replied Sir Charles stiffly, conscious that he was once again being made to look like the greatest sneaksby in nature. "I have since regretted my request of Lady Sylvia."

"I should hope you had, Charles! After what she did for me, we should thank her profusely rather than insult her!" She turned to glare at Miss Bitfort-Raines. "And how you could take it upon yourself to be so interfering, Claire, I cannot imagine!"

"Well, this is quite a pretty pelter you have gotten yourself into, miss," said Miss Bitfort-Raines acidly. "I think, Charles," she added, "that you would have done much better to have left her at Lansing as you planned to do."

"Well, I shan't be left at Lansing as though I were a parcel to be dropped off until someone is ready for me! I shall do as I please!" retorted Diana.

Then, ignoring her own words and her unannounced departure from Lansing, she added quite irrationally, "And if you think to rule the roast when you are married, Claire, I should tell you that my brother is very accustomed to calling the tune in our house. It will be most unfortunate if you attempt to take charge."

Miss Bitfort-Raines, her lips folded tightly, tightened her grip on her reticule and extended her hand to Sir Charles.

"I must bid you good-day, sir," she said icily. "It is clear to me that no one here is concerned with propriety of behavior. I believe that it is more than time for me to return to my own home."

Diana stood up abruptly. "I must say that I agree with you, Claire," she said frankly. "I believe that you have already said far more than you needed to."

"Well, of all the insufferable, meddling busybodies!" exclaimed Miss Redford as the door closed after her loving sister-in-law-to-be. "I am grateful, Charles, that you have the good sense to recognize her interference for what it is."

"Well, Diana," he temporized, "Claire did have your best interests at heart, although it is most unfortunate that she chose to go about matters as she did."

"I should just think it *was* the outside of enough, Charles! If you see no harm in my seeing Lady Sylvia, I scarcely think that Claire should take it upon herself to say otherwise!"

Sir Charles, who quite agreed that Miss Bitfort-Raines had overstepped herself in interfering, could not bring himself to agree that there was no harm at all in her time spent with Sylvia, so he tried to steer a middle course through stormy waters.

"It is most certainly a matter between the two of us, Diana. As you know, I do have some reservations about Lady Sylvia's behavior, although I am sure that it has been above reproach during the time you have spent with her."

"To be sure it has, Charles!" cried Diana indignantly. "How could anyone find fault with someone who does nothing save watch at the sickbed of a child? Claire astonishes me! Oh, Charles, my heart goes out to Lady Sylvia! She seems so alone."

Sir Charles, distressed by the news of the call paid by Miss Bitfort-Raines upon that lady, gratified his sister by promising to call upon Lady Sylvia immediately.

And he was as good as his word. He felt decidedly uneasy, for the memory of his last call was still vivid in his mind—and he was most reluctant to follow so close upon the heels of Claire's visit, particularly since Sylvia's state of mind was already questionable. Nonetheless, he felt that he must make the gesture. More than ever he regretted Claire's habit of taking too much upon herself, and he braced himself for a scathing rebuff from Lady Sylvia.

He was surprised by his reception, however. Amelia Mannering was in the drawing room when Pelton showed him in, and she advanced toward him with both hands outstretched.

"We are so grateful to see you, Sir Charles," she said fervently, and he noticed then that Gerard Mannering was also in the room. "Lady Sylvia needs the support of someone who has known her for a long time, someone that might be of more help to her now than either Gerard or I can be."

She paused to wipe her eyes, and Sir Charles stared down at her. "But what is this, Miss Mannering?" he asked. "Has Robert died?"

Miss Mannering shook her head, and her brother answered for her. "No, Sir Charles, although it seems that it must happen at any moment. Our concern is Lady Sylvia at the moment, however. She has not slept or eaten in several days, and neither of us nor your sister has been able to prevail upon her to do so. We fear that when— if—Robert dies, that she will break down completely."

Sir Charles nodded. Sylvia's emotions were always intense, so none of this was a surprise to him, although it was disturbing nonetheless. And of course there was no reason to think that she would listen to him about taking care of herself, but he could at least try.

"I will go upstairs and tell her that you are here," said Miss Mannering, withdrawing quickly, her brother following in her wake.

Sir Charles paced the room restlessly, wondering if Sylvia would consent to see him. Their last interview had scarcely had an amicable closing, and Claire had certainly done what she could to complete their alienation. He paused for a moment before a portrait of the present Marchioness, painted just after her marriage, and looked into her smiling eyes. The only striking similarities between the her and her daughter were their expressive eyes and their grace of movement. He thought for a moment of Sylvia and her early morning exercises and smiled to himself. The other trait they shared was not a physical one: it was simply that they cared not at all what others might think of them.

He heard the door open behind him and he turned, expecting to see Lady Sylvia, but it was Povey, heavy-eyed and wearing a worried expression, who stood there.

"Forgive me, Sir Charles," she said, closing the door quietly behind her, "but I wanted to have a word with you privately before Lady Sylvia comes down."

Sir Charles waited expectantly, but she seemed to have some trouble continuing.

"I hope that you will not think that I am overstepping myself, sir, but I can't think what to do next and there is no one else here that I know to turn to. Mrs. Simpkins calls, of course, and some of the other ladies—but Lady Sylvia will not see them and she would not thank me for talking to them."

There was another pause and then Povey rushed into words again, glancing toward the closed door. "I fear for her health, Sir Charles. Something must be done, regardless of the child. She simply will not take care of herself, sir. It is not unusual for her to fast a bit for her health, but she has not eaten for several days, nor exercised, nor behaved at all in a normal way. Try to do something for her, Sir Charles. It may be that she will confide in you."

"I will do what I can, Povey—but what is it that she should confide in me?"

In response, Povey shook her head. "It is not for me to say, sir," she replied, folding her lips tightly.

And before Sir Charles could ask anything else of her, she slipped quietly from the room, anxious to be gone before the arrival of her mistress.

He was still staring toward the door when Sylvia entered, and he was startled, not just by her sudden appearance, but by her physical state. Her cheeks looked hollow and her hair had lost its sheen. She was carefully arrayed, but her movements were slow and her eyes fearful.

He hurried to her side and guided her to a sofa, and she sank down upon it.

"Sylvia," he began, trying to decide what he should say first. "I would like to apologize to you for Claire's call. She should not have been so thoughtless as to come to you at such a time."

"No, it doesn't appear at all the thing to do, does it, Charles?" she agreed tonelessly, and he winced at her choice of words. Once again she was accusing him of being concerned only with appearances.

"It made me angry at the time, Charles, but that faded quickly enough. It really is of no consequence at a time like this."

He took her hand and patted it, unable to think of what he could say to this. He would have greatly preferred that she be outraged. That would have been a reassuringly familiar reaction. Her present lethargy—and her haunted expression—disturbed him, and he thought of Povey's words.

"Of course there are other things far more important, Sylvia. One of them is that you take care of yourself."

She shook her head. "How can that be important at the moment, Charles? Robert is the only one who matters now."

"Of course he matters now, Sylvia—which is precisely why you must take proper care of yourself," he returned, seeing his opportunity and seizing it immediately.

"How can you possibly do all that you think necessary for Robert if you haven't enough strength to do so?" he demanded in a bracing tone. "If you let yourself go like this, you can be in no proper condition to be certain that he is cared for as he should be. And who is to say that he cannot sense the attitudes of those about him, even though he does not appear conscious? Dr. Clayton has mentioned to me that he believes that such things are possible. What will Robert be receiving from you save a feeling of despair?"

Sylvia stared at him, her attention fully captured. Seeing this, he pressed his advantage. "I shall ring for Pelton to bring you some broth, and then you must rest, at least for a few hours. Then, when you go into Robert's room you will feel more yourself—and you will be of more help to him."

She allowed him to ring for Pelton and Povey appeared in his wake.

"I believe that I shall take the broth in my chamber, Povey," she said, rising to her feet and wrapping her shawl about her. "And then I shall sleep until seven if you will awaken me then."

She had realized that he was right about one thing: she must rest or she would again sleep when she should be watching over Robert. At this hour of the day Povey could still manage to stay awake and there would be several others in and out of the room as well. She must rest in order to protect Robert during the long watches of the night to come.

Povey directed a grateful glance at Sir Charles as Pelton left the room to give the cook directions. Sylvia turned to him and held out her hand. "Thank you, Charles," she said simply. "It was kind of you to come—particularly when you feel as you do about me."

Before he could protest her statement, she had left the room with Povey, and he saw himself out. Standing on the front steps of Danville House, he stared thoughtfully across at the plane trees in the square. He had helped her a little, and that was a satisfaction, of course. But where precisely did that leave him? he wondered wryly. Engaged to one eligible young woman and quite desperately in love with another—one who was married and completely involved in concerns of her own. His orderly, well-regulated life had once again been overset by Lady Sylvia Danville.

That very evening after taking her broth and a nap several hours in length, Amelia and Sylvia sat again at Robert's side, Sylvia devoting herself to bathing his forehead.

"He is on fire," she murmured, patting the small, thin hand and tucking it back under the covers. She sank hopelessly into her chair. It would soon be over.

Sylvia covered her face with her hands, trying to blot out thoughts of Laura and her pride in her infant son. Once more she reproached herself for taking Robert away from Egypt without consulting Carter. Little though she liked him, however would she be able to face him and tell him about her unforgivable carelessness?

Her mind wandered to the warnings she had received. Robert was most certainly in danger—but she could not believe that Charles was the dark man responsible for it. There were other dark men in the world, and Charles had shown himself to be more concerned with her welfare than she would ever have expected. She smiled to herself, amused. Perhaps that was what the gypsy meant when she told her that things were not what they seemed to be.

An hour or so later she jerked awake, horrified that once again, despite her rest in the afternoon, she had drifted off to sleep. A glance told her that Amelia was still soundly asleep. And then she realized what had awakened her.

Robert was twisting restlessly under the covers—and his forehead was drenched in perspiration! She leaped to her feet and held the candle over him, anxiously checking the covers and the pitcher at his bedside to be certain that this was not a repeat performance of last night's mischance. To her relief, the pitcher was full and Robert seemed slightly cooler to her touch.

"Amelia! Have Povey send for Dr. Clayton! It looks as though the fever has broken!"

Anxiously she hovered over the boy, trying to wipe his brow and to keep him from tossing the covers from the bed as he thrashed about. Never, she thought, would she have thought she could be delighted to see Robert so uncomfortable and restless. What would have terrified her a few days ago was now a most welcome sight.

When Dr. Clayton arrived, he confirmed her belief. The fever had indeed broken. The doctor administered a draught that would keep the child still so that he could rest.

"And now, ma'am, if I may say so, you must also get some rest," he said sternly. "I have a potion here for you as well."

Sylvia laughed. "It won't be needed, Dr. Clayton. I assure you that I will sleep like one of the dead for what is left of the night."

And so she did. Once assured that Robert was out of danger, she retired to her chamber and slept dreamlessly for the next thirty-six hours.

Chapter Sixteen

"Well, now that Dr. Clayton says that Robert is out of danger, will you be going to Greystone Park?" inquired Miss Redford a few days after his fever had broken. She had continued to pay her calls faithfully to Danville House, ignoring the protests of Miss Bitfort-Raines.

Her question sounded a little forlorn, for she had grown accustomed to the daily visits and thought that life would seem drab without Lady Sylvia.

"Yes, indeed," replied Sylvia with a smile. "I think that we all need the rest and change of scene. Gerard and Amelia are coming with us," she added, seeing her companion's surprise at the "we all."

"I am glad that you won't be going alone," Miss Redford replied sincerely. "It will be much more cheerful with them, I am sure." She reflected silently that her brother would not be pleased by the news, for he was still irritated by their presence at Danville House.

"I am certain that they will be pleasant company, and it is very kind of them to consent to come," agreed Sylvia, "for I know that they are fonder by far of the city. I have been casting about for ideas to amuse them while we are there," she continued, "and I decided that having a masquerade of our own would be enjoyable."

"A masquerade!" exclaimed Miss Redford. "That would be delightful!"

Sylvia smiled at her. "I was afraid that your unhappy experience would have turned you against all thought of a masquerade."

"Not at all! My misfortune could have occurred anywhere, and nothing is more charming than dressing up for a masquerade ball!"

"Then perhaps I may be able to persuade you to join us for the ball," replied Sylvia. "Greystone Park is not too far from London, and I had thought to have a house party for the occasion."

"I should love to come!" Miss Redford assured her. "And I should love to see Greystone Park as well."

"Do you think, Diana," said Sylvia hesitantly, "that your brother will give his permission for you to attend?"

"Of course he will!" said Diana, instantly taking fire. "He will not pay the least heed to what Claire says!"

"Will he not?" inquired Sylvia in some surprise. "I thought that—that Miss Bitfort-Raines spoke for Sir Charles as well as herself."

"Not at all," responded Diana firmly. "Claire takes altogether too much upon herself at times, and so Charles and I told her after she came to call upon you."

"You *both* told her that?" asked Sylvia, finding it difficult to credit what she was hearing. It was true that Charles had been very kind upon his last visit, the one just before Robert's fever had broken, but she had not thought that it heralded any change in his attitude, rather that it had been the gesture that he considered proper to make at the time.

"Indeed we did! And so, as you can see, Charles would make no objection to my coming to Greystone."

Sylvia was much less certain of this, despite Miss Redford's reassurances, and she added, "I plan, of course, to invite Sir Charles and Miss Bitfort-Raines as well."

Miss Redford's face fell. "Oh! Well, I can see inviting Charles, Lady Sylvia, but do you feel that you must invite Claire, too? I know that it is rag-mannered of me to say so, but we will have a much better time without her."

Sylvia chuckled. "I would offer no argument with that, Diana, but I fear that it would do nothing but set up your brother's hackles if we failed to include her."

Miss Redford nodded reluctantly. "I can see that that would be so—still, it would be so much pleasanter without her there to attend to everyone else's affairs."

"She will not be alone in doing so, Diana. I will be inviting Mrs. Simpkins and Lady Riverton as well."

Her guest brightened a little at this. "How clever you are, Lady Sylvia! That will answer very well, for both of them dislike Claire and they will keep her occupied by annoying her for at least a portion of the time."

Sylvia laughed, amused by Miss Redford's forthrightness. "And there will naturally be a host of others, Diana, so don't feel that we will be such a small party that we will be living in one another's pockets. Greystone Park is quite a large place, you know, so you will not be always with Miss Bitfort-Raines."

"You may depend upon that," responded Miss Redford earnestly.

Sylvia had been thoughtful after her departure. It might well be that she should consider taking Charles into her confidence. It was true that nothing else had happened since the strange occurrence in Robert's bedroom, but she had still been uneasy, and she and Povey had been very careful in their attendance upon Robert. Povey had moved her cot into Robert's room and slept there each night, the cot positioned directly in front of the door. Sylvia could think of no possible way that Charles could be connected with any of this, and it would be reassuring to talk matters over with him.

She had decided at last that a servant had been to blame for the attack, for she discovered that one of the new maids had been passionately devoted to the footman that Pelton had dismissed for taking the necklace. The malicious mischief done to Robert was exactly what she would have expected of someone seeking to avenge herself, and she had instructed Pelton to dismiss the maid as well. Once the girl was out of the house, she and Povey had breathed a bit more freely, although Povey maintained her post in Robert's room.

She smiled to herself. It had all turned out for the best after all. It seemed that the girl had unintentionally done Robert a kindness rather than a disservice, for the rapid cooling of his body had undoubtedly helped in his recovery. And now she was safely gone and they would be on their way to Greystone, far removed from gypsies and their warnings.

Lady Sylvia was in a merry mood when she returned to Greystone Park. Not only was she pleased to be home again, but she was grateful beyond the telling to be able to turn a recovering Robert over to the safekeeping of Nanny Reese, the unquestionably capable old woman who had cared for both her and her father. She felt that at last she shared the responsibility with someone else and could lean on the good woman's competence.

Nanny, small and bright-eyed and brisk, clucked as she looked him over. "Too thin, my lady, and that's a fact, but 'twill take no time at all to remedy that." And she had whisked Robert off to the refurbished nursery, now complete with the toys and clothes that Sylvia had sent ahead, there to ply him with porridge and nourishing soups and thick slices of bread and butter.

Greystone Park was a rambling estate, the earliest portion of it having been built in Tudor times. Only one wing remained from that era, however, and the rest was a rather careless patchwork of styles achieved during the interval of centuries as various Danvilles had indulged their fancies. The result might have been nightmarish, but was, instead, like the Danvilles themselves, eccentric and charming.

"Walking through Greystone Park is like reading a history book, except that one is seeing it rather than reading about it," one guest was heard to remark, wandering through one of the long galleries that had been added rather haphazardly to the establishment, this one to house the marble busts brought home from Greece and Italy by a Danville who had been an ardent classical scholar. It was clear to any visitor to Greystone that the current Marquess had come by his passion for antiquities quite honestly.

"But only a Danville could hold up his head and behave as though this were the finest palace in the country," Lady Riverton had retorted to the complimentary guest, "instead of an elegant rabbit warren."

Sylvia regarded it all with affection, from the ancient gatehouse to the cavernous Tudor library, from the Elizabethan knot garden to the two-hundred-year-old puzzle-garden with the sweet-scented roses at its center. Most of her life had been spent wandering the world with her parents, but that had made life at Greystone all the sweeter. Here everything remained the same, from the servants to the house itself. For Sylvia it represented order and stability and beauty.

She heaved a sigh of relief as she wandered through the gardens on her first day home. The puzzle-garden had always been her favorite place as a child, and she walked there now, unperturbed by the high, thick walls of shrubbery that enclosed her. She chose her turns unhesitatingly until she arrived at last at the stone bench in the center, where she could sit in the private sunny space and admire the scarlet roses carefully planted so long ago at the heart of the maze. Here she had always come for peace and privacy. She smiled. When Robert was a little older, she would show him the way.

Later that afternoon she retired to her father's study to inspect his precious cartons, carefully packed with his discoveries and purchases and notes, which she had had transported carefully from London. A quick survey showed her that several of the cartons had been opened and then somewhat clumsily tied shut again. Annoyed, she opened them to see if anything had been damaged.

The first one was filled to the brim with notes in her father's fine, spidery handwriting, and it seemed to be intact, although it was clear that some of the papers had been taken out and then replaced, for they were out of order. Her father was very precise about the organization of his notes, arranging everything by date and indexing all of the entries by topics. The others contained a variety of jewelry and vases and small collectables, all carefully packed, ranging from ancient scarabs to a much more modern string of blue beads. Although it appeared that some of the pieces had been unwrapped, the boxes were almost full and it seemed unlikely that anything had been taken, but Sylvia knew that there was no way of knowing whether or not anything was missing until her father arrived. The carter who had brought the boxes down from London had been employed at Greystone all of his life, so she knew that if anything were missing from them the theft had occurred before they had left London. It was an annoyance, but for the moment she locked the cartons in the study and put them out of her mind. She would address that problem a little later when she had more time.

The next few days slipped by happily enough. Robert loved his freedom at Greystone: there were so many rooms to wander through and rambling gardens to explore, although Sylvia was careful to see that someone was always with him, even here. She felt reasonably secure, but she was not willing to take any chances.

Robert had grown quiet and rather sober after his illness, and Nanny was intent upon cheering him up, for she believed firmly that children should be happy as well as healthy. She had been already disposed to be fond of him, for she knew that he was hers to care for, but the fact that he had not only lost his mother but had also been deathly ill had ensured her devotion. Robert, quick to respond to affection, loved her in return and followed her trustingly about the house.

Amelia and Gerard pottered happily through the gardens and the galleries while Sylvia met with the housekeeper and the bailiff and took care of some of the business of the estate. They also were busily making plans for the house party, and for the masquerade that was to be its chief feature. The three of them went riding each morning, Sylvia taking great pleasure in showing the Mannerings the estate and the surrounding countryside that was so much a part of her childhood and the amiable brother and sister responded enthusiastically.

It was on one such ride that they sighted a plume of smoke rising in the distance, and Sylvia had stopped to stare at it.

"Is there something wrong, Lady Sylvia?" asked Mannering, pulling up beside her and following her gaze.

"There is no cottage there," she replied, pointing toward the smoke.

"Perhaps we should investigate," he responded, turning his mount in that direction.

The ladies fell in behind him, following him along the path that led down into the green woodiness of a dingle, where they saw three wagons pulled together and a wood fire in the midst of them, with a kettle on to boil. A dog lay next to the fire and a woman bent over it, carefully feeding bits of kindling into it.

"Why, it's a band of gypsies!" exclaimed Amelia in delight.

The woman glanced up at the sound of voices, and disappeared quickly into one of the wagons. Sylvia felt her stomach muscles tighten as she took in the scene. There was no reason to fear the gypsies, of course, but she could not see any of them now without thinking of the warnings.

"Perhaps we should not interrupt them this early in the morning," she remarked, bringing her horse to a halt.

Mannering, not remarking her hesitancy, exclaimed with enthusiasm, "What a stroke of luck! Why don't we see if one of them can come to the ball and tell fortunes?

You said that was a great success at the masquerade you attended, Lady Sylvia."

The Mannerings were aware of the gypsy's warning at the ball—at least the portion of it referring to the fire—but they had, of course, no idea that Sylvia had become a nervous wreck thinking about the rest of the warning—and about her first one. They knew she had appeared distressed, but they had attributed it to Robert's illness.

Now, however, Miss Mannering noted Sylvia's sudden paleness and her obvious lack of enthusiasm for the plan, and she threw her brother a warning glance, saying, "I think, Gerard, that Lady Sylvia has had her fill of gypsies for the time being."

Sylvia had seen the look and tried to pass it off lightly. "It's of no consequence, Amelia," she had assured her. "And Gerard is quite right. The guests would love it."

Mannering, embarrassed by his lapse, said hastily, "Don't give it another thought, Lady Sylvia. I simply wasn't thinking of what had happened to you. I hope that I haven't distressed you."

She smiled, touched by his anxiety. "Not at all, actually. I am quite sure that Miss Bitfort-Raines had planned to use her fortune-teller to embarrass me. As it turned out, the gypsy did me a kindness by trying to warn me."

Mannering smiled back at her. She had shared with them the story of the gypsy's change of heart about telling her the fortune prepared by Miss Bitfort-Raines. "Perhaps this is your opportunity to avenge yourself upon Miss Bitfort-Raines," he said lightly.

"Gerard!" exclaimed his sister. "You can't be serious!"

"Why not?" he asked, amusement in his voice. "We wouldn't do anything malicious, of course. Just embarrass her a little bit. I daresay that we wouldn't do anything as mischievous as she planned to do to Lady Sylvia—and think of the amusement that having a fortune-teller would provide the guests."

The three of them looked at one another and, with one accord, started once again down the path to the camp. Sylvia had looked about intently to see if Madame Zeena were present with this group, but she saw no sign of that lady.

She was amused by the idea of teasing Miss Bitfort-Raines by giving her a dose of her own medicine. She had thought of having the fortune-teller say something to the effect of "Beware of twisting the truth; it will catch the twister within its coils!"

The woman who had been tending the fire emerged from one of the wagons as they came closer, and they explained their needs to her. She informed them that she could read palms and that she would come on the night of the ball. They did not inform her of the special fortune planned for Miss Bitfort-Raines, indeed Lady Sylvia was not certain that she would go through with it, but they entertained themselves on the ride home with possible messages and the reactions they would receive from that young lady.

Still, entertaining though these notions were and amused though she was by the Mannerings, she discovered that she felt uncomfortable because of the appearance of a gypsy camp so close to Greystone. It was foolish, of course, for there had always been occasional passing groups of the travelers in this area. Still, she had seen altogether too much of gypsies and fortune-tellers in the last few months of her life.

The first arrivals for the house party were Arthur Ashby and Boots Symington, who were honored by their invitation to such a hallowed pile as Greystone Park, and who had made a special trip to Bond Street to purchase a magnificent top for Robert. They were followed closely by Lady Riverton and Mrs. Simpkins, who had decided that she could tolerate Augusta's slights for the sake of riding at no expense in a well-sprung carriage. The gentlemen retired to the gardens to inspect Robert, whom they now considered their own especial charge, while Sylvia showed the ladies to their rooms.

Lady Riverton looked Sylvia up and down, her eyes glittering with magpie brightness. "Heard you were in pretty queer stirrups, my girl," she said frankly. "But you look to be in fine fettle now. I'm glad to see it."

"Thank you, Lady Riverton," said Sylvia, smiling. "And I'm glad to see you looking so well."

"*I* always look well," she retorted. "It's Ophelia here that becomes sickly at the blink of a cat's eye!"

Mrs. Simpkins, who prided herself upon her sickliness as her one claim for attention, preened herself a little. "I *do* have a delicate constitution," she said. "Alfred, my dear husband, always said that—"

"He always said that you were liverish and needed a good tonic," finished Lady Riverton, who delighted in finishing other people's stories, preferably inaccurately.

"He always said that I must take every precaution, for I could become deathly ill over trifles that could not overset others in the slightest," Mrs. Simpkins finished with dignity, ignoring Lady Riverton's cackling.

"Then you must take every care, Cousin Ophelia," responded Lady Sylvia. "And feel free to ring if you need anything."

"You need never fear that, my girl," Lady Riverton

assured her. "When Ophelia has the opportunity, she makes certain that she is waited on hand and foot."

The rest of the party arrived gradually, but by late afternoon there was a full house. Sir Charles was strolling about the grounds when he saw Robert and Sally enter the knot garden. He followed them, eager to have a closer look at the boy.

As he neared them, Robert bent over to inspect the white pebbles that bordered the hedges of blue-leafed rue, running his fingers through them as Sally stood watching. He was a handsome boy, dark-haired and dark-eyed, and Sir Charles caught himself searching the boy's face for any similarity to Sylvia. He could see none, but that, he reminded himself, was not unusual. Children did not necessarily resemble their parents closely. At any rate, Robert might well look like his father. And Sir Charles found his mind wandering to the absent Carter Blackwell. What could possess the fellow to allow his wife and child to be so long alone, particularly when he had been informed that his son lay near death?

"I see that Robert has been enjoying Greystone," he remarked casually to Sally, approaching them more closely.

A little flustered by being thus addressed, Sally nodded wordlessly.

"Does he spend much of his time outside?" he inquired, hoping that this time he might draw a response.

Sally nodded again, but managed to add, "As much as he can, sir."

Sir Charles glanced about him. "This is a very large place. Has he gotten lost yet?"

Sally shook her head vehemently. "Oh, no, sir. That would never be allowed. Lady Sylvia doesn't allow Robert to go anywhere without one of us. Why, she won't even have him left alone in his own room, not even at night. Either Povey or I sleep in his chamber."

This caught his attention, and he looked about him as though studying the garden. "You must have been accustomed to doing things that way in Egypt," he remarked casually.

Sally shook her head even more forcefully. "In Egypt Robert ran wherever he pleased in the household, and in the garden, too."

"And perhaps someone slept in his chamber there because he was afraid of the dark," he ventured, still fishing for information.

"Robert is never afraid of the dark, sir," she replied. "Why, he can get up and walk about in the pitch blackness and not be afraid."

"Can he indeed?" responded Sir Charles thoughtfully. This was a strange turn of events. What could Sylvia be afraid of? Another kidnapping? It must be the warning that was troubling her again—although it was possible that something else had happened. He wondered for a moment if he might be able to speak with her about it, but, upon reflection, decided that she would not welcome his interference.

Sally was thinking over her words and she hastened to make a slight amendment, not wishing to be less than honest. "Well, there was a time when Robert was a bit afraid of the dark, Sir Charles."

He looked up at her words and she lowered her voice a trifle, moving a little away from Robert. "Just after his mother died, he wished to have someone with him and the light on as he was going to sleep. But after a few weeks of having Lady Sylvia sit by his side, he was able to go to sleep normally. And of course he sleeps all the time with his lamb."

Sir Charles stared at her in disbelief. "His mother died!" he said blankly.

Worried by his expression and wondering if she had done something amiss, Sally hastened into speech again. "Why, yes sir. I thought that you must know that. I hope I haven't said something that I oughtn't."

He smiled grimly. "Not at all. You have done everything just as you should," he assured her.

Sylvia's behavior was so utterly typical of her that he longed to seek her out immediately and shake her until her teeth rattled. She had caused this entire brouhaha over nothing. A moment's reflection showed him the injustice of a portion of this. She had not actually caused the entire tempest in a teapot. It was true that others had leaped to the wrong conclusion, but she had done nothing to disabuse them of the notion when she could have done so with ease.

He bent down beside the boy and helped him to make a large pile of pebbles, receiving a bright smile as a reward for his efforts. He noticed, too, that a silver locket hung under the boy's blouse.

"Have you a picture there?" he asked gently.

Robert fingered the locket and nodded.

"That holds a picture of his mother and father," volunteered Sally. "Shall I open it, Rob, and show the nice gentleman?"

The child nodded again, and Sally bent forward to open it for him. The miniatures showed a sweet-faced girl and a handsome man.

"They are lovely," said Sir Charles sincerely, closing

the locket gently and smiling at the child again. "Have you a picture of your lamb?"

Robert shook his head and chuckled a little at the idea of having a picture of his lamb.

"Perhaps I can come to the nursery sometime and meet your lamb," said Sir Charles gravely, quite as though he were asking to come to meet a most important individual.

"Well, that would be lovely, wouldn't it, Rob?" said Sally coaxingly.

Again the boy chuckled and ducked his head.

"Well, I shall take that as an invitation," announced Sir Charles. "I shall come to call tomorrow." He stood up and bid them a good afternoon, amazed that it was now so easy to speak to the child when he knew that he was not Sylvia's son.

"Well, Charles, what a very attractive picture that was," said Miss Bitfort-Raines, a distinct edge in her voice.

He had joined her on the terrace and was staring down at the knot garden where Robert was still playing.

Irritated by his lack of response, she continued, jealousy betraying her into ill-considered conversation. "It is a piece of great good fortune that the boy has dark hair and eyes," she remarked brightly.

"And why is that, Claire?" he inquired, knowing that she would continue until he had satisfied her with a response.

"Why, because when you and Lady Sylvia are wed, people who don't know you will readily believe that you are Robert's father. His coloring is much like your own, you know."

His lack of response to this made her feel secure enough to continue her chatter. "It would be best, I think, if all of your children were dark-haired. After all, it is important that they be handsome, and I don't particularly admire red hair. It is not a very distinguished color."

He stared out across an expanse of smooth green lawn to the south. Lady Sylvia was walking toward them, her hair glinting in the sunlight.

"It is odd that you should think that, Claire," he said in an absent tone, as though his mind were otherwise engaged. "I think that there is scarcely any color so lovely."

Having succeeded only in giving herself pain, Miss Bitfort-Raines retired to her chamber to dress for dinner. Sir Charles remained on the terrace, hoping that he would have an opportunity to speak with his hostess, but she managed to avoid him very neatly—so neatly that he was certain that she was doing so deliberately. Finally, he was able to single her out from the crowd gathering on the terrace.

"Robert looks very well, Sylvia," he remarked casually, glancing in the direction of the knot garden. "Life in the country seems to be agreeing with both of you."

Her eyes followed the direction of his gaze and she smiled. "Yes," she replied simply. "Robert loves it here, too."

He noticed that her gaze became fixed at a point beyond Robert and Sally, and he looked in that direction to see what had caught her attention. A footman stood at the edge of the garden, his eyes too on Robert and Sally. When he suddenly glanced up and saw that he was being observed, he turned abruptly and hurried away. Sir Charles smiled to himself. So Lady Sylvia was a strict mistress; that was scarcely what he would have expected.

"I was a little surprised to discover that his father has not yet joined you," he ventured.

Her eyes clouded slightly. She too had wondered at the absence of Carter Blackwell. "I don't know where he is," she admitted. "My last letter from mother said that they had received the news of Robert's illness and sent word to him immediately. He should have arrived even before the letter, but I haven't heard from him."

"I'm certain that he will arrive soon," said Sir Charles confidently, noting her worried expression.

"But where could he be, Charles?" she asked. "He would come directly to Robert."

He had no answer for her, still wondering about the identity of Carter Blackwell, and she was once again growing fearful. What if something had happened to Carter on his journey? He had undertaken it only because she had been responsible for Robert's removal and the subsequent illness. If he had suffered some mischance, that would also be on her head. She was discovering that feeling guilty could become a way of life.

"I should never have taken Robert without his permission," she said flatly. "If something has happened to Carter, it will be my fault."

"Nonsense!" replied Sir Charles briskly. "He is a grown man and very capable of taking care of himself, I am certain. Something has merely happened to delay him. Doubtless he will arrive at any moment."

She gave him a grateful look. "I shall hope so, Charles." And she drifted away from him in the direction of Robert and Sally.

He watched her leave, thinking how fortunate a man Carter Blackwell was to have such a son. He suddenly wondered, too, just what Sylvia's feelings for the gentleman were. He had been so relieved to discover that Robert was not her own son that he had quite overlooked the fact that she had the child in her custody and that she was obviously deeply concerned about his father. The sudden happiness that had engulfed him at his discovery evaporated just as quickly.

He wondered too if something more had happened to cause her to be so careful of Robert, or if she had just become so guilt-ridden that she felt she must watch his every step. And why would she not confide in him if something more had occurred to frighten her?

As he pondered these unpleasant thoughts, he heard an all too familiar voice, and turned to see Lord Wilmington engaged in conversation with Lady Riverton. That gentleman glanced up and caught Sir Charles's eye, bowing ironically.

Sir Charles turned back toward the garden abruptly. He had no desire to be in company with Wilmington, and still less did he wish to see him with either Sylvia or Diana. Robert was not the only one who needed watching.

Chapter Seventeen

The next morning at breakfast, Sir Charles was annoyed to see Lord Wilmington again, this time in company with Amelia Mannering. He was seated next to Sylvia and he managed to speak to her in a low voice.

"Why did you invite Wilmington?" he demanded in a whisper.

She smiled at him pleasantly. "Because, Charles, he is a charming gentleman whose company ladies enjoy, and because he is fond of all things Egyptian and wished to look at my father's collection. He has come to visit us several times in Egypt, you know."

He did know that all too well. He had, in fact, before discovering the truth of Robert's identity, searched the boy's face carefully for any resemblance to that gentleman. He had of course failed to find any and had been somewhat ashamed of the thoughts that had caused him to look. It was possible, he supposed, that Wilmington's motives were as simple as she had indicated, but his knowledge of the man led him to doubt it. His distrust of Wilmington grew with each day that passed.

The ball was to be that evening, and Sylvia had

planned to have her guests dine *al fresco,* so she spent the majority of the morning supervising the arrangement of tables in a delightful walled garden and the decoration of the ballroom for the masquerade. The guests amused themselves by wandering among the gardens and across the smooth lawns and getting in the way in the ballroom as footmen and maids and gardeners scurried about, transporting part of the gardens to the interior of the house.

Pots of bright flowers and screens of greenery began the transformation of the ballroom to a summer garden. A brightly striped tent was set in a corner remote from the orchestra so that the gypsy would be able to make her fortunes heard amidst the sounds of festivity. Sylvia had been a little more considerate in her plans for Claire Bitfort-Raines than that lady had been for her: Miss Bitfort-Raines would receive her fortune in the privacy of the tent.

During the confusion of the morning, Sylvia had tried to keep an eye upon Robert, for he appeared fascinated by all of the activity and kept wandering away from Sally. The new footman troubled her somewhat; it seemed to her that he kept turning up in places where he had no business to be. She was trying not to allow it to distress her too much, for she knew that she had been so on edge that small occurrences could very easily seem more important than they were.

She wished again for a fleeting moment that she could confide in Charles. It would be a comfort to hear someone say to her that she was imagining things, that gypsy prophecies were not to be believed, that the kidnapping and the strange attack during Robert's illness should be dismissed as flukes of fortune. But, she reminded herself sternly, there were altogether too many strange events occurring for her to ignore them. She had Robert to consider, and the prophecies had, after all, been correct on several counts. There *had* been a danger that she had saved them from at the Bitfort-Raines's ball, and there *had* been danger to her and to Robert. Therefore, she could not lightly dismiss the matters of the dark man and the warning against trusting those she thought she knew. Unfortunately, that seemed to include virtually everyone.

So she would put her trust in no one. And she would be profoundly grateful when Carter Blackwell arrived and took responsibility for his son. There were too many small, unsettling things still happening, even here at Greystone. Aside from the problem of the bothersome footman, the gatekeeper had reported more strangers at the gates than usual, even a group of gypsies passing by. She was made uneasy by these reports, even though she was certain that the gypsies were merely those that they had called upon in the dingle. She smiled a moment as she thought of Claire Bitfort-Raines. Her revenge against that lady would be modest, but satisfying.

She was busily arranging flowers in the ballroom when Sally hurried in. "Lady Sylvia!" she called anxiously. "Lady Sylvia, come quickly!"

Sylvia dropped the flowers she was working with and ran to the door. "What is it, Sally? Has Robert hurt himself?"

"He is in the maze, Lady Sylvia!" cried Sally, wringing her hands. "I tried to get him out, but I couldn't find the way. I could hear him, but I couldn't reach him! Oh, my lady, I am so sorry! He is crying for you!"

She and Sylvia hurried toward the maze, followed closely by Ashby and Symington and one of the garden-

ers. When they arrived there, however, Sir Charles was
emerging from the tall shrubbery with Robert sobbing on
his shoulder.

"He is quite all right, Sylvia," said Sir Charles, patting
the boy on the back. "We were just about to go up to the
nursery with Sally so that I could meet his lamb, were we
not, Robert?"

Robert, his shoulders still shaking, lifted his head and
nodded firmly.

Sylvia stared at them in astonishment. So far as she
knew, Charles had no particular fondness for children,
and that he should put himself out to this extent was
amazing. She could see, too, that she was not the only one
amazed. Miss Bitfort-Raines stood close by, her cheeks
red and her eyes blazing. She turned and walked away as
Sir Charles and Robert started toward the house with
Sally.

Sylvia watched them leave very thoughtfully. She knew
that she should feel grateful to Charles, but it did seem
strange. And he had been present in the park at the time
of the kidnapping, and he had evinced a most unusual
interest in Robert. And he was, of course, a dark man. A
dark man who was not behaving in a manner that she
recognized.

"Are you quite well, Lady Sylvia?" asked Gerard Mannering, who was standing close beside her and looking at
her in some concern. "Perhaps you should sit down and
rest," he continued, leading her to a nearby bench.

He saw that she was watching Sir Charles and Robert
disappearing into the interior of the house. "Robert was
not hurt, merely frightened," he said gently, misinterpret-
ing her anxious expression. "You need not be worried
about him. And he looked quite happy with Sir Charles."

"Yes, he did, didn't he?" she remarked wonderingly.

And she looked at Gerard Mannering's kindly face—his kindly, dark-eyed face, framed by hair so dark that it was almost black. Her hand shook as she lifted to her lips the glass of lemonade one of the maids brought for her. She was surrounded by dark men.

"Is there something wrong, Lady Sylvia?" he inquired anxiously. "You don't seem to be yourself today."

He did not add that she had not seemed herself for a number of days. He had hoped that he and Amelia would be able to be of service to her, to help restore her spirits after her ordeal with Robert, but she didn't seem to be recovering as quickly as they had expected. She had seemed almost euphoric when they first arrived at Greystone, but that mood had dissipated almost immediately.

"Well, it is scarcely to be expected that Lady Sylvia *can* be herself when she is working like a madwoman, Mannering," said Lord Wilmington, ignoring the glance of distaste with which the younger man greeted him.

"Come along with me, my dear lady," he said, offering her his arm, "and I shall engage to see that you are soon feeling much more the thing. A stroll through the Egyptian gallery, an island of calm away from this madness, should restore you."

Sylvia stared at him as though mesmerized, rising and taking his arm without question. Yet another dark man, she thought to herself. It was madness indeed. There was not a single man that she could trust.

"Forgive us for abandoning you for a moment, Mr. Mannering," she said quietly as she rose. "Perhaps Lord Wilmington is right and I just need a few moments of quiet to calm my nerves."

Mannering stood aside, reluctant to see them leave

together, but knowing that he had no right to interfere. He watched intently as they disappeared into the house together.

And Sylvia discovered that Wilmington had been right. A few minutes in his company, falling into their established custom of light flirtation, calmed her so that a return to the activities in the gardens and the ballroom did not seem as overwhelming as it had earlier. And the cool dimness of the gallery in which her father had so carefully arranged his Egyptian artifacts helped to restore her peace of mind. They paused before one of two of the items so that she could tell Lord Wilmington something of their history, and just the familiar routine of doing so soothed her, making her think of her parents and her childhood.

"And do you think that your parents will stay much longer in Egypt, dear lady?" Wilmington inquired casually as they inspected a small charm in the form of a hedgehog.

"They will be arriving in England in September," she responded.

"I was thinking of the longer span, my dear. Do you think that they will continue to live in Egypt for a portion of each year as they have been doing?"

"I should imagine so," said Sylvia idly, picking up the hedgehog and smiling at it. "The ancient Egyptians respected the hedgehog for his ability to hibernate and then appear refreshed each spring. They felt that he was worthy of honor because of that."

"Not a very handsome beast, however," observed Wilmington, holding up his glass to look at it more closely. "Did your father find this at a market, or did he discover it in some dusty tomb?"

Sylvia shrugged. "I couldn't say, Lord Wilmington. He acquired quite a number of charms last autumn while he and Carter were away. It could have been discovered in either manner."

"Has the Marquess found any more information to help him relocate the tomb he was so interested in when I last visited?" inquired Wilmington, stooping over to look at a miniature footstool of ebony and cedarwood, its top inlaid with ivory.

Sylvia smiled. "No, nor do I think he will. The man who led him to the general area where he found it disappeared from his village and Father has never found him again to record the directions. It has been a source of great annoyance to him."

"I can imagine that it would be. Your father takes all of this very seriously." He paused for a moment beside a small glass case that displayed a collar of minute gold and faience beads, its blue still startlingly vivid.

"The necklace that you wore to the masquerade was much like this one, was it not?" he inquired.

"Yes—almost exactly, in fact. There are a good many replicas of antique pieces available in Cairo. They have some wonderful craftsmen."

His reference to the masquerade recalled her to a sense of her duties, and together they returned to the ballroom so that she could see that the decorations for the evening's festivities had been completed. The effect of the flowers and greenery in the ballroom was as charming as she had hoped it would be, and it was with a feeling of satisfaction that she went to the nursery to spend an hour with Robert and Nanny.

She rode out to the gypsy camp later that afternoon to make certain that her arrangements for the evening were understood. She was smiling as she left, for a group of young girls had been dancing, and she had stayed to watch them, feeling her spirits lift with the lithe grace of their movements. For a brief time the feeling of oppression had disappeared and she had almost felt that she could enjoy herself in a normal manner. As she left the dingle in which they were camped, she was smiling and humming a little of the gypsy melody she had just heard.

"Well, Sylvia, are you now planning to run away with the gypsies?" inquired an amused voice.

"Charles! I didn't see you there in the shadow of the trees. Were you following me?" she exclaimed, her displeasure clear.

"Of course not," he responded, amazed that she would think such a thing. "I was merely out for a ride. Why would I be following you?"

Then, feeling that he had been too abrupt, he added with a smile, "Naturally, I don't mean to imply that following you would not be a pleasure. You are still as lovely as ever." And he meant what he said, for the light of the setting sun on her hair made it appear that her face was framed by an aureole of reddish gold.

"And you are still dealing in Spanish coin, Charles," she returned, unimpressed by his compliment.

He fell in beside her on the ride home, even though it was obvious that she had no desire for his company.

"You didn't answer me, Sylvia," he said lightly. "Are you planning to run away with the raggle-taggle gypsies?"

"Why not?" she responded. "It is precisely what you would expect me to do, is it not? It would make another lovely *on-dit* for the *ton.*"

"My heart would go out to the gypsies if you did run away with them, Sylvia," he retorted. "They would not know what they were asking for and would doubtless return you immediately."

Sylvia laughed reluctantly, but said nothing more, and they rode in silence for a while. Then Sir Charles glanced at her impassive profile and smiled. "I met Robert's lamb this morning," he said pleasantly. "I felt quite honored."

"You should be," she answered briefly. "Robert has not taken kindly to strangers on this trip, and that lamb is his most prized possession."

"That and the miniatures he wears in his locket," said Sir Charles dryly. "He seems quite proud of those as well."

Sylvia glanced up at him sharply. "So you saw those!" When he did not reply, she rode on, again falling silent for a while. "His mother's name was Laura," she said finally. "And I was extremely fond of her. His father's name is Carter Blackwell."

"Is he any relation of old Colonel Jackson Blackwell?" Sir Charles inquired.

She nodded. "He is a nephew. And since Laura's death he is a very wealthy nephew."

Sir Charles considered this news carefully. So Carter Blackwell was an eligible young man, now a wealthy young man, and he had a son that Sylvia already treated as her own. He found that news less than palatable, but he knew that he had no right to cavil. After all, he was to marry Claire in September.

"I had wondered if you might be planning to have a fortune-teller for your ball tonight," he remarked casually, thinking of his own visit to Madame Zeena.

She glanced up at him sharply, startled by his remark. "As a matter of fact, I have employed one. That is what

I was doing at the gypsy camp. Whatever made you think of it?"

He shrugged. "I suppose I was thinking of Claire's ball, for seeing the gypsies brought it all back to mind again. Will you have her tell your fortune?" he asked curiously.

Sylvia's laugh was brittle. "I believe that I have had my fortune told quite enough," she retorted.

He stopped suddenly and reached out to stop her mount as well. She looked at him indignantly, but he spoke before she could.

"What is troubling you, Sylvia?" he asked, looking at her gravely. "You were far too distressed by what happened to Robert yesterday. A little boy getting lost in a maze when there are crowds of people about is not something that would normally frighten you. What was the real problem?"

For a moment she was tempted to tell him, but then she remembered Claire and the gypsy's warning and turned her face away. "It was nothing of consequence, Charles," she said in an off-handed voice. "And we should be getting back to Greystone."

Annoyed by her refusal to tell him anything and his lack of any real right to require it of her, he could not refrain from saying, "It seems to me, Sylvia, that you might very well run away with the gypsies just to cause more gossip. Why on earth did you allow the rumor that Robert is your child to begin?"

She shrugged, knowing full well that that response would aggravate him more than anything else. "Who can really tell why they do anything? It was just a whim," she said, her whole manner bespeaking boredom.

"Just as it was a whim to take away Carter Blackwell's son without permission?" he asked acidly. "How very like you to put your own desires above every other consideration."

"And how like you, Charles, to carp and criticize when you know nothing of the situation!" she retorted. "I am sure that you go down on your knees each night and give thanks that we did not marry so that you are not in any way responsible for my behavior! And how grateful you must be to have a paragon like Miss Bitfort-Raines, who will always do the proper thing and never embarrass you!" she added bitterly. "What a comfort she must be to you!"

Anger again overcame him. This tactic was so typical of Sylvia: carrying the battle into his own territory and crediting—or discrediting—him with thoughts that were not his. Of course, he reminded himself with a flash of honesty, he had indeed thought just those things, so she was perhaps partially justified in her remarks.

That thought infuriated him still more, particularly as he thought of how Claire, whom he had indeed considered a paragon, had behaved badly and caused at least a portion of Sylvia's misfortune. There is nothing more treacherous than a mixture of righteous indignation and angry guilt. Sir Charles discovered that as he pulled her roughly toward him and kissed her soundly.

Sylvia jerked away from him, but instead of slapping him and galloping away as he fully expected her to do, she sat looking at him for a moment until her anger was fully under control, and then said sweetly, "And you told me that poor Lord Wilmington was too free with the ladies. Perhaps *you* had best go back and spend your time with your fiancée, Charles. I fear that Miss Bitfort-Raines would scarcely regard this as proper behavior." And she turned away from him and started briskly back toward Greystone.

Inside, however, she was still shaking with anger, anger caused by his presumptuousness both in speaking to her as he had and in kissing her. But she was angry too, she confessed to herself as she rode home, because she had wished for him to kiss her.

By the time she reached Greystone, she was calm enough to face the others without showing distress. Lord Wilmington and Gerard Mannering were both awaiting her arrival, and she thought, as she watched them approaching her across the lawn as she walked up from the stables, that either of them would be a better bargain that Charles Redford. Mannering—insofar as she could tell—was a frank and open gentleman, a man to be trusted—if he were not dark, and Wilmington—well, Wilmington was a frank and charming rake, a man who made no pretense to be anything other than what he was. Charles Redford, on the other hand, was neither frank nor open nor charming.

And it was most unfortunate that she was still in love with him. How was it possible that her head could make such a cool appraisal of her situation but that her heart should refuse to accept any such assessment?

From the corner of her eye, she saw Claire Bitfort-Raines waving to Sir Charles and then rushing out to lace her arm through his, drawing him into a close conversation. Smiling brilliantly, Sylvia turned to Lord Wilmington and extended her hand.

Taking in the situation at a glance, that gentleman smiled knowingly and bowed. "I am, as always dear lady, at your beck and call," he assured her.

And together they strolled toward the maze. Once

more an oblique glance assured her that Sir Charles was following their progress, and she leaned toward Lord Wilmington and laughed, quite as though he had said something incomparably witty.

Wilmington leaned down to her, his eyes sympathetic. "I had no idea, my dear, that things were so serious between you two."

Sylvia managed to look surprised. "Why, whatever do you mean, Lord Wilmington?" she inquired innocently.

"Oh, it's to be that way, is it, my dear?" he inquired in amusement, leading her to the opening of the maze. "Then I had best warn you, Lady Sylvia, that when Henry VIII led a lady into a puzzle-garden, he had no intention of having her find her way out again any time soon."

He paused for a moment. "And I am so very like him, dear lady. I don't know whether you had remarked that or not."

"Like Henry VIII?" she asked in mock astonishment. "Surely not, Lord Wilmington! You are a man of good figure, while poor Henry was a man of considerable girth."

"You are, of course, quite correct," he conceded. "That was not the similarity I was thinking of, however."

"Indeed? And what did you have in mind, my lord?"

"Why, just that both of us are of a poetic nature, lovers of beauty. And, in this case, both of us lovers of puzzle-gardens for precisely the same reasons."

Sylvia laughed, the sound of it rippling across the open expanse of grass so that Sir Charles could be sure to hear it. Then, certain of his attention, she said to Lord Wilmington as she tapped him playfully on the arm, "You frighten me, my lord, truly you do! I don't know that I can trust you!"

And she allowed him to lead her into the maze, noting with satisfaction that Sir Charles was staring bleakly after them.

Chapter Eighteen

Their stroll through the maze was brief; indeed, it was more of a trot than a stroll and Lord Wilmington spoke with some asperity as they left the puzzle-garden.

"I think, my dear, that we could at least have dallied for a few moments on one of the benches instead of racing through it as though there were a prize to be had at the end."

She smiled at him apologetically. "I am sorry, my lord, to have taken advantage of you so shamelessly, but I did have to hurry back here so that I could superintend the last-minute preparations for the ball tonight. I had not really planned on the time necessary for a walk through the maze."

"At least not until you saw Sir Charles," he pointed out tartly. "I think that young man has a great deal to answer for. Not only is he boring beyond permission, but now he is also responsible for my being raced about as though I were being prepared for Ascot."

She laughed lightly. "It is good of you to be so pleasant about my abuse of you, Lord Wilmington. I apologize again."

"Nonsense, my dear," he replied, softening a little. "At least you did not consider me too elderly to make the journey through the maze. I had feared from some of your comments that you considered me just slightly younger than Methuselah."

"Not at all, my lord. You wrong me," she protested. "And I plan to take shameless advantage of you tonight as well. I shall expect you to dance with me several times."

"It will be my pleasure, my lady," he said formally, bowing low to her. "And now, if you will excuse me, I am going to my room to have a glass of warm milk and a nap so that I may recruit my strength for the evening hours."

His playful manners always relaxed her, and Sylvia was able to prepare for the ball with a lighter heart than she would have thought possible earlier in the day. She had decided to wear the Cleopatra costume once again, if only to irritate Sir Charles. Povey carefully arranged her hair and Sylvia painstakingly lined her eyes in the old Egyptian manner. After slipping into her narrow gown and her thin sandals, the final step was putting on the jewelry that would complete her costume. Going to the chest that contained the jewelry, Povey opened a drawer and then turned around abruptly.

"Have you already taken your jewelry out, my lady?"

"No, of course not, Povey. There was no need to do so until it was time to wear it." She looked up at her maid's face. "What has happened?" she asked, filled with misgiving.

Povey gestured silently to the open drawer and Sylvia rose to inspect it. The velvet cases used to hold her jewels were tumbled wildly about, one or two of them open.

"Some of the pieces are gone, my lady," said Povey.

"The drawer was almost filled when I unpacked your things."

She pulled open the drawer below it, but there was no sign of any of the cases. Carefully, they opened the cases that remained in the drawer and inspected their contents.

"Can you tell what is missing, my lady?" asked Povey anxiously.

Sylvia nodded, closing the last case slowly. "Most of the Egyptian pieces are gone," she said slowly. "My diamonds are still here, and Mother's set of emeralds. Why would those not be taken, Povey?"

Povey shook her head. "More to the point, my lady, who would have taken them?" She hesitated a moment and then added, "It must be someone here, my lady. It could hardly be a thief who happened to come here and happened to know that you have that particular jewelry. A stranger would have been noticed, at any rate."

Sylvia sank down onto her chair. "Of course he would have been, Povey," she agreed, and she thought for a moment of the strangers at the gate that the servants had mentioned—and the gypsies.

"We will not mention this to anyone just yet, Povey," she said abruptly.

"Just as you wish, my lady," said Povey, looking a little troubled by her decision. "But what will you do about your costume tonight? People will be expecting to see you in your Egyptian jewelry."

"And so they shall," she replied briskly. "Come along with me, Povey. We will borrow some of the pieces from my father's collection."

And together they went down to the gallery that she and Lord Wilmington had strolled through just that afternoon. Taking out a key, she carefully unlocked the small case holding the necklace so like her own, then selected from other cases the pieces needed to complete her costume.

In the privacy of her room she fastened the collar firmly into place, her mind racing. Why would anyone take these pieces and leave the diamonds and emeralds? This was obviously no ordinary thief, and could scarcely be one of the servants, even if she had been willing to suspect one of them, for there would assuredly be no reason for one of them to take an Egyptian piece rather than the diamonds which would bring an excellent price instantly.

She had sent Povey down to request that Lord Wilmington and Amelia begin the ball for her, saying that she would join them as soon as possible. As she made her way down the stairs, she looked eagerly through the doors opening into the ballroom, refusing to acknowledge to herself that she was looking for Sir Charles. It was true, however, that her heart sank as she entered the ballroom and realized that his Roman toga was nowhere to be seen. Miss Bitfort-Raines, attired once again as Marie Antoinette, was dancing with Arthur Ashby, who looked as though he had been sentenced to two weeks in the British Museum.

"You must forgive me, my dear, for not wearing my toga or my—my whatever-it-is that pharoahs wore," said Lord Wilmington, joining her to survey the crowd. He was swathed in a black domino, looking vaguely sinister.

"I knew that you would come again as Cleopatra and I desperately wished to be properly attired to partner you," he continued apologetically, "but my legs are not, I fear, my best feature, and I felt that it would be wiser to be more discreet this time."

"You look splendid," said Sylvia comfortingly. "There

was no need to feel that you had to dress in such a manner."

"I could not help but notice how taken you were by Sir Charles's attire at our last masquerade," he explained, watching her with bright eyes through the slits in his mask, "and I feared that I could not equal his fine figure in a toga."

Sylvia flushed slightly, but managed to laugh lightly. "You were quite mistaken then, sir," she returned. "I believe that Sir Charles merely fancies himself in the role of Marc Antony. Power has always held a great charm for him."

"Then he's no different from most men, my girl!" said Lady Riverton sharply, punctuating her words with a sharp tap of her cane. Her eyes took in Sylvia's costume at a glance. "I took a liking to your gown at the Bitfort-Raines's masquerade. Just the sort of thing that I would have worn when I was a girl!"

"I daresay, Augusta," said Mrs. Simpkins dryly. She was sedately attired as an aging shepherdess. "The only thing that surprises me is that you are not wearing it tonight."

"Well, I could have done so if I had wished to, Ophelia!" snapped Lady Riverton. "But whoever heard of Cleopatra leaning on a cane? If you can answer me that, then I'll put on a gown just like this one and wear it for the evening."

"And she would, too," said Mrs. Simpkins in disgust as Lady Riverton, sighting new prey across the room, hobbled away in that direction. She was not yet out of earshot yet, however, and she turned at Mrs. Simpkins' words.

"Of course I would, Ophelia!" she called. "That gypsy was quite right in her assessment of me—said that I was a woman of spirit and taste! I suggest that you stay out of the fortune-teller's tent, though, Ophelia. You might not like what she tells you!"

And cackling happily at this sally, she disappeared into the crowd.

Sylvia brightened. At least the fortune-teller had come and was obviously plying her trade. And she had made at least one guest happy. Across the floor stood Miss Bitfort-Raines, no longer with Arthur Ashby, who had gratefully made his escape, but with Lord Digby, whom she had engaged in grave conversation.

Does she never smile, Sylvia wondered, seeing the serious expression on the other woman's face. It was, after all, a masquerade and not a lecture on the arts. She could not wait to see Miss Bitfort-Raines's expression after *her* visit to the fortune-teller.

Glancing about the room, she still saw no sign of Sir Charles and, strangely enough, Lord Wilmington had disappeared. Arthur Ashby came to claim her hand for a dance, and he was ably followed by Mr. Symington, who was determined to atone for the poor showing he had made the day of the attempted kidnapping. Both gentlemen had been faithful in calling upon her and Robert, and, although neither of them were particularly to her taste, Sylvia felt obligated to be kind to them for their attentiveness.

An hour slipped by and there was still no sign of her missing guests. She had seen Amelia dancing, but Gerard, Sir Charles, and Lord Wilmington were all still absent from the festivities. Puzzled, Sylvia decided that she would check their rooms, but went first to the gypsy's tent so that she could see if Miss Bitfort-Raines had yet had her fortune told. If not, she would give the gypsy a clear description of the lady.

She was obliged to wait her turn for a visit with the gypsy, who was clearly proving popular with the guests. They emerged from her tent laughing and recounting the tales of her predictions to the waiting group.

Finally, her turn came and Sylvia entered the darkened tent, lighted only by one wavering candle. Before she could ask about Miss Bitfort-Raines, the old woman reached out and took her hand, turning the palm toward the candle flame.

"You will marry a tall, dark man, my lady, and your life will be a long and happy one with many children."

The voice sounded vaguely familiar to her—but not like that of the old gypsy woman she had hired—and she tried to focus more clearly on the face in the shadows.

"Will I not marry a tall, dark *stranger?*" inquired Sylvia, determined to hear more of the voice.

"No, my lady, not a stranger, but a man you already know—and love," came the reply.

Sylvia, certain now of the fortune-teller's identity, reached forward and jerked away the scarves draped about the gypsy's hair and face, revealing Sir Charles's laughing eyes. She turned to leave, but he caught her hand and pulled her close to him in the darkness.

"Just what game are you playing at, my lady?" he demanded in a low voice, his lips next to her ear. "Why have you been pretending that Robert is your child? And why did you run away from me this afternoon?"

Sylvia struggled in his arms, but her struggle was half-hearted, and all resistance stopped when his lips met hers. Her arms slipped around his neck and for a breathless minute she was only dimly aware of the orchestra playing and the people dancing outside the tent. Then she felt his warm breath and the slight movement of her hair as he murmured against her cheek, "Marry me, Sylvia—marry me!"

She heard his low words, but could scarcely credit her ears. She drew back to stare at him, but before she could say a word, the flap of the tent was suddenly pulled back and Gerard Mannering rushed in.

"He's gone, Redford!" he gasped, letting the flap fall behind him and almost collapsing at Sylvia's feet.

"Who is gone, Gerard?" she demanded. "And since when are you hand-in-glove with Sir Charles?"

"It is Wilmington, Lady Sylvia," gasped Mannering, trying desperately to recover his breath.

"Wilmington!" she exclaimed, turning upon Sir Charles. "Lord Wilmington was here at the beginning of the ball—and even if he has left, what concern would that be of yours, Charles?"

"It isn't jealousy, my dear, if that is what you're thinking," responded Sir Charles with a grim smile. "It is much more serious than that."

Sylvia flushed, glad of the darkness, for that was precisely what she had been thinking. "Then what has he done, Charles, that is so serious?" she demanded.

"We believe he is a French agent," said Sir Charles. "We have been watching him for months, even when he visited your family in Egypt. And when he began to spend so much time with you, I suspected that he might have a particular interest in you for more than personal reasons."

"How very ungallant of you, Charles!" said Sylvia dryly. "What, pray tell, could he have been interested in, if not me?"

"I'm not absolutely certain about that," Sir Charles

admitted, "although it must, I think, be tied to your interests in Egypt. Just because Bonaparte was forced to leave that country doesn't mean that he has relinquished all hope of regaining it."

"You are mad, Charles!" she exclaimed. "We are at peace with France. Have you forgotten that?"

"Only for the moment," he assured her. "Bonaparte is not prepared to give up his dreams yet—and his dreams still include the wealth of Egypt and the link to the East."

"And you, Gerard," she said, turning to Mannering, who had by now regained his composure. "Since when have you been working with Sir Charles?"

"Oh, that was a very recent event, Lady Sylvia," he assured her, smiling. "Sir Charles had noticed that I was being very watchful of Lord Wilmington—not because I thought he was an agent, but because I thought that he was a questionable party because of his reputation."

"Wilmington kept a very careful eye on me because he knows of my ties to Whitehall," Sir Charles explained, "but he had no reason to be suspicious of Mannering, who was able then to keep a much closer eye on him. And Mannering was kind enough to say that he would assist me in this matter."

He scrutinized Gerard as keenly as the guttering candle would allow. "Are you ready now, Mannering?" he asked.

Mannering nodded, pulling himself to his feet and bowing apologetically to Sylvia. "Forgive us for leaving again so abruptly, Lady Sylvia."

The two of them left together, and Sylvia tried to gather her thoughts. The very idea that Lord Wilmington might be a spy seemed preposterous. And yet, as she thought back, she remembered his distaste for Charles and his political views, a distaste that might very well have been more than personal.

Looking around the tent, she wondered for a moment what had happened to her real fortune-teller. Charles had undoubtedly paid her and sent her on her way so that he could do his impersonation for the evening. Few things seemed to her as out of character as his behavior this evening. To dress up as a gypsy—and to propose marriage to her when he was already engaged! She shook her head. He had asked her what her game was, but she decided that he must be playing some deep game of his own. At any rate, she was certain that the proposal was anything but sincere—despite the passionate sincerity of the kiss. But how unlike Charles it was to do anything that even *appeared* to be in questionable taste.

Still wondering, she blew out the candle and left the tent. The ballroom was now almost empty as the revelers went in to a supper of champagne and lobster patties. Hurriedly fixing a plate of refreshments for Nanny, she went upstairs to see if Robert had been able to sleep through the sounds of festivity. The nursery was far removed from the masquerade, but Robert was always keenly responsive to atmosphere, and she feared that he might still be awake.

She opened the door to the nursery gently and slipped quietly in. Nanny Reese was dozing quietly in her rocking chair, her mending in her lap. In the corner of the chamber was Robert's small trundle bed, the covers rumpled.

Sylvia set the plate down on the work table next to Nanny and tiptoed to the side of the bed. For a moment she stared down at it in disbelief. It was empty!

"Robert!" she called, thinking that he might have wandered into the next room, the old schoolroom that was now his playroom. Opening the door to it, she carried a candle in to search it. Returning to the bed chamber, she realized that her calling had not awakened Nanny, who still slumbered quietly.

"Nanny, wake up!" she said, gently shaking the old woman's shoulder. When there was no response, she dropped to Nanny's side, fearful that she might be dead. Upon closer examination Sylvia could see that she was alive, but her breathing was irregular. Nor could any amount of shaking make her awaken.

Hurrying down the hall to the small chamber where Sally slept, she rapped loudly on the door.

"Sally!" she called. "Sally, wake up and go to Nanny! Something's wrong with her. I'm going to look for Robert."

Sally's frightened face appeared at the door about the time Sylvia reached the stairway, and she waved the little maid in the direction of the nursery. "Go quickly, Sally! I'll be back as soon as I can!"

And she hurried downstairs to her own chamber for a cloak. The evening had cooled and she was going out to search the gardens and be certain that Robert had not wandered away by himself. If he had awakened while Nanny was asleep, he might very well have decided to go exploring on his own, and the gardens had won his heart.

Once in her room she snatched a cloak from the wardrobe, not pausing to ring for Povey, and turned back to the door. A large square of white caught her eye, and she stopped to go back to her dressing table. Hesitantly she opened the note, written in black ink in a large, bold hand, and read it. Then, unable to believe her eyes, she read it once more.

The letter instructed her to bring the box of notes her

father had sent from Egypt to the lane beside the gypsy camp at midnight—and to come alone if she wanted to see Robert again. She did not need to look at a clock to know that midnight was almost upon her.

Chapter Nineteen

Sylvia paused only long enough to change from her costume into a riding dress and then made her way quickly to the stable. Only minutes after receiving the note, she was moving briskly down the road in her phaeton, grateful for the full moon. Next to her on the floor was the box of notes from her father's study. Since most of the stable hands had been occupied with the horses and carriages of guests from the neighborhood, she was able to slip out without anyone taking particular note of her.

As she approached the gypsy camp, a caped figure stepped forward from the shadows of a copse.

"This is as far as you must go, dear lady," Lord Wilmington called to her. "There is no need to exhaust yourself by traveling too far."

"How can you stand there and call me 'dear lady,' Lord Wilmington?" she demanded. "How could you have had a hand in any of this? You have played the part of a gentleman and yet you have proved to be a kidnapper and a thief! And to think that I accused Sir Charles of only appearing to be a gentleman!"

Wilmington's voice sounded pained. "Those are such

hard words to use, Lady Sylvia. Surely there is no need for such harshness between friends—and to compare me to that tedious young man is really too much for me to bear."

He extended his hand to assist her from the phaeton, but she ignored it and sprang lightly down.

"I don't see how you can have the effrontery to refer to our friendship when you could do this to Robert!" A sudden thought shook her. "Were you behind the first kidnapping attempt, Lord Wilmington?" she demanded.

He shook his head. "I am grateful that I need not take responsibility for that botched effort, my lady. The man that was employed for that was most certainly less than competent. I pride myself on being more careful."

"And the other accident when Robert was ill—leaving the window open and soaking his covers—was that your doing as well?" she asked.

Wilmington looked puzzled. "I know nothing of that," he replied.

Sylvia's hands trembled on the reins. "But why have you done this tonight, my lord?" she cried. "What had we done to you?"

He sighed. "A man must live, Lady Sylvia—and I fear that I live very expensively—much more expensively than my modest fortune will allow. And so I must take measures to make up the difference."

He smiled at her gently and took her hand. "And I am most sincere when I say that I find you charming, my lady. I greatly regret that I was forced to take such measures."

Sylvia snatched her hand away. "So Charles was right!" she exclaimed. "You are a spy! You are doing all of this for money!"

Wilmington sighed more deeply and his smile disappeared. "Redford again! I told you that I found him a most tiresome young man—and altogether too obsessed by the thought of king and country."

"Did you take my jewelry, Lord Wilmington?"

"Again, my lady, allow me to apologize for being forced to take such measures—but they were truly necessary. I did not have time to examine them, so I took all of the pieces—for I must have proof, you see."

Sylvia wished to question him further, but the child's welfare was the more pressing matter.

"Where is Robert?" she demanded, ignoring her desire to know more of his activities and trying to peer into the shadows behind him. "I thought that I was to find him here."

"Most certainly I never told you such a thing," he replied. "If you will do me the kindness of standing to one side, my lady."

And he caught her by the elbows and swung her aside, then stepped into the phaeton and took up the ribbons. Bowing to her briefly, he said, "I hope that you will forgive me, my lady, for leaving you to make your way home alone. If it is any comfort to you, I have infinite confidence in your ability to do so."

"I had no notion that you were so cowhearted, Lord Wilmington," she said angrily, wishing that she had her riding crop. "You are going to leave me afoot—and take the notes and my jewelry—without keeping your part of the bargain. That is scarcely the role of a gentleman!"

Her voice rose as she thought again of the missing child. "Where *is* Robert? You must tell me!"

"That is where you are wrong, dear lady. I do not feel

Mona Gedney

at all that I must," he replied gently as he pulled away in the phaeton.

Sylvia watched in despair as he drove briskly away. What could he have done with Robert? There was no assurance that the child was still at Greystone, but she had no choice but to walk back and begin the search there. She did not know what else to do.

Suddenly, however, she remembered the gypsy camp, just a bit farther down the road. Gathering up her courage, she turned and began to walk briskly in that direction, using the moonlight to guide her steps. Perhaps they would lend her a horse so that she could ride home.

When she arrived, most of the camp was in darkness, but a fire burned low in the midst of the gathering of wagons and a man sat close beside it. He leaped lightly to his feet at the sound of her approach.

"Pardon me," she said hesitantly as she approached him. "I know that it is late, but I have been robbed of my horse, and I need a ride back to my home. I will be willing to pay well anyone who will take me there—or lend me a horse."

The man surprised her by acting as though hers was an everyday request. "I will harness my cart," he said briefly, and turned to the copse where their horses were tethered.

"I don't suppose that you have seen a man with a young boy tonight, have you?" she inquired hesitantly when he returned. "The child is very young—only three—and he has dark hair and eyes and his name is Robert. The man, Lord Wilmington, is rather tall, with dark hair, and he is wearing a black domino."

The man looked up sharply at Wilmington's name. "Lord Wilmington?" he asked, and she nodded. The gypsy walked to the nearest cart, and she could hear the sound of voices, one of them suddenly raised almost to a shout.

He returned with a young boy. "Frederick will drive you home," he said briefly. "And the boy that you are searching for is asleep in that cart," he added, nodding to the cart closest to the fire. "We did not see a man with him. He was alone when we found him."

"May I see him?" she exclaimed joyfully, almost afraid to believe that it could be true.

The man nodded again and led her to the cart, holding a lantern high enough so that she could distinguish Robert's sleeping form. "I cannot thank you enough, sir," she said fervently when they were outside once more. "However did you find him?"

"We found him crying in the woods," he replied. "And my mother insisted that we take him in."

"How kind of her!" Sylvia exclaimed.

"Not at all, lady," said a deep voice. Startled, Sylvia peered into the shadows, and Madame Zeena stepped from the shadows into the circle of firelight. "I knew when I first saw him that the child was good luck for us. We could not do other than take him in. It was necessary."

"All the same, it was good of you to do so," said Sylvia, extending her hand to the gypsy.

The older woman took it, but did not immediately release it. Instead, she looked at Sylvia gravely. "The danger has not passed, lady. I told you that there was danger for a child—and for you. That is still true."

Sylvia sat down abruptly upon a log that had been pulled close to the fire. "Are you certain?" she asked, no longer willing to act as though the gypsy's warning was merely a theatrical gesture.

Madame Zeena nodded. "You must walk carefully. Do not believe all the things you see, lady."

"I have already learned that," replied Sylvia bitterly, thinking of Lord Wilmington. She had considered him nothing more than an amusing flirt, and once again it was no fault of hers that Robert had not been a victim of her blindness.

Before they left the camp, the man who had spoken with her first and two others, all on horseback, joined them. "Which way did the lord ride?" he inquired.

Sylvia looked at them in surprise, then pointed to the east. He bowed gravely in thanks and the three of them left, moving at a steady clip down the road.

The ride back to Greystone was peaceful, with Robert sleeping quietly in the back of the cart, until they turned onto the main road. There they met a party of riders, Sir Charles and Gerard Mannering at its head.

"Where have you been?" demanded Sir Charles. "We have been serarching the grounds since Sally told me that Robert had disappeared and you had gone to search for him."

"I have been doing exactly that, Charles!" she snapped. "Searching for him! And I have found him!" she said, indicating the sleeping child behind them.

She glanced at the others, then said in a low voice, "And I must speak with you privately, Charles. Ride ahead with me."

His look was questioning, but he did not pursue the subject while the others were near. Once they had pulled ahead of the others, he turned to her expectantly. "Well, Sylvia—what have you to tell me?"

"Charles, it was Lord Wilmington who kidnapped Robert—and he admitted to being a spy! He left a note telling me where to meet him and to bring with me the box containing my father's notes."

Sir Charles's eyebrows drew together. "Your father's notes?" he said sharply. He stared at her for a moment. "What do those notes contain, Sylvia?" he asked.

She shook her head. "Just his observations during his travels and descriptions of some of the pieces he has collected. I can't imagine what Wilmington expected to find, Charles. He didn't say anything that would explain why he wanted it. And we must get those notes back, Charles!" she said anxiously. "My father will be distraught by their loss!"

"And he released Robert when you gave the box to him?"

Again Sylvia shook her head. "He took the box and my phaeton and left. It was only by accident that I found Robert. I walked to the gypsy camp to see if someone could help me, and there he was."

"Robert was at the gypsy camp?" asked Sir Charles, his attention suddenly diverted from the notes. "How did that happen?"

"Lord Wilmington must have just abandoned him in the woods, and they heard him crying," she replied. Sylvia paused a moment, then added hesitantly, "It was the strangest thing, Charles. Madame Zeena, the gypsy from Claire's masquerade found him, and she insisted that they keep him because she said that he would bring them good luck . . . and she told me that the danger still exists for Robert and me."

"Did she indeed?" said Sir Charles, his eye kindling. "I believe that we will look into that." And he felt that he was nearing the source of the problem. Here were the gypsies again, involved once more with the problems, and talking

about their "danger." Probably they were working with
Wilmington. Madame Zeena was undoubtedly a part of
the problem—and perhaps the cause of some of the danger—and he had every intention of taking care of it before
something truly disastrous occurred.

Sylvia studied his face, and decided that she would not
add the portion Madame Zeena had told her about still
using caution—and that things were not what they
seemed to be. Sir Charles was probably exactly what he
appeared to be—but she no longer felt certain of anything.

"I will carry Robert up to the nursery," said Sir
Charles, as they came to the house. "Povey and Sally are
waiting for him there. You must come with me to reassure
him."

"And how is Nanny?" she asked anxiously.

"She will be all right," he responded, "but she was
drugged, you know."

Sylvia's eyebrows shot out of sight. "What do you
mean, Charles?" she demanded.

"Just what I said, Sylvia. Something had been placed in
her tea."

"But she will recover?" Sylvia asked anxiously.

Sir Charles nodded. "I suggest that in the meantime we
take ourselves to the nursery. I have no intention of letting
you or Robert out of my sight for the rest of the night."

And Sir Charles meant exactly what he said. Robert
was soon asleep in his trundle bed with Povey seated
grimly beside him, and a cot was made up next to him for
Sylvia. She protested, but it was to no avail.

"You just be sensible for once, miss," commanded
Povey. "Lie down and sleep and Sir Charles and I will
stay just as we are. Nothing else will happen tonight, you

may rest assured of that." And her knitting needles rattled threateningly, as though daring any dragon to come near her charges.

Realizing that there was nothing else she could do, Sylvia gave up the argument and lay down, after checking once more to see that Robert was safely tucked in beside her. It was reassuring to see Povey seated between her and Robert and Sir Charles on guard at the door. For the first time in what seemed a long, long while, she was able to relax completely, and she slept dreamlessly through the remainder of the night.

She awoke refreshed, to find that Robert had awakened earlier and was eating his breakfast by the window with Povey, while Sir Charles still sat by the door, watching her. The events of the night came rushing back to her, and she looked again to be certain that Robert was safely there.

"Is Nanny well this morning?" she asked anxiously.

Povey nodded. "But she is angry because she is not being allowed up just yet. The doctor told her that she was to rest today, but she told him that she had to get up so that she could find out just what happened to her yesterday. She was fearfully upset when she discovered that Robert had been taken while she was asleep."

"I daresay the doctor will have trouble keeping her in bed then," said Sylvia, smiling. It sounded as though Nanny was herself again. "It would be too bad for Lord Wilmington if Nanny learned he was responsible for drugging her. He wouldn't fare well."

Povey nodded in agreement. "He wouldn't stand a chance. I should like to see it."

"Nanny need not worry about it, I will engage to see to

it myself that Wilmington doesn't fare well," said Si
Charles, still seated in his position at the door.

Startled, both ladies looked up, having momentaril
forgotten his presence. Sylvia looked at him speculativel
Could he truly be other than he seemed, she wondered
At the moment he seemed sincerely concerned about he
and about Robert. Then she gave herself an interna
shake. Of course he could appear interested in their wel
fare when he felt quite otherwise—who could mask hi
feelings as well as Charles? He could appear to be any
thing he wished.

Gerard Mannering arrived at the door of the nursery
and Sir Charles stepped out into the passageway to speal
with him, the two of them conversing in hushed voices
Determined not to be excluded from events occurring i
her own home, Sylvia wrapped herself in her dressing
gown and joined them.

He and two of the stable hands had spent the last few
hours of the night searching for Lord Wilmington, at the
request of Sir Charles, but they had found no sign of him

"He is probably on a packet for France by now,"
sighed Mannering.

"Well, I must apologize, Charles, for believing you
suggestion about his being a spy was so outrageous," said
Lady Sylvia. "It is clear that I really knew nothing about
the man. If he would kidnap Robert, he is beyond my
understanding. And to rob my father, whom he claimed
to regard as a friend!"

There was nothing comforting that the two gentlemen
could offer. Sir Charles thanked Mannering for his help
agreeing with him that too much time had elapsed at this
point, and that Lord Wilmington was undoubtedly
beyond their grasp by now. Mannering excused himself,

going to his own chamber to change before going down to breakfast.

The morning was uneventful. After she had dressed and visited Nanny to assure herself that the old lady was indeed herself again, Sylvia went down to join her guests at breakfast and to give them a carefully edited version of last evening's events. Only the Mannerings were aware of what had actually happened. The others accepted her story easily, finding it quite believable that Robert had frightened them all by wandering away in the night after Nanny had been taken ill.

Miss Bitfort-Raines, however, was rigid with anger. There was no explanation that she would find satisfactory. She confronted Sylvia and Sir Charles in the library as they conferred in low voices with Gerard Mannering.

"Well, Charles," she said, her color high as she entered the room. "I thought that I would find you with Lady Sylvia. It appears to me that you are unduly concerned with her welfare. In fact, I believe that you were not in your room all night. When I sent Niles to you with a message, your valet informed her that you were not there."

"I was in the nursery, Claire," he said in a pacific tone, hoping to avert what appeared to be a rising storm. "It was some time before we found Robert and restored him to his nursery and sleep."

"It seems to me that there are others who could have taken care of the child once he was found," replied Miss Bitfort-Raines coldly. "I take it that you were in the nursery also, Lady Sylvia?"

Sylvia nodded briefly. "And, if you will excuse me, I am returning there now." And she moved quickly to the door, closing it quietly behind her.

Gerard Mannering, murmuring that he too had mat
ters to attend to, retired discreetly, leaving Sir Charle
and his lady in possession of the library.

The outcome of that interview was quite clear, for ar
hour later Miss Bitfort-Raines departed for London in her
carriage, quite alone except for Niles. Sir Charles, having
determined that their engagement was no longer a livable
arrangement, had allowed Miss Bitfort-Raines to vent her
wrath upon him and to warn him of all of the evils that
an attachment to Sylvia Danville would expose him. He
had listened quietly, and when she had finished her tirade
he had simply asked her, "And so you wish to end the
engagement, Claire?"

She had stood staring at him a moment, and then torr
the ring from her finger, flinging it down on the tea table
beside her. "You are a fool, Charles Redford!" she had
exclaimed, then turned and hurried from the room.

As he had pocketed the ring thoughfully, he reflected
that there was a great deal of truth in her words. Any
connection with Lady Sylvia would undoubtedly involve
him in any number of unforeseen adventures. And he
admitted to himself that he did not find that appealing.
Nonetheless, he had discovered that the prospect of seeing
her only at a distance was even less appealing. Least
acceptable of all, however, was the thought that he might
have no opportunity to be with her again, even though he
was no longer engaged. There was no guarantee that she
would find him any more acceptable now than she had
four years ago.

Lady Sylvia retired once more to the nursery. Povey
had resigned her post to Nanny for the moment and taken
herself off to bed, informing them that she would be back
to sit with Robert through the night once more. Sir

Charles, although no longer stationed at the door, appeared frequently just to see that all was going well.

It was not until the afternoon that the butler came in to inform Sylvia that Carter Blackwell had arrived and was awaiting her in the library. She did not notice the questioning glance that Sir Charles directed toward her at the announcement, for she was too filled with relief. Carter had finally arrived and Robert was playing safely in the nursery. Her nightmare of having to greet him with the news that some accident—or worse—had befallen his son would now be laid to rest once and for all. Sir Charles watched with misgiving as she left the room, her eyes alight and her step lighter than it had been for days. It seemed to him that she was entirely too happy to receive Robert's father, and once again he found himself wondering if there was more to their relationship than she had indicated.

Nor was he reassured when Sylvia escorted that gentleman into the nursery later that afternoon—too much later, it seemed to Sir Charles, who had remained there waiting for them to appear. What could they have had to say to one another that would have taken so long?

In the meantime, he and Robert had constructed several building block towers, sending them crashing down one after another, with Nanny and the lamb as an appreciative audience. When Sally had brought in Robert's biscuits and milk, Nanny had poured him a cup of her tea and together they had picnicked in the nursery. Sir Charles had had no experience with small children, but he had discovered that Robert was an entertaining companion. He would not have begrudged his time with the boy if he had not been so keenly aware that Sylvia was spending that same time with his father.

It was with relief that he heard the door open and Sylvia's familiar voice. "Look who is here, Robert," she called.

The boy looked up from his biscuit and saw his father standing in the doorway, but it did not appear to Sir Charles that there was any particular recognition on his part.

"Come here, Robert! Come and give your father a hug!" called the handsome young man who had entered with Sylvia, bending down and opening his arms. Robert did not rise, so Nanny set him on his feet and gave him a little push in that direction.

"Come along, Robert," called Lady Sylvia encouragingly.

Focusing on Sylvia, the boy smiled and ran to her arms, neatly dodging his father's embrace. If Blackwell were discomfited, he gave no sign of it, but instead lifted Robert from Sylvia's arms and gave him a brief hug before setting him down on the floor again and bending down to speak to him.

After Blackwell had duly greeted his small son, who then hurried back to Nanny and Sir Charles and the blocks, he followed Sylvia to the group, extending his hand to Sir Charles, who rose to meet him.

"I have heard, sir, that I am indebted to you for watching over Lady Sylvia and my son," he said, his smile dazzlingly white against the bronzed skin that indicated his long hours under the Egyptian sun.

"Not at all," murmured Sir Charles. "I really have done nothing."

"Charles, this is Carter Blackwell, of course," interrupted Lady Sylvia. "And, Carter, Sir Charles Redford."

She looked down at Sir Charles's teacup on the floor

and Robert standing and waiting amongst the blocks. "I see that you have kept busy, Charles," she said in amusement. "That was very kind of you."

She turned back to Carter. "We haven't allowed Robert to go out today, and so it was particularly kind of Sir Charles to give some of his time to play with him."

Blackwell nodded in agreement, but Sir Charles felt that he was not as pleased by this as he might have been. Instead, he patted Robert on the head, ignoring the fact that the boy drew away immediately and attached himself to Sir Charles's elegant buckskins.

"It is very kind indeed, Sir Charles, and I don't intend to impose upon your good nature any longer. Please feel free to rejoin the other guests. Perhaps a ride would blow away the cobwebs of the nursery."

Sir Charles, resenting the casual dismissal, bowed briefly. "A ride does sound like a good idea," he agreed. "Your servant, ma'am," he said, bowing briefly to Sylvia as well and turning to the door.

"And Redford," called Blackwell after him. "Don't worry about standing guard tonight. I shall see to it myself and you may have a good night's rest."

Further irritated by this, Sir Charles made his departure. There was no reason for his feelings, he told himself rationally. Robert was, after all, his son, and he had known Sylvia longer than he himself had—and had closer ties. Still, when he glanced back at them before closing the door of the nursery, he was profoundly annoyed to see Blackwell place his hand possessively on Sylvia's arm as they talked to Nanny. He closed the door with a smart snap and made his way to the stable. A ride to clear his head definitely seemed in order.

Certain of his errand, he turned his horse toward the

gypsy camp. It was time to look more closely into the matter of Madame Zeena. He placed no stock in gypsy fortune-telling, but he did have a firm belief in their resourcefulness. He was convinced that they—probably employed by Wilmington—lay behind at least one of the kidnappings and the fire. Perhaps now he would find out a little more about the matter. Wilmington had gotten beyond his grasp, but they could still be questioned.

The ride gave him a chance to grow a little calmer. There was no point in wasting his time thinking of the handsome Carter Blackwell and the way that he looked at Sylvia, nor about her fondness for his child and her distress at the thought of having to tell him that something had happened to Robert. None at all. Sylvia Danville would always do as she pleased, and he knew it. She would always do the thoughtless thing, the scandalous thing—and he knew that. The disconcerting thing was that he no longer cared. He simply wanted to marry her.

When he arrived at the point in the road nearest the gypsy camp, he turned off, following a path down into the trees below. To his chagrin, however, there were no gypsies. They and their wagons were gone, leaving only the traces of their fires in the dell.

He rode slowly back toward Greystone, stopping at an inn along the way to see if he could discover any news of them and the direction they had taken. Perhaps they had removed themselves far beyond the reaches of Greystone and this would mark the end of Sylvia's problems now that Wilmington was already gone.

As it happened, he didn't have to make any inquiries. The gypsies were already under discussion in the taproom and he listened as he sipped his ale.

"He was in a rare taking," a man at the table next to

him was saying, puffing on his pipe between comments. "They had lashed him, you know, laid bare his back and done it proper."

"I heard that he had been lashed across the face as well," said his companion.

The man with the pipe nodded. "Twice," he said gravely. "Once across each cheek. They wanted to mark him, I think. It was a punishment."

"For what?" asked the other eagerly.

"For attacking one of their young women," was the reply. "The way I heard it, they have been tracking the nob for months to give him a taste of his own back again."

"How did you find out all this?" asked his friend curiously.

"Seems that one of the footmen over at Greystone where the nob was staying was one of the gypsies. He got a job there when they heard the nob was a-coming to stay there for a while. They've kept one of their people close to him all the time, one way or another."

Sir Charles turned to them abruptly. "I am Sir Charles Redford—and a guest at Greystone Park," he announced. "Can you tell me the name of the gentleman that was lashed?"

The two men stared at him and then at one another. The one with the pipe moved restively under his gaze. "I heard that his name was Lord Wilmington," he admitted finally.

Sir Charles nodded to himself. It was what he had guessed, of course, not just because of Wilmington's absence, but because it fit with everything he knew of the man. Only a coward would attack a woman. He undoubtedly deserved more than the lashes, and Sir Charles was surprised that the gypsies had stopped with that.

"Where did you take him?" asked Sir Charles. "To the closest surgeon?"

"Didn't take him nowhere, governor. Didn't want to be mixed up in it at all," replied the man with the pipe. "I should imagine he took himself off to the nearest saw-bones, though. He was a proper mess."

"And where would I find the nearest surgeon?" inquired Sir Charles.

He was directed to a village some five miles away, and he hurried from the inn, hoping to apprehend Wilmington at the surgeon's. Upon his arrival at that gentleman's establishment, however, he discovered that Wilmington had not been seen there, and Sir Charles returned as quickly as possible to Greystone to share this latest development with the others and to make immediate arrangements for continuing the search.

It was still imperative, if Wilmington were somewhere within reach, to stop him, recover the box of notes, and question him closely. He would once again press Manner-ing and the stable hands into service to cover all of the surgeons within a two hour ride of Greystone.

Chapter Twenty

"But do you really think that you might still find him?" Lady Sylvia asked Sir Charles as he and Mannering sent word to the stable hands and prepared to depart.

Sir Charles nodded grimly. "If he was lashed as severely as the gossips at the inn say he was, he won't be riding for a day or two—and he will have to have some help with the cuts. I had thought that the gypsies were working with him in this, but I see now that they were just following him for their own purposes."

Sylvia shivered. "I know that he deserved to be punished, but surely not in such a barbaric manner."

"The gypsies believe in very direct methods," answered Sir Charles. "He was fortunate to have gotten off that easily. They could have done worse."

"Don't tell me how," returned Sylvia, turning away.

"I am not certain how long we will be gone," continued Sir Charles, "but I want to know that you and Robert are safe, so you must swear to me that you will remain inside until we return. Don't walk in the gardens or even on the terrace."

"Oh, really, Charles! What is there for us to fear now?"

"Probably nothing. But I want to be certain. Do you promise me that you will do as I have asked?"

"I will be here, Sir Charles," interceded Blackwell smoothly, seeing that Lady Sylvia was bristling, "and I guarantee that I will not leave her side."

With that slender comfort Sir Charles was forced to be satisfied, for the stablehands appeared and it was time for them to be underway. He was dissatisfied, though, for Sylvia had not given her word. Still, he would be gone for a relatively brief time, he told himself, and surely all would be well until he returned.

Sylvia and Carter Blackwell watched them ride away, then walked slowly back to the library.

"My poor guests," murmured Sylvia, glancing out the window at young Ashby and Symington strolling through the knot garden. "Their hostess has abandoned them and they are having to fend for themselves. At least Amelia is with them and doing her best to see that no one wants for anything."

"I am sure they are getting along, Sylvia," said Blackwell, linking her arm with his as they stood looking out the window. "People expect a house party to be casual, with plenty of time to themselves to ride and amble about the grounds."

Sylvia had noticed the small proprietary gestures he had been making, quite as though their relationship was a more personal one than it was, and she did not like them. Disengaging her arm, she walked across the room to straighten a picture frame.

"If that is what they expect, then they are very contented people," she said cheerfully, "for they certainly have the time to do those things. And there are plenty of servants to help them."

She stood there, gazing at the picture thoughtfully. "It seems strange to think that I had a gypsy employed here, and that his purpose was to watch Lord Wilmington. It makes me wonder how many other things I have not been aware of." She suddenly remembered the footman that she had let go in London and wondered if there had been a similar connection.

"But the strangest thing, I think, is that Lord Wilmington wanted my father's notes. I cannot imagine what he hopes to do with them."

Blackwell turned toward her, his eyebrows lifted. "He took your father's notes?" he demanded. "I assumed that the fellow wanted money, and I was about to ask how much he had required so that I could repay you."

Sylvia shook her head ruefully. "No, Carter—money I could understand. But he specifically wanted the box of notes. Why would he be interested even in reading them?"

Blackwell stared at her for a moment. "For the tomb, of course," he said.

"The tomb?" she echoed blankly. "Surely you don't mean the tomb that my father has been trying to find again? *He* has not found it yet. How could someone else expect to do so?"

"Your father very carefully recorded a description of the location when he visited it, but since he hasn't been able to find the guide who led him to the valley in the first place, he has not been able to locate it again," explained Blackwell earnestly. "If someone knew exactly which valley to go to and had your father's description, he could locate that tomb in an instant—and who knows how rich a find it might be! Your father thinks that it may well be a treasure trove. He brought back a necklace that he recovered in the area and he hopes to be able to identify the period of the tomb by that."

"But Wilmington isn't interested in digging up tombs!" protested Sylvia. Suddenly, however, her eyes widened and she slowly added, "But we know that he is a spy—and that might be what this is all about."

Blackwell looked puzzled. "What are you talking about, Sylvia? What does being a spy have to do with the tomb?"

"Sir Charles told me that the war with France isn't really over, and that Bonaparte still has his eye on Egypt. And of course he requires a huge amount of money for his campaigns! What better way to fund an army than recovering a king's ransom from a tomb! If that tomb that my father located is untouched by vandals—and as rich a find as he thinks it may be—then it would be of great interest to the French!"

"This is beginning to sound like a fairy tale," said Blackwell in disbelief. "Boney is going to dig up tombs to fund his campaigns?"

"It isn't farfetched at all, Carter!" insisted Sylvia. "Just think about Denon's journals. Why, I just purchased those volumes for my father two weeks ago in London! He describes his travels with the French army while they were in Egypt, and heaven knows Bonaparte brought a whole collection of experts on Egypt with him when he tried to invade five years ago. He has people who would know how to use the information that my father recorded!"

She could see that he was still not disposed to believe her, so she said firmly, "You may stay here if you wish, Carter, and wait for the others to come home, but I am going after Lord Wilmington."

He had stretched out comfortably on a sofa, but at her

words he leaped to his feet. "What are you talking about, Sylvia? Sir Charles and Mannering are taking care of that!"

"They don't know where to look," she said confidently. "Wilmington isn't dull-witted; he knows that we would check with all of the surgeons if we heard that he had been injured. But he must have medication for those cuts, so I daresay he has made inquiries and found out about Bess."

"Bess? Who is Bess?" demanded Blackwell.

Sylvia started for the door. "She is the local herb-woman, Carter—our white witch. Now, if you will forgive me, I'll just run upstairs to put on my riding dress and be certain that Nanny and Povey are with Robert."

"But you aren't supposed to go outside!" he called down the passageway after her.

"*I* didn't give my word!" she called back, and he heard the slamming of a distant door.

When she came down the stairs, her riding crop tucked under her arm, it was quite obvious to Carter that she had no intention of listening to reason.

"Well, I said that I would not leave your side, and I won't," he sighed. "Even if this proves to be more than I had bargained for."

As they left the house, he once again placed his hand on her elbow, as though to guide her, and this time she stopped a moment and gently removed his hand.

"I prefer to walk alone, Carter," she said, smiling pleasantly.

"I see," he replied slowly. "Does that mean in every way, Sylvia?" he inquired. "I had hoped that, with Laura gone . . ."

"If you are asking me if there is any possibility of our

marrying, Carter, the answer is no. I know that we should not suit."

"I am not so certain of that, Sylvia," he replied.

"But if I am, Carter, that is half the battle lost," she said, smiling again to try to take the sting from her words.

It was clear from his expression that she hadn't managed to do so, and their ride to Bess's cottage was a quiet one. Since her phaeton was gone, they had taken the gig, and Sylvia had reluctantly relinquished the ribbons to him. Their stop at Bess's cottage was brief and when Sylvia emerged, she ran quickly down the path to the front gate.

"We have him, Carter!" she exclaimed as she seated herself in the gig. "Bess says that a boy came from the Angel Inn, asking for salves to heal open cuts. It's a tiny little place with only three rooms, just the kind of spot where Wilmington would think that he would be perfectly safe. What a surprise our arrival will be!"

The Angel Inn was as small as Sylia had described it, and it was tucked alongside a little traveled road. There they found Wilmington reclining on his bed in the tiny upstairs bedroom.

"Do come in," he said genially when they appeared at his open door. "There is no privacy here. The owner and his wife come and go as they please. We have had any number of interesting conversations about how I will pay my shot when I am able to travel."

Sylvia stared at him, distracted first by his wounds, which had been covered with heavy salves and bandages, and then by his words.

"Why should there be a problem, Lord Wilmington?" she inquired. "Have you no money? I shouldn't think that would bother you. Surely there is someone from whom you could take it."

"Bitterness does not become you, Lady Sylvia," he said reproachfully. "You need to cultivate a more positive attitude toward your fellow creatures. It is *I* who have a right to be bitter!"

"You!" exclaimed Sylvia. "Why should you be bitter? Was my horse not fast enough? Did the phaeton break an axle?"

Wilmington shook his head, ignoring her bitterness this time. "Do you think that if I had your horse, Lady Sylvia, that I would still be here? Here where I can be attacked and taken at will? It is I, good lady, who has been the victim. You see that I have been physically assaulted—that should have satisfied their barbaric instincts—but it did not. Next they robbed me, taking my horse and phaeton—"

"*My* horse and phaeton," interrupted Sylvia firmly.

"—and my money and jewelry," continued Wilmington, ignoring her, "and, the lowest blow of all, my box of notes."

"You mean *my* jewelry and my *father's* box of notes!" exclaimed Sylvia, outraged by his appropriation of the property of others. "What did you mean, Lord Wilmington, when you said that you needed my necklace as *proof*? Proof of what?"

"Proof that your father had found a rich tomb, of course," he replied. "That, along with the notes, would have brought me a rich reward from the Frenchies—and their gratitude, of course. Who knows what it might have won for me? But now, of course, thanks to the thieving Romanies, I have no hope of such riches."

It was obvious that he felt his own wrongs deeply, but

he could not be brought to recognize his own wrong-doing, and eventually Sylvia and Blackwell gave up any hope of bringing him to a sense of his crimes. Satisfied that he could go nowhere in a hurry, they felt that they could leave him and go in pursuit of the box of notes.

"And so the gypsies took the notes as well?" inquired Sylvia.

Wilmington nodded his head. "Just as prettily as you please. They just plucked me of everything, whipped me, and then rode away."

As Sylvia and Blackwell made their departure, he called after them, "And if you have the opportunity, get back my jewelry, too. Some of it has sentimental value."

"They will not be allowed to escape with your father's notes, Sylvia," said Blackwell reassuringly as they climbed into the gig. Relieved that he now seemed to be taking a more personal interest in the matter, she directed him to several of the larger inns on the main road, hoping to discover where the gypsies might be going next. It wasn't until their third stop that they met with success. There one of the men in the taproom had heard it said that they were going to the fair in Middleton, the next village, where they would tell fortunes and perhaps sell some of their horses.

"Do you suppose that we should send a message back to Greystone so that the others know where we're going if they return before us?" Sylvia asked Blackwell.

"No, I don't think we need trouble ourselves with that," he replied. "It won't be a long ride to Middleton. Then we can recover the notes and turn back toward home."

Shrugging, she gave way to him, and it was not long until the fair came into sight. A Punch and Judy show was in progress and a noisy crowd had assembled to enjoy it, while another group had gathered to applaud a group of acrobats. As they rode farther, they saw a string of horses being inspected by prospective buyers and several familiar wagons pulled up at the edge of the green.

There Sylvia found the man she had spoken to at the camp the night before. He smiled and doffed his hat.

"I see that Frederick got you home safely, lady. Is the little boy well?" he asked.

"Yes, indeed, thanks to you and your mother," she said, smiling. "And I understand that you found Lord Wilmington and—spoke—with him."

His eyes gleamed in appreciation at her choice of words, but he nodded gravely.

"Did you by any chance find a box filled with papers among his things—and some jewelry?" she asked anxiously. "He robbed my father of his work, and me of my jewelry."

The man stood perfectly still for a moment, then nodded. The other men and boys were watching him carefully. He went to one of the wagons and brought out a small bag and the box, still tied together, and presented them to her with a bow. Blackwell took the carton from her and carried it back in the gig.

"Our apologies, lady," he said. "I think that perhaps there has been a misunderstanding about the lord's carriage and horse as well. Was it yours, lady, and the lord had taken it from you?"

She nodded.

"It will be brought to your home," he promised. "When the fair is over, one of our young men will drive it there."

"Thank you," Sylvia said gratefully, extending her hand. "You have been most kind."

"You must still beware of those you think you know, lady," intoned a deep voice from their tent. It was Madame Zeena who stepped forward from the shadows.

Sylvia smiled at her. "You were right, Madame Zeena, but that episode is over. I am ready now to get on with my life—without any warnings hanging over me. All of those problems are behind me."

As Blackwell and Lady Sylvia rolled away in the gig, Madame Zeena stood at the edge of a crowd of fairgoers and watched them, shading her eyes with her hand against the brightness of the setting sun.

Sylvia sat with the box, heavy though it was, on her knees. She had worried about facing her father and telling him that his precious notes had disappeared. Once again fortune had smiled on her and she would be able to restore his work to him. Perhaps now she would be able to relax and forget the warnings that she had received. They had all been taken care of. Perhaps now she could seriously devote herself to recovering from the spell of Sir Charles Redford. After all, that was why she had come home to England.

So deep in thought was she that she paid no attention when Blackwell turned off the main road and down a narrow lane. It wasn't until he brought the gig to a stop that she became aware of what had happened.

"Is there something wrong, Carter?" she asked. "Why have we stopped?" She looked around and continued, "And why did you turn off the road?"

Blackwell smiled apologetically and held out his hand. "I am afraid that I need to take the notes, Sylvia," he said gently.

She stared at him blankly. "Do you mean that *you* are

going to take them, Carter?" she cried. "Why would *you* betray my father? You love him!"

He nodded. "I am fond of your father, Sylvia. And of your mother, too, naturally. But there are other matters to consider."

"What matters?" she cried. "What are you talking about, Carter?"

"I have a number of important things I wish to accomplish in my lifetime, Sylvia," he said dreamily. "Your father has been of great assistance to me, but I must get on with the work myself, and I need more money to pursue my interests. I have found the man who can guide me to the valley where your father found the tomb, but unfortunately one cannot dig up tombs in the midst of the desert without a very large amount of capital—so I must be practical. You are an heiress; therefore, we will be married this afternoon, Sylvia."

She stared at him, open-mouthed. "You must be mad, Carter!" she exclaimed. "I am not going to marry you!"

He smiled again. "Oh, yes, I think you will." He patted his jacket pocket. "I have the special license right here, and I have made arrangements with the gentleman who will perform the ceremony."

Sylvia was beginning to feel that he might indeed be mad, so she explained this situation to him in a patient voice. "I am touched that you wish to marry me, Carter, and it was very farsighted of you to get the special license—but, Carter, I don't wish to marry you. Don't you understand that?"

"Oh, yes, I understand. But you will marry me, you know. You must think of Robert."

"What do you mean by that?" she asked, genuinely puzzled.

"If you don't marry me, Sylvia, I shall be forced to kill him," he replied gently.

She dropped the box of notes from her knees as she looked at him, her eyes widening in fear as it dawned her that his wits truly were disordered. "But he is *your* son, Carter! Why would you harm him?"

Blackwell looked her as though she were simple-minded. "Why, Sylvia, you know that Laura's land and fortune are Robert's—and that I am merely his guardian. Unless, of course, something happens to him. In that case, they will be mine."

He looked at her thoughtfully as he considered the matter. "I had thought, you know, that that would be the easiest matter—to simply have an accident befall him. But it didn't work out. First that young Mr. Ashby interfered, and then paying the maid to give him a good soaking merely appeared to aid in his recovery. Ironic, wasn't it?" he asked, as though asking her to share in his amazement.

Sylvia gripped her hands firmly together and assumed a practical tone. "Well then, Carter. If that was your plan, why did you not merely wait until Robert was in your care and then—eliminate him?"

"Why, it would have been much more suspicious, of course, had it happened while he was in my care. If he were your charge, I would be beyond suspicion. Also," he continued, a smile softening his handsome face, "it occurred to me as I was watching you that marrying you would give me even more money. Because, sooner or later, I would have Robert's inheritance, too."

Sylvia had begun to shiver, and it was not merely because the sun was setting and the afternoon warmth was slipping away. Next to her sat a man who was un-questionably mad—a man that spoke of killing as most people spoke of taking afternoon tea. He knew that she would never allow him to marry her and take control of her fortune—so she was quite certain what he had in mind. And if she flatly refused to marry him, he would undoubtedly kill her—and then go home and murder his son.

He noticed her shaking and wrapped her shawl around her shoulders. "I think, my dear, that we should go directly to the rectory, don't you?"

She forced herself to smile and nod her head. "You are so clever, Carter," she said in an admiring tone. "I had no idea that you were so needle-witted."

He expanded visibly under her praise, and she decided to risk another question, forcing herself to sound merely interested, as though the whole matter were an academic question.

"When you have my father's notes and use them to find the tomb, how will you explain that?"

He smiled again, pleased to be able to expand upon his plan. "There will be no need to explain things to him," he said gently. "Your father and mother—like you—will meet with a tragic accident. With the Danville fortune as well as Laura's, I will be able to uncover a lost world." His face looked radiant. "People will write of my work for hundreds of years."

He turned to her, still smiling. "So you see, Sylvia, it will all work out beautifully."

"You will forgive me if I don't see it in just that light, Carter," she said dryly, unable to continue her charade.

He laughed lightly. "I do enjoy your sense of humor, Sylvia. I shall miss it."

They had just resumed their journey down the lane when there was a shout from behind them. Sylvia, casting

caution to the winds, waved and screamed for help.
Blackwell, looking back, saw Sir Charles and Mannering
galloping after them. Cursing, he lashed the horses with
his whip, but it was obvious that they would not be able
to outrun their pursuers. He jerked the horses to a halt
and, to Sylvia's horror, drew out a pistol. He stood up in
the gig, brandishing the gun, and had just reached down
for her when a shot rang out, and Blackwell fell where he
stood, dead before he struck the ground. The horses,
startled, gathered themselves to bolt, but Sylvia had
enough presence of mind left to grab the ribbons.

When she looked up to see who had fired the shot, she
saw Sir Charles. He leaped from his mount and into the
gig beside her, while Mannering bent over Blackwell.

"Are you all right, Sylvia?" he demanded, cupping her
face in his hands and looking at her intently. "Did he hurt
you?"

She shook her head, discovering in horror that her
lower lip was trembling and she was just before crying.
"No, Charles—but it was terrible! He is mad, Charles,
completely mad! He wishes to do the most horrible
things!"

Mannering looked up grimly. "Well, he won't be doing
them now, Lady Sylvia," he assured her. "It is all over."

Sir Charles folded her in his arms and held her close as
she poured out her story.

"I think that he lost all sense of right and wrong, my
dear," he said as she finished it. "He simply didn't care
about anything except the glory of making a great discovery. The poor fool!"

She looked up at him, caught by his tone as he murmured the last words. "He thought that he had to have a
fortune and search for an even greater fortune in the

desert—he thought that would be a great discovery," he explained. "What Blackwell didn't realize is that it isn't necessary to go to such extremes to make a great discovery. I have made one right here in England—I learned it the other day."

Still she said nothing, waiting.

"Shall I tell you what it is?" he asked.

Sylvia nodded, afraid to say anything.

He smiled down into her eyes and said softly, "That I don't want you ever to leave me again, Sylvia. You may do any outrageous thing that you wish—except leave me."

"I came back to England to cure myself of you, Charles," she confessed. "I was certain that if I looked at you closely enough I would see all the reasons why I shouldn't love you."

"And did you?" he asked, smoothing back her tumbled hair.

She nodded. "I saw every one of them, but—"

"But what?" he prodded.

"But they didn't make me stop loving you."

She lifted her eyes to the evening sky, now streaked with scarlet, and she was startled to see Madame Zeena in the distance, seated in Sylvia's own phaeton. The fortune-teller nodded and smiled.

"Did Madame Zeena help you find me?" she asked, her eyes wide.

Sir Charles nodded. "Mannering and I were able to trace you to the fair, and she had watched you as you left. In fact, she was just leaving in the phaeton to follow you as we arrived."

Sylvia smiled back at the gypsy and waved. Madame Zeena waved back and turned the phaeton toward home.

"She will take it back to Greystone," explained Sir Charles.

Sylvia watched her depart with a lightening spirit. Surely now it was all over. It occurred to her that the warning had been a more extended one than she at first realized. Not only had Wilmington and Carter not been what she had thought, but also Sir Charles himself was not what she had thought him. I am a most regrettable judge of character, she thought ruefully.

"Are you quite sure that you wish to marry me, Charles?" she asked earnestly.

His response was fully as satisfying as she could have wished, and she snuggled next to him as he turned the gig around to take them home. Suddenly, however, a most unpleasant thought struck her and she sat bolt upright.

"Robert!" she exclaimed. "Charles, what shall we do about Robert?"

"Claire said it herself," he said complacently.

"Said what?" Sylvia demanded.

"That it was most fortunate that my coloring is dark. Robert will look a great deal like my own child."

"And that is what you wish to do? Take Robert as our own son?" she asked, amazed at this new side of his character.

He nodded. "Then, if you grow too sedate, I shall have to rely upon Robert—and the other children—to create a scandal. I should hate for life to grow boring."

She smiled and rubbed her cheek against the late afternoon roughness of his. "We will do our best to keep your life interesting, Charles," she promised.

And it may be noted that they—Sylvia and Robert and the other children, Amelia and Gerard and Adrian and Richard—did precisely that.

ABOUT THE AUTHOR

Mona Gedney lives with her family in West Lafayette, Indiana. She is also the author of four previous Zebra regency romances: A LADY OF FORTUNE, THE EASTER CHARADE, A VALENTINE'S DAY GAMBIT and A CHRISTMAS BETROTHAL. She is currently working on her next regency novel. Mona loves hearing from her readers and you may write to her c/o Zebra Books. Please include a self-addressed stamped envelope if you wish a response.

ZEBRA'S REGENCY ROMANCES
DAZZLE AND DELIGHT

A BEGUILING INTRIGUE (4441, $3.99)
by Olivia Sumner

Pretty as a picture Justine Riggs cared nothing for propriety. She dressed as a boy, sat on her horse like a jockey, and pondered the stars like a scientist. But when she tried to best the handsome Quenton Fletcher, Marquess of Devon, by proving that she was the better equestrian, he would try to prove Justine's antics were pure folly. The game he had in mind was seduction — never imagining that he might lose his heart in the process!

AN INCONVENIENT ENGAGEMENT (4442, $3.99)
by Joy Reed

Rebecca Wentworth was furious when she saw her betrothed waltzing with another. So she decides to make him jealous by flirting with the handsomest man at the ball, John Collinwood, Earl of Stanford. The "wicked" nobleman knew exactly what the enticing miss was up to — and he was only too happy to play along. But as Rebecca gazed into his magnificent eyes, her errant fiancé was soon utterly forgotten!

SCANDAL'S LADY (4472, $3.99)
by Mary Kingsley

Cassandra was shocked to learn that the new Earl of Lynton was her childhood friend, Nicholas St. John. After years at sea and mixed feelings Nicholas had come home to take the family title. And although Cassandra knew her place as a governess, she could not help the thrill that went through her each time he was near. Nicholas was pleased to find that his old friend Cassandra was his new next door neighbor, but after being near her, he wondered if mere friendship would be enough . . .

HIS LORDSHIP'S REWARD (4473, $3.99)
by Carola Dunn

As the daughter of a seasoned soldier, Fanny Ingram was accustomed to the vagaries of military life and cared not a whit about matters of rank and social standing. So she certainly never foresaw her *tendre* for handsome Viscount Roworth of Kent with whom she was forced to share lodgings, while he carried out his clandestine activities on behalf of the British Army. And though good sense told Roworth to keep his distance, he couldn't stop from taking Fanny in his arms for a kiss that made all hearts equal!

Available wherever paperbacks are sold, or order direct from the Publisher. Send cover price plus 50¢ per copy for mailing and handling to Penguin USA, P.O. Box 999, c/o Dept. 17109, Bergenfield, NJ 07621. Residents of New York and Tennessee must include sales tax. DO NOT SEND CASH.

ELEGANT LOVE STILL FLOURISHES —
Wrap yourself in a Zebra Regency Romance.

A MATCHMAKER'S MATCH (3783, $3.50/$4.50)
by Nina Porter

To save herself from a loveless marriage, Lady Psyche Veringham pretends to be a bluestocking. Resigned to spinsterhood at twenty-three, Psyche sets her keen mind to snaring a husband for her young charge, Amanda. She sets her cap for long-time bachelor, Justin St. James. This man of the world has had his fill of frothy-headed debutantes and turns the tables on Psyche. Can a bluestocking and a man about town find true love?

FIRES IN THE SNOW (3809, $3.99/$4.99)
by Janis Laden

Because of an unhappy occurrence, Diana Ruskin knew that a secure marriage was not in her future. She was content to assist her physician father and follow in his footsteps . . . until now. After meeting Adam, Duke of Marchmaine, Diana's precise world is shattered. She would simply have to avoid the temptation of his gentle touch and stunning physique — and by doing so break her own heart!

FIRST SEASON (3810, $3.50/$4.50)
by Anne Baldwin

When country heiress Laetitia Biddle arrives in London for the Season, she harbors dreams of triumph and applause. Instead, she becomes the laughingstock of drawing rooms and ballrooms, alike. This headstrong miss blames the rakish Lord Wakeford for her miserable debut, and she vows to rise above her many faux pas. Vowing to become an Original, Letty proves that she's more than a match for this eligible, seasoned Lord.

AN UNCOMMON INTRIGUE (3701, $3.99/$4.99)
by Georgina Devon

Miss Mary Elizabeth Sinclair was rather startled when the British Home Office employed her as a spy. Posing as "Tasha," an exotic fortune-teller, she expected to encounter unforeseen dangers. However, nothing could have prepared her for Lord Eric Stewart, her dashing and infuriating partner. Giving her heart to this haughty rogue would be the most reckless hazard of all.

A MADDENING MINX (3702, $3.50/$4.50)
by Mary Kingsley

After a curricle accident, Miss Sarah Chadwick is literally thrust into the arms of Philip Thornton. While other women shy away from Thornton's eyepatch and aloof exterior, Sarah finds herself drawn to discover why this man is physically and emotionally scarred.

Available wherever paperbacks are sold, or order direct from the Publisher. Send cover price plus 50¢ per copy for mailing and handling to Penguin USA, P.O. Box 999, c/o Dept. 17109, Bergenfield, NJ 07621. Residents of New York and Tennessee must include sales tax. DO NOT SEND CASH.